Readers love the Ryder & Loveday series

'Insanely brilliant'

'I absolutely loved this book'

'Faith Martin, you've triumphed again. Brilliant!'

'If you haven't yet read Miss Martin you have a treat in store'

'I can safely say that I adore the series featuring Dr Clement
Ryder and Probationary WPC Trudy Loveday'

'This book is such a delight to read. The two main
characters are a joy'

'Yet another wonderful book by Faith Martin!'

'As always a wonderful story, great characters, great plot.
This keeps you gripped from the first page to the last.
Faith Martin is such a fantastic author'

FAITH MARTIN has been writing for nearly thirty years, under four different pen names, and has published over fifty novels. She began writing romantic thrillers as Maxine Barry, but quickly turned to crime! As Joyce Cato she wrote classic-style whodunits, since she's always admired the golden-age crime novelists. But it was when she created her fictional DI Hillary Greene, and began writing under the name of Faith Martin, that she finally became more widely known. Her latest literary characters, WPC Trudy Loveday and city coroner Dr Clement Ryder, take readers back to the 1960s and the city of Oxford. Having lived within a few miles of the city's dreaming spires for all her life (she worked for six years as a secretary at Somerville College), both the city and the countryside/wildlife often feature in her novels. Although she has never lived on a narrowboat (unlike DI Hillary Greene!) the Oxford canal, the river Cherwell, and the flora and fauna of a farming landscape have always played a big part in her life – and often sneak their way onto the pages of her books.

Also by Faith Martin

A Fatal End

FAITH MARTIN

ONE PLACE. MANY STORIES

HQ
An imprint of HarperCollins*Publishers* Ltd
1 London Bridge Street
London SE1 9GF

www.harpercollins.co.uk

HarperCollins*Publishers*
1st Floor, Watermarque Building, Ringsend Road
Dublin 4, Ireland

This paperback edition 2022

1

First published in Great Britain by
HQ, an imprint of HarperCollins*Publishers* Ltd 2022

ISBN: 9780008410551

MIX
Paper | Supporting
responsible forestry
FSC
www.fsc.org   FSC™ C007454

This book is produced from independently certified FSC™ paper
to ensure responsible forest management.

For more information visit: www.harpercollins.co.uk/green

Printed and bound in Great Britain by
CPI Group (UK) Ltd, Croydon, CR0 4YY

This is dedicated to loyal readers everywhere.
Be assured, every author really appreciates you.

Prologue

Oxford 1963

It was the first Saturday of September 1963. Playing on the radio in someone's front room, Billy J. Kramer and the Dakotas were singing their latest number-one hit, 'Bad to Me', and the sound filtered out through the open window into the warm streets of the city.

In the cinemas, the latest posters were advertising the upcoming attraction of *The Great Escape*, featuring the American heart-throbs Steve McQueen and James Garner.

But what really floated the boat of the teenagers now was the new wave of popular music sweeping the land, and Oxford – like most major cities – was only too happy to cater to their wants and needs with open arms … and open hands.

For just two shillings, you could venture down the left-hand side of the High Street where a rather disreputable alleyway would take you to the Forum, or you might prefer to hang out at the Carfax Assembly Rooms, which had played host to the Beatles the year before they became nationally famous.

But for those ultra-modern young girls and boys who liked to think of themselves as being a cut above the lily-livered masses and made of much sterner and rebellious stuff, the Bootleggers Club in Walton Street was the place to go. Delicious rumours circulated that real criminals could sometimes be found there, and the bar staff were notoriously lax when it came to estimating a youngster's age. All the best up-and-coming bands played there too, and it was satisfyingly dark, dingy and – better yet – hated by local city councilmen who were always trying to get it shut down. And somehow never quite managing to do it.

That particular Saturday night started out at the Bootleggers Club much as usual. By seven o'clock the first of the bands had begun to perform on the small stage. Already the room, not the biggest in the world, was packed. The band – a motley group of likely local lads calling themselves the Undergrads – were doing their best, but apart from a toe-tapping basic beat, they had little else going for them.

Not that that fact worried Felix Simpkins much. As manager of the club, he cared little about the quality of the entertainment, so long as the youngsters came in their droves, paid the entrance fee and drank his booze. Besides, he knew the first few acts were always the worst. Later on, the big draw – the Rainbirds – would take to the stage in the prime nine to ten p.m. spot, and even Felix, who had a tin ear, could tell they were in a different class from most of the long-haired rabble.

In the basement below, where the acts went to change, drink and relax in a makeshift common room so squalid that even the rats thought twice about going in there, Ray Reason smoked from a pack of Players and watched his fellow Rainbird member Marty Cuthbertson picking gently on his Watkins Rapier. Marty, like every other kid with the drive to become a pop star, dreamed one day of owning a Gibson or a Fender, and just like everyone else, had to make do with what he could afford.

Ray, at nineteen, was blessed with brooding good looks, with black hair and blue eyes. He liked to call himself the lead singer, but the truth was, he and Marty usually shared the singing. That was because Marty was the band's songwriter. He was also, by the tiniest of margins, the band's best guitar player too, a fact that Ray would never willingly admit out loud. But Marty was too tall, too lanky, too goofy-looking to really set the hearts of their female fans alight.

No, it was because of Ray that the band was getting a reputation as the next big thing. And when the next posters went out to advertise one of their gigs, come hell or high water, the band's name would have changed to 'Ray Reason and the Rainbirds'. He'd been talking about it to rest of the lads for ages, insisting that it sounded better. Just look at the current number one! It wasn't 'the Dakotas', was it? No, it was Billy J. Kramer and the Dakotas. And the new Mersey sound that was all the rage – was it 'the Pacemakers'? Or was it *Gerry* and the Pacemakers? He'd even pointed out that his own name (he really had been christened Raymond Reason) was the ideal name to go with 'Rainbirds'.

But Marty wasn't having it, and that pushy cow of a girlfriend of his wasn't having it either. But Ray would win in the end. He always did.

Outside, a young female fan, almost (but not quite) too young to get past even the Bootleggers' lackadaisical doorman, was instead prowling around the back passageways, looking for a window that she could climb into.

In the main dance hall, Lindy-Lou Kempson listened to the Undergrads murder a revamp of an old Buddy Holly song and tried not to wince. She was steadily drinking vodka, although she knew she really shouldn't be. At eighteen, she'd only started drinking a few months ago, when she discovered the Bootleggers Club and began dating Ray. Now she stood against the wall at the back of the dark, cramped, heaving room and felt sick.

She was also beginning to feel quite desperate. What if her boyfriend didn't stick by her? A very pretty girl, with long brown hair and big pansy-brown eyes, she was the daughter of a respectable middle-aged couple, who'd come, originally, from Torquay. And she knew her parents would be shocked and furious if they knew that she was 'in trouble'.

Jennifer Renfrew, who delighted in calling herself Jenny Wren, was watching Lindy-Lou from behind a crush of silly giggling girls who couldn't be much older than fourteen. She had spotted Lindy-Lou almost immediately upon entering the hall but was studiously avoiding her. Instead, she pushed her way through the little group of starry-eyed teenagers and made her way out to a side door, where she emerged into a dim and smelly corridor. The lavatories were out here, and she noticed the light in the gents' wasn't working again. Wrinkling her nose in disgust, she stepped quickly past them. Trust that penny-pinching and obnoxious Felix not to get it fixed.

She walked quickly down the unsavoury corridor towards a dog-leg turn. Just beyond it, a narrow iron spiral staircase descended to the basement, from which she could hear voices wafting up. She knew they belonged to the players in the bands who were hanging out down there as they waited for their turn on the stage, and nervous laughter and cigarette smoke leaked upwards in equal measure.

She hoped Marty had worn that new shirt she'd got him. It showed off his fair hair just right, and would make him stand out under the stage lights. He needed all the help he could get to make sure that Ray didn't hog the audience's attention.

She negotiated the tight space of the staircase and turned to the only large doorway down there. As she paused on the threshold, looking around for her boyfriend, she saw Ray first, lounging on a sofa that had half its stuffing spilling out, and drinking thirstily from a pint glass of beer.

She ignored his sardonic grin as their eyes met, and she wound her way through to where Marty was sitting, picking out yet another new tune on his guitar.

Jenny knew Ray wanted to take over as leader of the band, but he'd do it only over her dead body. Marty was the songwriter, he could play the guitar like Eddie Cochran and his voice was as good as Ray's any day of the week.

Outside, a large Bentley pulled up beside the entrance to the club and a man climbed out, surveying the brightly lit but appallingly ugly little building with a wry smile.

Titus Crowther-Beauley was thirty-nine years old but looked a lot younger. He dressed well and lived well. He was five foot seven, with dark brown hair and eyes, a legacy from his now-deceased Italian mother. His father – a minor, penniless lord – lived in genteel poverty in Scotland, in a crumbling fortified manor house that Titus avoided like the plague.

Well-educated but cash poor, Titus had had the brains, good sense, charm and ruthlessness necessary to make his own name – and money – choosing to inhabit the world of television, theatre, film and now the music industry. Agent and in some cases manager of nearly a hundred stars – no matter what their metier – he had a good eye and ear and had risen to become an acknowledged star-maker.

And he very much enjoyed being fawned over and feted by good-looking aspiring actresses, desperate film directors and fashion magazine editors alike.

Tonight, he'd come to the Bootleggers to listen again to a band that his spotters had first picked up on as a possible contender for the next big thing. On the whole, he'd been impressed by his first sight and sound of the band, and had cautiously sounded them out, to see if they already had management. He'd made no promises, but not surprisingly most of them had been very excited by his interest, although he had encountered unexpected reticence from one member of the band. Nevertheless, he'd gone to see them again, and had once more been happy with their performance.

Now he'd all but made up his mind to add to them to his stable, his instinct telling him that, potentially, they might turn out to be a nice little gold mine for him. And as for the lone dissenter, well, he was sure that little problem could be dealt with, if it became necessary.

The man on the door, mightily impressed by his motor, almost bowed him into the dingy club's interior. Titus only hoped things didn't become too manic tonight. When word got around (and it soon would, like wildfire) that he was there and maybe talent-scouting, things had the potential to get silly. Once or twice, his presence had nearly caused a riot at am-dram productions and singing contests, as acts desperate to catch his attention came (in some cases literally) to blows in order to impress him.

From the main room a heavy beat was throbbing and Titus took a deep breath before plunging into the world of hypersexual teenage girls and gyrating dancers. He doubted he'd get a decent drink in this backwater and only hoped that the Rainbirds would be as good as the last time he'd seen them.

And so that Saturday evening at the Bootleggers progressed, more or less, as it had done many times before. Acts came and went, long-haired young men sang sometimes incomprehensible songs, and girls and boys kissed under the cover of darkness, drank too much and (in some rare cases) discreetly imbibed things other than alcohol.

Except this time, and before that particular night was out, an ambulance would have to be called and a dead body would have to be removed.

And a soon-to-be-grieving family would get a knock on their front door and learn that their lives would never be quite the same again.

Chapter 1

Dr Clement Ryder looked over his packed coroner's court with slightly watery grey eyes that missed nothing. There was a preponderance of girls in their late teens clogging up the public galleries, but in the circumstances, Clement didn't regard that as particularly surprising.

At just over six feet, and now nearing his sixtieth birthday, the former surgeon turned city coroner was an impressive figure. With thick silvery-white hair and matching bushy eyebrows, he was dressed impeccably in his favourite dark blue suit, and everyone who felt his gaze on them automatically sat up a little straighter. To begin with, he'd never lost that cool, almost otherworldly confidence of a man who had regularly wielded a scalpel on a helpless human body. Plus, there weren't many people in that room who were unaware that Dr Ryder was someone of power and influence.

That particular Wednesday morning, with the courtroom clock showing that it was just coming up to half past ten, Dr Ryder was observing his latest jury with a slightly weary eye.

Yesterday, he'd opened the inquest on the death of Raymond Reason – a musician found dead at the Bootleggers Club, halfway down a set of spiral iron stairs, having apparently fallen down them. All the witnesses had been questioned, and the medical evidence had been duly given. Unfortunately, they'd started late, and the medical evidence had thrown up some rather complicated issues (picked up on and thoroughly questioned by Clement himself) and so they'd had to reconvene today.

Which meant that the members of the public who had been called upon to do their civic duty and act as coroner's jury were anxious not to waste any more time than they had to in order to get things over and done with. And, unless Clement was totally misreading them (and Dr Ryder very seldom did *that*) they were itching to deliver a verdict of accidental death and then swarm out of the courthouse to hearth and home, work or the nearest pub, depending on their various priorities.

And there was very little that he could do to stop them, much as he might like to.

As a former surgeon, he had listened closely and, far more importantly, *understood* the medical evidence given by the pathologist. Namely, that Ray Reason had received *two* blows to the head, with the *second* one being the fatal injury. But he was not sure that the jury had noted the significance of this, even though he'd tried his best to bring it to their attention with his questioning of the medical expert.

He sighed and straightened a little in his chair. The remainder of the evidence available had now been dealt with, and he had only to give his summing up.

Unluckily for him, he was frustratingly aware that he had no real legal or ethical way of directing them towards the verdict that he thought *should* be brought in. In his opinion, the way and means by which Raymond Reason had met his death could bear much more investigation. But even he had to admit that the evidence simply wasn't there to bring in a verdict for murder by person or persons unknown. Not yet anyway.

Which meant that he could only let the inquest continue to take its due course and finish doing his job in a fit and proper manner. He was damned if he was going to give anyone the opportunity to say he hadn't done his job properly – especially since he might not have his job much longer.

Pushing that thought determinedly aside, he now eyed the jury one by one. Consisting mostly of men with just one lone woman (a rather bored-looking housewife), they all respectfully looked back at him, careful to hide their impatience.

Clement, aware that he was about to have to try and explain to them the difference between a verdict of accidental death and a verdict of death by misadventure, knew that very soon their impatience would give way to total consternation. Because even lawyers and doctors had trouble grasping the difference.

Not that it would matter much in the long run, he thought wryly. Either verdict wouldn't be the right one in this case.

'Ladies and gentlemen of the jury,' he began dryly and politely. 'You have now heard the evidence, and it is up to you to deliver your verdict on how Mr Raymond Reason met his death on Saturday last. Remember, we are only concerned in this court with establishing the *identity* of the deceased – which has, I'm sure you'll all agree, been done to your satisfaction – and *cause* of death. Now, there is no doubt that Mr Reason died due to blunt-force trauma to the head, resulting in a catastrophic brain injury. You will, no doubt, have listened very attentively to the evidence of the doctor who performed the post-mortem.'

As had Clement. *Very* carefully indeed. It was perhaps not surprising, given his former profession as one of the country's top surgeons, that Clement had understood far more than his jury the true significance of the head wounds that the musician had sustained at the Bootleggers Club. Unfortunately, these were not sufficiently suggestive, in themselves, for him to feel justified in confusing the jury by trying to explain their import in the hope that they'd then bring in a verdict of murder by person or persons unknown.

Besides, as he'd just pointed out, their job was simply to say

9

who had died, and how. And Mr Reason had definitely died because of injuries to his head.

'Now, there are several verdicts you may consider,' he continued. 'For instance, suicide.'

Somewhere in the public gallery there was a slight quiver of interest. Probably members of the press, scenting a scandal or a story, Clement thought with distaste. He hurried to squash any such notions.

'But in this case, the deceased was a young man with everything to live for, had showed no signs of depression or despondency to any members of his family or wide group of friends. Nor had he left a suicide note. And you may conclude, besides, that throwing yourself down a short flight of spiral stairs would hardly be likely to guarantee one's own demise.'

The housewife on the jury nodded at the logic of this.

Clement sighed. 'There is also open to you the option of bringing in a verdict of murder by person or persons unknown,' he said, and again a little wave of excitement rippled across the full courtroom.

He paused hopefully, but not even the most intelligent members of his jury seemed to take the hint.

With a grim internal smile, Clement pressed on. 'Which leaves you to consider that Mr Reason met his death either accidentally or by misadventure,' he concluded in resignation.

'Now—' he leaned a little forward in his chair, his face becoming totally impersonal '—I need you to attend to me very closely.'

The oldest member of the jury, a man in his early seventies, blinked nervously, and surreptitiously put his hand to his ear to turn up his hearing aid a notch.

'The law regarding the difference between accidental death and death caused by misadventure can be rather complicated,' he began, and saw his clerk roll his eyes at this massive under-statement. 'In order to bring in a verdict of *accidental* death, you must be reasonably convinced that neither the death *nor* the acts which brought it about were intended.'

At this, four people on the jury blinked, three of them shot the person next to them a quick, blank look and one looked frankly panicked.

'For example,' he rushed on, 'take prescription medication. A person takes something, say an aspirin, for a headache. But they have a bad reaction to it, which causes them to die. That the person died was *unintentional*, but the act of taking the medication *was* intentional. That was not then a truly accidental death.'

Seeing the housewife frown, he tried again. 'Where death can be said to be *truly* accidental, it is in the sense that there was no intentional act which caused that death.'

The old man with the hearing aid very distinctly reached up and turned it off. Clement sighed, but persevered. 'Misadventure, on the other hand, is an *intended* – albeit lawful – act, where death is the *unintended* outcome.'

Now, even the alert young professional types on the jury were looking confused.

Clement was by no means convinced that Ray Reason had died as a result of either accident *or* misadventure. But he was resigned to the fact that the evidence so far could only justify the citing one or the other. So he bit the bullet and did the only thing he could do, in the circumstances, and gave them the push they needed.

'Accidental death reflects death following an event over which there is no human control. If it is your belief that Mr Reason fell down the stairs, hitting his head and causing his death, then you must return a verdict of accidental death.'

The housewife looked relieved. So did the rest of them.

Clement, with a sigh, asked them if they wished to retire in order to discuss the matter and bring in their verdict. But as he suspected, they wanted only to get it over with. As he watched they hastily consulted, selected a foreman, whispered their consent to a unanimous verdict and stated with confidence that Mr Raymond

Reason had met his death due to accidentally falling down an iron spiral staircase, whereupon he had hit his head, causing him to die.

Clement, somewhat wryly, thanked them for their diligence and dismissed them.

In the public gallery, a lot of pretty young girls wept and had to be consoled by other weeping young girls. A few newspaper men scribbled copy that would no doubt later appear in their respective newspapers, bemoaning the tragedy of dying young.

And Dr Clement Ryder, after completing his paperwork and grabbing a very hasty lunch, set off towards the nearest police station to make one Inspector Harry Jennings a very unhappy man.

It wouldn't be the first time he'd done that. But as he strode down the street, blind to the dreaming spires above him and the subfusc-clad students weaving their way around him, he did wonder if it would be the last.

Chapter 2

Inspector Harry Jennings looked up as a peremptory rap came on his office door. But before he could give permission to enter, it was thrust open.

Since he knew no subordinate would ever dare to march in on him without permission, he was expecting a superior officer to enter. But he was not particularly surprised, after a split second of recognition, to see that it was the city coroner instead.

In his early forties, Harry Jennings had thinning fair hair, a big nose that was the bane of his life and hazel eyes. Unmarried, he was still trying to find himself a wife, but for some reason, even though he could offer a nice little home (a rented council house towards Cowley way) and a nice and steady income, the good women of Oxford weren't exactly beating a path to his door.

He had hopes of gaining a promotion soon, however, and had been assiduously working towards that aim. The last thing he needed to see right now was the troublesome Dr Clement Ryder cluttering up his office. The man inevitably brought problems with him.

In the past, the coroner (with the help of one of Jennings' own very junior officers) had been instrumental in uncovering and investigating several deaths that had turned out to be not as

13

cut and dried as the police department had originally thought. Which meant that, along with the kudos that inevitably resulted by presenting the city with yet another successfully solved murder case, also came the internal embarrassment of having had their fat pulled from the fire by the ever-vigilant – and extremely competent – coroner.

It was perhaps not surprising that any visit made by Clement Ryder to the police station instantly gave Inspector Jennings a severe case of the heebie-jeebies.

'Inspector, I need a word with you,' Clement said flatly.

The words caused the Inspector's already despondent heart to sink even further, but he smiled stiffly and invited the old vulture (as he was widely known, but never to his face) to take a seat. As Clement duly folded himself into the chair, the Inspector's mind was frantically trying to anticipate any possible slip-ups they might have made. But for the life of him, he couldn't think how any of their current cases could have attracted the old man's attention.

'It's about the Ray Reason case,' Clement began briskly, helping him out.

'Who?' Jennings responded blankly.

'The inquest on the musician found dead at the Bootleggers Club. I've just come from conducting the inquest.'

Jennings sighed, quickly trawling his memory for the facts. 'This is the young layabout who drank too much and toppled down a nasty flight of stairs, yes?' he mused aloud. Although his department had investigated it, he had assigned it (as a low-priority case) to his right-hand man, Sergeant O'Grady. From the brief reports he'd read, it had seemed a simple enough, open-and-shut case. Some young lad with aspirations to make it onto the radio, wailing out some of that so-called music that was becoming so popular with the youngsters nowadays, had drunk a bit too much at a sleazy nightclub and taken a tumble down the stairs. Cracking his head on the way down. Nothing particularly controversial with that, surely?

He knew that the Bootleggers Club was a thorn in their side, and that a lot of his colleagues had been trying to get enough evidence against the manager to have it shut down for a while now. They suspected under-age drinking on a large scale, and call girls probably did a bit of business there too, and they suspected a spot of dope might be involved. But much as everyone might want to see Felix Simpkins behind bars at last, there had been nothing to indicate that he'd had anything to do with a death on his premises. In fact, logically, if Simpkins had wanted someone dead, the last place he'd have it done would be in his own club.

Nevertheless, the Inspector now eyed the city coroner warily. 'You say you've just held the inquest? What was the verdict the jury brought in?'

'Accidental death,' Clement said reluctantly, but his eyes were twinkling just a little. He knew the way the Inspector's mind worked, and was already anticipating the little skirmish that would come next. And Clement Ryder did enjoy a little skirmish now and then.

'Ah, that's all well and good then,' the Inspector said, his shoulders relaxing just a little. 'So I can cross it off our books.'

'I'm afraid not,' Clement said quietly and firmly.

The Inspector bit back an impatient sigh. Couldn't this bloody coroner just ever let well enough alone? 'If the jury brought in a verdict of accidental death, I'll be recommending to my superiors that we close the case,' he countered, equally firmly, and in a valiant attempt to nip in the bud whatever it was the old vulture was angling for.

'In which case, I'll just have to ask them to open it again,' Clement warned him flatly.

For just a split second, Harry Jennings was about to open his mouth and say that, in which case, the powers that be would thank him politely for his opinion and send him on his way. But then reason – and sanity – returned, and he left the words unsaid. Because both of them knew that if he was determined to

15

make waves, Dr Clement Ryder wouldn't hesitate to do so. And that he had the clout to make those waves whoppers.

For a start, a peer of the realm, no less, had good reason to believe that his son owed his life to this man and WPC Trudy Loveday, the constable who'd worked that case with him. And then there was the sticky fact that his own Superintendent had asked the coroner to investigate a case that had cleared *his* son – posthumously – of murder.

And if all that wasn't enough, there was the undeniable fact to be taken into account that the old vulture certainly did have a nose for smelling when something wasn't quite right. And that, if ignored, he was perfectly capable of going off and investigating without any supervision at all, getting them into all sorts of mess.

No, on the whole, the top brass preferred to have someone keeping a close eye on the coroner when he was in the mood for one of his escapades. And if they had a serving police officer working the case with him, then at least they could take all the credit if (and when) it came to something.

Admitting defeat, the Inspector sighed heavily. 'All right then. Let's have it. What is it about the Reason case that has your nose twitching?'

Clement smiled coolly. 'Is Constable Loveday about?' he asked casually.

Harry again sighed heavily. 'She is,' he agreed. It came as no surprise that the coroner wanted her services yet again, and although he knew he was going to offer them – eventually – it was not in Inspector Jennings' psyche to give up without at least a token fight. 'And if I think she's needed, I can always assign her to assist you again. But I need to know what it's all about first.'

Abruptly, Clement became weary of all the fencing. It had been amusing for a while, but now he was impatient. 'I'd rather not have to explain things twice. It'll save time in the long run, so why don't you just get her in here, and I'll explain the problem to you both?'

Jennings felt a flash of resentment as the temerity of the man shot through him, but was politic enough to tamp it down. Instead, his lips twisted wryly, and he got up and walked to the door. There, he opened it and called through to no one in particular in the outer office, 'Ask Constable Loveday to come to my office at once, will you?'

Chapter 3

WPC Trudy Loveday, called from her seemingly never-ending task of filing in the records office, tugged on the hem of her tunic to make sure that it was straight, tapped on the door of Inspector Jennings' office and waited until he called out for her to enter.

When he duly did so, she stepped smartly into his office, her face a picture of polite respect. Then she spotted Dr Ryder sitting in the chair opposite her superior officer's desk, and her face broke out into a spontaneous, excited smile.

She was smiling because it had been a long while since she'd last seen her friend and mentor – January, in fact – and she was glad to see him. And she was excited because every time the coroner bearded her Inspector in his office it was usually because he wanted something. And the 'something' was nearly always semi-official permission to pursue a possibly criminal matter that had attracted his attention. And whenever Dr Ryder wanted to stick his nose into something, he needed an official police presence in order to do so.

She was under no illusions that it had been the luckiest day of her professional life so far when Inspector Jennings had assigned her to work in tandem with the coroner. For, since the first time they'd joined forces, they'd solved no less than seven murders, and unless she mistook the grim look on the Inspector's face, they were about to start looking into an eighth.

'Take that silly grin off your face, Constable,' the Inspector said irritably, and at once Trudy returned to an attitude of polite respect, all but standing to attention.

'Yes, sir. Sorry, sir.'

Jennings sighed heavily once more, reluctantly but silently acknowledging that it probably wasn't fair to take out his frustration with the old vulture on a lowly constable who was unable to fight back. 'Sit down,' he said to her, a little less abruptly. 'Dr Ryder has just dropped by to bring to our attention …' Here he paused and shot the coroner a flat look. 'But perhaps I'd better let him explain,' the Inspector said with a wry emphasis that Trudy didn't quite understand. But she understood her place enough to bring out her notebook and get ready to take notes.

The Inspector caught the conspiratorial and friendly look that passed between the two, and leaned back in his chair, praying for patience. Either that, or that during the next lightning storm, the coroner was struck by divine intervention.

'Certainly. I've just held the inquest on the death of a Mr Raymond Reason,' Clement began. 'Do you know the case?'

'This is the member of a local pop group who was found dead at the bottom of the stairs in a nightclub where he'd been performing?' Trudy asked, nodding. 'I've read about it in the papers. He was very young, wasn't he?'

'Just turned nineteen,' Clement said heavily. 'And you've not quite got your facts right. He wasn't found dead at the foot of the stairs, but more or less halfway down them.'

Trudy, who was now nearing her twenty-first birthday and felt, after three years in the police, very grown up indeed, sighed. To her, nineteen meant he'd still been almost a boy.

She was a pretty girl: tallish, slim, with a mass of long dark curly hair that she kept ruthlessly restrained and confined under her police cap. She had big brown eyes and long eyelashes that suited her heart-shaped face, and a small smattering of freckles that tended to become more prominent in the summer months, and of which she often despaired.

'Last Saturday night the police were called to the Bootleggers,' Clement continued smoothly, 'after a barman at the club named John Rix had discovered Mr Reason's body halfway down a fairly short set of wrought-iron spiral stairs. You need to make a particular note of that, as it is, in *my* humble opinion—' here he shot a quick scowl at the attentively listening Inspector Jennings '—rather significant.'

Trudy nodded. 'Where was this staircase located exactly?'

'The club has one main dance hall on the ground floor where the acts perform, with a bar area along one side. Off the main room is a series of smaller rooms, consisting of a storage room, a pair of conveniences, the manager's office and a rather filthy kitchen,' Clement said, with a slight moue of distaste.

'The building is old and, as is usual with a building of that age, rather higgledy-piggledy, with twists and turns here and there, and grimy windows leading off to the back alley. About midway between the various back rooms, there is a short spiral staircase – perhaps twenty feet in height or so – which leads down to a basement area. This basement area contains what you might expect: a boiler room, a coal bunker where the coal is delivered, and a much bigger room – probably a former wine cellar – that the club has furbished (and I use that word very lightly) as a common room. This rest area is somewhere for the various acts to hang out when they're not on stage, relax, have something to drink or eat and so on. There are also a couple of screens for them to use if they have to change into costumes or such.'

'So it seems likely that Mr Reason had gone down the stairs to use the common room? What time was this?' she asked, her notebook already possessed of several pages of her neat shorthand.

'He was found at just before nine o'clock. His band … Sorry,

I can't remember at the moment what they were called,' Clement said, hoping that neither Trudy nor – worse – the Inspector would make anything of his memory lapse. 'His band was due to take their turn on the stage in around ten minutes or so.'

'He might have gone down to the common room to change?'

Clement shrugged. 'I don't think so. The manager of the club testified that most of the rock bands came already dressed for their performances. More likely he was just rounding up the rest of the group. Or perhaps he'd gone down for another drink. Some of the performers liked to have a few to steady any nerves or bouts of stage fright, apparently, and the bar staff kept them well supplied with bottles of beer,' Clement said dryly.

'He'd been drinking, in other words,' Jennings put in heavily. 'Not surprising, is it? Young whippersnapper who thought a regular job wasn't good enough for him, and with dreams of becoming the new Cliff Richard or what have you. You can hardly expect that sort to be sensible!'

Clement nodded. 'Perhaps. The post-mortem found he had some alcohol in his system, but not enough to say that he was drunk. And, in my humble *medical* opinion—' he again emphasised his own area of expertise ironically '—certainly not enough to make him so unsteady on his feet, or be so disorientated that he'd be an obvious candidate for falling down the stairs. Especially tightly wound spiral stairs, which are harder to fall down than regular stairs.'

'Because it's almost impossible to fall from the top to bottom of them in a single go, you mean,' Trudy said, nodding in understanding. 'Which explains why he was found halfway down?'

'Precisely,' Clement said, glad to see that she'd lost none of her quick wits since they'd last met. 'His head was nearest the bottom, his feet and legs caught up in the spiral angle above, preventing him falling any further,' Clement confirmed. 'You can see the actual police diagrams and all the testimony from the case back at my office later.'

'Let's not get ahead of ourselves,' Jennings felt obliged to put in. 'You haven't said anything yet that says the jury wasn't right to bring in a verdict of accidental death.'

Clement nodded. 'I'm coming to that. It's the medical evidence that I don't like. And neither did the doctor who performed the post-mortem,' he added for good measure.

This made Jennings shift uncomfortably on his seat. Because when it came to technical or specialist evidence, he knew, the police had no other option but to take an expert's professional opinion seriously, and well the old vulture knew it!

'Know this pathologist, do you? A friend of yours perhaps?' Jennings intimated slyly, still seeking a way out. He wouldn't put it past the old man to get a crony to back up his own theories, if it suited his book.

'Never met him before, actually,' Clement said blithely. 'He's a new chap, apparently, working out of the Radcliffe Infirmary. First time he's given evidence in my court.'

Jennings, defeated, sighed. 'Go on,' he said forlornly.

'According to his findings, Raymond Reason had several bruises and abrasions on his body, all about where you would expect to find them, if the human body came into contact with wrought iron. There is a clear bruise, almost in a straight line for instance, on the underside of his left forearm, where he probably landed heavily on it. As you know, a falling man or woman will usually try to save themselves by flinging out a hand or an arm and trying to get a hold of something, or, failing that, prevent injury to their face by trying to land hands downwards.'

'Yes, I'm aware of that,' Jennings interrupted impatiently. 'But again, so what? You're only confirming that your medical man discovered just what you'd expect of someone who had fallen where his body was found.'

'Yes. It wasn't *that* that Dr Reigate had an issue with,' Clement said through slightly gritted teeth. 'If you'd let me finish? It was the head injury the dead man sustained that was causing him trouble. Or should I say, the *two* head injuries he sustained,' Clement added quietly.

The Inspector drew in a sharp breath. Now they were coming to it. 'He hit his head twice?'

'Yes. The first injury … do you want precise medical terms?' Clement broke in his narrative to ask, a wicked little glint in his eye that had Trudy hiding a smile.

'No, no spare me that,' Jennings said hastily and predictably. 'Just explain it without all the fancy Latin words or bamboozling sentences that you types seem to enjoy so much.'

Clement nodded gravely. 'Very well then. Simply put, Mr Reason sustained two head injuries. The first fractured his skull, but almost certainly, not fatally. It would have rendered him instantly unconscious and caused a concussion, and he'd have had to undergo a spell in the hospital, and suffer some minor side effects from it. Temporary memory loss of the incident, perhaps, and the usual headaches. But, given that he received medical treatment within twelve hours or so, there was no reason why he shouldn't have made a good recovery.'

'I take it the second injury was different?' Trudy prompted gently.

'Hmm? Oh, yes, that was different,' Clement said. He rubbed a hand tiredly across his brow, and Trudy wondered what was distracting him. It was not like Dr Ryder to be anything other than brusque and efficient.

'The second injury was much more forceful, and resulted in bleeding on the brain that led to death within five minutes or so.'

'Well?' Again, the Inspector interjected impatiently. 'What difference does it make which head injury killed him? I still can't see the problem. He'd had a bit too much to drink, was excited about prancing about on stage and stumbled down an awkward set of stairs and bang! He hit his head twice, and there you go. Bob's your uncle.'

Clement smiled wryly. 'Yes. But how did he manage to hit his head twice? That's what I'm wondering.'

23

Both Trudy and the Inspector looked at him curiously. With a sigh, Clement reached out, waggling his fingers for Trudy's notebook. Unquestioningly, she handed it over and he tore a clean page off, then reached across the Inspector's desk and nabbed a pencil from his desk set.

'Look, this roughly represents the set of stairs where Mr Reason died,' Clement began, rapidly sketching. 'At the top, a waist-high railing surrounds the entrance to the stairs, so that the unwary can't just wander into them and take a tumble. After that, a "cage" of sorts follows the steps down. There are two twists – mark that – seven steps apart, in the actual set of stairs.' As he talked, he continued making marks on the piece of paper. 'X marks the spot where he was found, feet pointing up, head pointing down, meaning that he was going *down* the stairs, not up, when he sustained his injuries. Clear so far?'

He handed the sketch first to Trudy – which caused Inspector Jennings to go slightly red-faced in temper – then after she'd absorbed it and nodded in understanding, he passed it to the Inspector.

Jennings all but snatched it from his hand and scowled down at it. 'Obviously there's a point to all this?' he said, forcing himself to look insouciant. He knew that the coroner had a first-class brain, and it galled him to know that the clever old sod had picked up on something that he hadn't. Paradoxically, he had to admit that it gave him a certain sense of satisfaction and pride that the city had someone in office as perspicacious as Clement Ryder. He might be the old vulture, and at times a right pain in the posterior, but he was on *their* side – that is, the forces of law and order.

Like all policemen, Inspector Harry Jennings hated to see criminals get away with anything – but especially with murder.

'All right. Mr Reason was five feet eleven inches tall,' Clement began. 'Given that he was found halfway down the stairs, he must have begun to pitch forward almost instantly – otherwise, he

24

wouldn't have come to rest only halfway down, and before the second of the spirals. You agree?'

'Yes, that's logical enough,' Jennings agreed cautiously. He'd always had a fear of appearing foolish in front of either his superiors or his subordinates – and with WPC Loveday and Dr Ryder he was in double jeopardy!

'So, the first question is, why?' Clement said. '*Why* did he fall almost on the first step? Usually people fall down spiral staircases because of the tight angles of the steps, and you catch your feet and over you go. But not in this case. Here, Raymond Reason started to take a header right at the outset.'

'You think he was pushed?' Trudy put in, her breath catching in excitement.

'It might explain why he pitched down head first, yes.'

'He could just have tripped over his own big feet just as he reached the stairs,' Jennings pointed out with a savage smile.

'Yes, he could,' Clement agreed calmly. 'But it's the first thing that sounds alarm bells. Now, for *whatever* reason,' he continued, 'the dead man falls immediately. He throws out his hands to try and save himself, but can't. He barks his shin (as evidenced by the bruises Dr Reigate found on him) and lands painfully on his arm. It would have hurt like blazes – falling down wooden stairs is bad enough, but there's no bounce or even a bit of "give" in wrought iron. Despite his best efforts, his head hits one of the stairs and he'd see stars, and probably pass out immediately. That's the first blow to his head. Now, because of the second spiral, his body is caught and held by the narrowness of the steps and the cage surrounding it. Hence, he is found halfway down by the barman.'

'So how did he come by the second blow to his head?' Trudy said, catching on at once.

'Exactly. How?' Clement said, nodding at her approvingly.

'Just a minute, couldn't he just have hit his head again? He could have gone head right over heels or something,' Jennings protested.

'How? He was in a tight and confined space, remember,' Clement objected. 'He'd fallen down far enough for his head to come to rest just past the first spiral, not past the second. To have gone head over heels after the initial tumble would have required a lot of forward thrust in order to catapult the rest of his body over his head. He'd have had to be going at a tremendous speed in order to do so. He'd have had to take a running jump at it! And that, you have to admit, is unlikely.'

Jennings studied the rough sketch again, trying to picture it. 'OK, so he fell, barked his shins and arm, and bounced his head off a step – either one of the downward-facing steps, or the one that would now be above him from the twist in the first spiral. Yes, well, why not this? He falls, hits his head once on the *downward* step, then it sort of ricochets back and he hits it a second time on the step that's now *above* him? That might account for it, mightn't it?' he demanded.

Clement surprised him by nodding. For some reason, the Inspector had expected him to be scornful of his theory.

'It's something that occurred to me too – and I think to Gideon Reigate. But it doesn't hold water, I'm afraid. Firstly, it's very unlikely that a man can hit his head twice in the manner you describe. A human body isn't made of rubber and doesn't bounce in quite the way you describe. However, I'm not saying it's totally impossible,' he added quickly, as he saw that the Inspector was about to open his mouth and argue. 'You and I have both been around a while, and seen a few peculiar things in our time. I can't state with certainty that it *couldn't* have happened that way. Just that it was unlikely.'

Mollified, both by the old man's acknowledgement that they were both experienced men of the world, and by the fact that Clement Ryder's undoubtedly superior brain had also considered the theory that he himself had thought of, Jennings nevertheless frowned.

'So what's to say it didn't happen, just this one time?' he persisted.

'Because, Inspector, if it had happened that way, the wound produced would have been very different,' Clement tried to explain. 'Say Mr Reason fell and hit his head on a downward step, then somehow his head snapped up to hit the stair above him, the wounds would have occurred *on different parts of his skull.*'

Jennings blinked and thought about it for a moment, then reluctantly nodded. 'Yes. I can see how that would be,' he conceded. 'And I take it the two wounds occurred in the same area?'

'Yes, roughly speaking. There was a difference of less than half an inch or so,' Clement agreed gravely.

'But isn't it possible that he fell, hit his head on the downward step, then, with his body still not coming to a full stop, somehow went up on his head and hit it a second time on the same downward step? Before coming to a full stop and settling back down, I mean?' Jennings asked. More because he was now definitely curious, rather than because he was still trying to score points off the old man.

'You're forgetting, it was the *second* wound that was fatal. Not the first,' Clement said.

'I don't quite understand that,' Trudy said, seeing that her Inspector didn't either, but wasn't about to say so in front of Dr Ryder.

'Think, Trudy,' Clement urged her. 'Which impact would have been the stronger one? The first one, when he fell with the maximum amount of speed, and his whole weight behind him? Or the second one, when most of the downward momentum would already have been spent? And don't forget, a ricochet is losing power all the time.'

'Oh I see. In that case, it would be the first blow that killed him, not the second!' she said, nodding.

'Wait a minute though,' the Inspector said. 'How come you're so sure in what order he got these bangs on his bonce? Perhaps the first blow was the killer blow, and the second one the lesser one?'

Clement smiled. 'Dr Reigate demonstrated, very clearly with

the X-rays, that the second blow intersected the first one. In other words, the second crack in his skull – the fatal blow – came *after* the first, as the fracture line clearly overlaid it.'

'Damn!' Jennings said.

'Quite,' Clement said, lips twitching. 'Somehow, our Mr Reason managed to go down the stairs, right from the start almost head first, fall, hit the central front top of his head and knock himself out. Then somehow managed to bang his head a second time, in pretty much the same place but with much more force, whilst being confined in a very small space.'

There was silence for a moment as all three digested this.

'What did the jury make of all this?' Trudy asked curiously.

'Dr Reigate only gave the dry medical facts,' Clement temporised.

'But you explained it to them? What you've just told us?' Trudy pressed.

Clement gave a small, slightly helpless shrug. 'No, because there was no point in confusing them,' he said reasonably. 'Neither Dr Reigate nor myself were – or are – in any position, *yet*, to explain just how exactly Mr Reason died in the way he did. Which is why we need to dig a little further. Isn't that right, Inspector?'

He looked challengingly at the Inspector who instinctively scowled.

'After all,' Clement continued smoothly, 'I could have, with just a little time and effort, made it clear to the jury where my suspicions lay, and steered them into delivering a verdict of murder by person or persons unknown. Which would have left the police with no room to manoeuvre at all, and no other choice but to set up a full-scale inquiry. Which, if it turns out to be a storm in a teacup, would leave us all with egg on our faces. But this way, WPC Loveday and I can look at it quietly and discreetly and see if we can't clear it up without a big fuss. You might say I've done you a big favour,' he added with a wolfish grin.

In truth, Clement didn't really care if the police were

inconvenienced or not. He was honest enough to admit to himself that he simply wanted the chance, one last time, to do some sleuthing with his bright and ambitious protégé whilst he still could.

Soon enough, his life would have to change – and not for the better. But for now, none of his sadness showed on his face as he smiled, hawk-like, at the deflated Harry Jennings.

'Fine,' Jennings finally agreed flatly. 'I'll have to run it past my superiors, of course …' he said wearily, already knowing that they'd have to give the green light – or face the unpalatable prospect of the city coroner making them all look like fools. 'Constable, I expect you to keep me thoroughly apprised,' he said, fixing Trudy with a gimlet gaze.

'Yes, sir,' Trudy said smartly. She waited until they had both stepped outside the Inspector's office before giving a huge grin of triumph.

The sight of her happy face made Clement's heart ache a little. As far as she was concerned, this was just the start of another of their adventures. For him though, it was a swan song.

'What do we do first?' she asked eagerly.

'To my office to gather up the files, then I think we'll take them back to my place to work on them. We'll have fewer interruptions there.'

Chapter 4

Vincent Ryder looked up from his book as he heard his father's Rover P4 pull up outside the house. The coroner lived in a Victorian house overlooking the park, and Vincent had many fond memories of growing up here as a child, with his twin sister Julia.

Since moving away from home nearly ten years ago, he'd come to appreciate the beauty of the city he'd grown up in, and it hadn't taken much to persuade himself that he really *did* want to take his summer holiday break here this year.

Of course, at the back of his mind, he also knew that he'd come to see how his father was doing.

Back in January, when the whole country had been in the grip of a vicious winter, he'd found himself snowed in with his parent after spending Christmas with him. And it was as a result of that enforced and prolonged period of closeness that he'd come to slowly understand that his father was not a well man.

Oh, being Dr Clement Ryder, he'd hid it well. And, as it turned out, had been managing to hide it well for a number of years, for it was not in his nature to ever acknowledge or give in to weakness.

At first, Vincent hadn't wanted to acknowledge his niggling and growing doubts, for – like most children – Vincent had always thought of his father as immortal and invincible. And given Clement's personality, perhaps he could be forgiven for continuing to sort of believe it, well into his adult years.

But the occasionally trembling hands (in a man who'd once been a surgeon) and his tendency to trip, even when there was no obstacle underfoot, finally forced Vincent to confront him and demand to know what was going on.

And, very reluctantly, his father had obliged him, telling him just why he'd been forced to retire from medicine, and retrain to be a coroner. Because he had Parkinson's disease.

Vincent, an architect, had no idea what that was or what it meant, and stiffly, not quite meeting his son's eyes, Clement had had to explain it to him.

Along with losing his mother, that day rated as one of the worst times of Vincent's life.

But his father, with his usual brusque manner that made it clear that any pity or sympathy would be anathema to him, had assured his son that he still had many good years left in him yet. Although there was no cure for his illness, there *were* things that he could do to slow the decline, and as a medical man, he knew just what they were, and was doing them. And slowly, bit by bit, he'd managed to mitigate his son's shock and dismay.

But Clement had also made it clear that there was nothing Vincent could do, and that he fully expected his son to return to his own life and his own world, and not to make a fuss. He'd also extracted a reluctant promise from Vincent not to tell his sister just how things were either. Julia, he'd insisted, had her work cut out for her as it was, looking after her husband, home and young children. She didn't need anxiety about her father added to her burden. After all, what could she actually do, except worry?

And so Vincent had agreed to toe the line. He'd duly gone back to Cheltenham, and telephoned a little more often, and came over every other month or so for the odd weekend. And whenever he did so, he pretended that nothing was wrong, as his father clearly wanted.

And if Vincent's request that he spend his summer holiday this year in Oxford had made his father hesitate slightly, Clement had nevertheless happily agreed.

It was tacitly understood, however, that his health would not be up for discussion.

Now, as he watched his father climb from his car, Vincent felt a familiar pang, deep in his chest. He watched as Clement reached down behind him to pull his walking cane from where it had been lying beside the driver's seat. He made a show of using it as a fashion accessory, but Vincent knew he carried it now in case he stumbled.

Then he saw the passenger door open and a police cap emerged, followed by the figure of a tall, slender girl.

Trudy!

Vincent felt another pang in his chest, but this time, its origin came from a very different place than that produced by the sight of his ailing father.

He'd only been in town two days, but Clement had already mentioned that he wasn't satisfied with the way his latest inquest was going. He'd confided that he had even been toying with the idea of getting the police to look more deeply into the death of some musician or other, and now it looked as if he'd actually done so.

And, of course, he'd asked for Trudy Loveday to help.

When Vincent had first met Trudy back in January, he hadn't been best pleased to discover that his father had somehow been roped into doing what he thought of as police work, and he had (unjustly as it quickly turned out) blamed the young WPC for it.

But then he too had been drawn into the fascinating case of a man found dead and frozen in his crashed car on New Year's Day. He had quickly come to see that his father was, and always had been, the driving force behind being allowed to 'investigate' some cases that aroused his curiosity.

Not that this had surprised him much. His father had always loved solving puzzles, and always managed to get his own way.

For a very short while, Vincent had worried that the pretty WPC might have turned his father's usual rock-like head, but that fear too had quickly evaporated. You'd have to have been blind not to see that Clement looked on the young police officer as his protégé and that she looked upon him only as a father figure and mentor.

Now he put the book down and walked quickly out to the front door, opening it for them just as they approached.

Trudy looked up, slightly startled as the door opened for them as if by magic, and spotted Vincent. And he was gratified and immensely glad to see that her face lit up in a spontaneous smile of welcome.

'Vincent! I didn't know you were here,' Trudy said warmly.

'My son's taking his summer holidays with his old man,' Clement said, a shade dryly. Of course, the coroner knew full well that Vincent's visit wasn't down entirely to him enjoying a holiday on the cheap. But so far, at least, he hadn't caught his son being overly solicitous towards him. Which was just as well.

'That's nice,' Trudy said, and meant it. She herself was very close to her family, and she didn't like to think that Dr Ryder might sometimes feel lonely, living by himself.

'Trudy, lovely to see you,' Vincent said politely. It wouldn't do for him to sound too pleased to see her, after all. Having just reached his thirtieth birthday, he was feeling a little sensitive to the fact that this girl was at least nine years his junior.

Then he caught the glint of amusement in his father's knowing eye, and flushed slightly. 'Come on in, I'll put the kettle on,' he added woodenly.

Not noticing his sudden awkwardness, Trudy nodded and stepped inside. Vincent, who was his father's height but of a more wiry build, pressed himself against the wall so that she could pass by easily. With light brown hair that could look gold under certain lighting, he had his mother's hazel eyes with flecks of green. He hadn't ever thought of himself as a vain man, but right then, he rather wished he had the more dashing looks of someone like Stewart Granger or Cary Grant.

Again, he saw his father's flickering glance of amusement and shot him a withering look in return.

'Would you prefer tea or coffee, Trudy?' Vincent called pleasantly.

'Tea please,' Trudy called back.

Vincent, still slightly flushed, retreated quickly to the kitchen,

Clement, highly amused, carried on into the living room, the Ray Reason case files tucked firmly under his arm.

Unless he missed his guess, things were going to get very interesting indeed in the next few days.

Chapter 5

'You're basically basing your whole "it-wasn't-an-accident" theory on the fact that Ray Reason hit his head twice?' Vincent said cautiously. Half an hour had passed, during which time Clement, Trudy and Vincent had gone over the case files. Somehow, it had been established – without anyone actually saying so – that Vincent would be helping them investigate the musician's death. There was a precedent for this, since he'd played a small part in helping them conclude their last case together.

'Not just that,' Clement said now, tapping the paper folder thoughtfully. 'You've got to take into account the fact that *you've* only read the dry black-and-white transcripts of the witness statements, whereas I had the advantage of watching and listening to them give their testimony on the witness stand.'

'And you thought some of them were lying?' Trudy asked curiously. She wasn't questioning his prowess, since she'd back his instinct and judgement any day of the week, she was just making sure that she didn't miss anything.

Clement, though, was fair and impartial enough to give that some obvious thought before he gave a small shrug. 'Let's just say, I got the feeling that a number of them were very relieved when they'd finished giving their evidence. And even more relieved when my follow-up questions were over.'

'Well, Dad, that really needn't mean anything sinister,' Vincent said, with a dry smile and a quick, conspiratorial glance Trudy's way. 'You may not realise it, but you can come across as being rather … er … intimidating at times.'

Seeing Clement give his son a long look, Trudy hastily tried to smooth things over. 'And don't forget, Dr Ryder, that you're used to being in a court, so you feel more or less at home there. But for most witnesses it's their first time coping with something judicial. And the atmosphere and pomp and everything can be rather overwhelming. Having to take an oath can make some people very nervous anyway. They were probably just afraid of doing or saying the wrong thing somehow, or making a fool of themselves or somehow landing themselves in trouble.'

Clement smiled. '*Et tu, Brute?*' he said.

Trudy, who had no idea what the words meant, blinked nervously.

Clement made a show of relaxing back in his seat. 'Despite what you two youngsters may fondly imagine, I'm not totally unaware of how people think, feel and act, given certain circumstances. I was only a surgeon for twenty-five years, and have only been dealing with the bereaved, the injured, the wronged and the wrongdoers, for the past six.'

Both Vincent and Trudy looked abashed at this gentle – but apposite – reprimand.

'So perhaps you might just give me the benefit of the doubt,' Clement went on, half amused, half not, 'when I say that I think I'm pretty good at spotting when someone's holding something back.'

'Of course you are, Dr Ryder,' Trudy said at once. 'So who was it who aroused your suspicions exactly? And how?' She knew that drawing him back into the specifics of the case was the best way of soothing his irritation, but she was also desperate to know what else the wily coroner knew that she didn't.

'For a start, the manager of the club.'

Trudy nodded. 'I don't know much about the Bootleggers, but I know it was raided a few times by some of my colleagues and nothing came of it. It's still open and doing business. But I can always check the records and see what I can find out about it.'

'Good, that's a starting point,' Clement said. 'But I don't need police confirmation to know that our Mr Felix Simpkins is a wrong 'un,' he said dryly. 'It's no great secret that he's an Oxford villain, born and bred. I remember hearing round and about that he had been something big in the black market during the war. That sort usually end up in jail at some point or other, so I think you'll find that he was probably in and out of prison fairly regularly in his youth. Which might explain why he only manages, rather than owns, the club. No one would have given him a licence. But presumably he's kept his nose relatively clean during his later years, since I can't see the real owners of the club giving him the job otherwise.'

'Do we know who the real owners are?' Vincent put in.

'Not offhand, but I'm assuming they aren't exactly lily-white themselves,' Trudy said angrily. 'There are people about that we, the police, know are outright crooked, but they don't have a stain on their character. My Inspector has a real bee in his bonnet about them, and I don't blame him. And they have a habit of hiding behind lower-grade crooks like Mr Simpkins when it comes to running their businesses.'

'Right! So a chap like that isn't going to like giving evidence, even if it is only to a coroner's court,' Vincent pointed out practically. 'And it's hardly surprising that you thought he was being shifty. Having a punter die in the club he manages must have given him a nasty turn. He might have been worried he'd lose his job for a start.'

'Oh he was a worried man, all right,' Clement confirmed with a grim smile. 'And yes, I dare say his masters weren't happy with the bad publicity a dead body gave the club. But I still say he was suffering from more than just the usual jitters. I'd be prepared to bet a shilling or two that he knew something specific that he was holding back.'

'So do we start with questioning him?' Vincent asked, then looked at Trudy as she gave a soft snort of amusement. 'What?'

'Oh, we can *talk* to him,' Trudy said. 'But we won't get anything out of him,' she predicted.

Clement glanced at her with a look that was both oddly approving, but also a little sad. She had certainly come a long way since he'd first known her, he mused, when she'd been just nineteen and as innocent and green as grass. And although he'd always known that that couldn't continue, and that life in her chosen career would inevitably harden her and give her a more realistic and cynical view of the world, it still gave him a pang to see it happening.

But he ruthlessly squashed any feelings of sentimentality. Soon she'd be truly on her own, and she wouldn't have him to help or guide her. And she would need all her newly acquired toughness in order to survive both the ridiculous prejudices of her own colleagues and the machinations of the criminals she'd be pitted against.

He sighed and, catching his son watching him closely, turned the smile into a grin. 'Trudy's right. I doubt we can expect much cooperation from the likes of Felix Simpkins.'

'But there was someone else, wasn't there, who you thought was holding back?' Trudy said perspicaciously.

'Yes. Two, actually. Ray Reason's girlfriend Linda Kempson, and another member of the band. Both were there because they knew the deceased and to give testimony as to the timeframe of what happened that evening, and both seemed to answer some of my question with, shall we say, very carefully chosen words.'

'Don't all witnesses choose their words carefully?' Vincent put in.

'I wish!' his father said, this time with a genuine grin. 'No, you'd be amazed at some of the things I hear. But usually, most witnesses are honest and to a degree spontaneous. The first few questions you put to them may make them flutter a bit with nerves, but as a general rule, once you get past that and strike up a rapport, you can tell that the answers they give are genuine. But both the dead man's girlfriend and his fellow band member kept a very tight hold on their tongues.'

'You think they actually lied about what happened the night he died?' Trudy asked, and Clement frowned thoughtfully.

'No,' he eventually said, surprising both the younger people, who'd expected a very different answer. 'It was more that I felt they were very careful to make sure that the answers they gave were satisfactory – to them.'

'As opposed to helping your court get at the truth,' Trudy said. Yes, she could quite see why that would ruffle Dr Ryder's feathers. If there was one thing that made him irascible (and many things did) somebody trying to put one over on him would probably head the list.

'So what *did* happen that night? According to your witnesses anyway?' Vincent asked. Although he'd read the notes, it wasn't the same as listening to it actually being described out loud. Already he was beginning to feel the thrill that came with the pursuit of the truth, and once again, he could understand why his father enjoyed himself so much when it came to his forays into solving crimes.

It was such a pity that he was going to have to give them up now.

'Let me explain the set-up at the Bootleggers, as far as it was explained to me,' Clement began. 'The club is in Walton Street and has always been popular with, shall we say, the more grubby side of Oxford's citizenry. Ironically enough, it's because it enjoys this bad reputation that it has become so popular with the growing youth culture. In recent years it's attracted the more daring teenagers who want to drink and dance and listen to pop.'

At this, Vincent had to grin. He didn't know that his father even knew who the Beatles were, let alone the short term for popular music.

'The club, obviously, is very keen to accommodate them. Felix Simpkins isn't the sort to see a potential whole new income stream slip through his fingers. Every Saturday night, he sells them booze and stolen cigarettes at outrageous prices, and to keep them entertained, brings in local pop bands to perform on the stage.'

Here he paused and reached into his jacket pocket to pop a strong breath mint into his mouth. He'd become used to sucking on them as they masked his breath. Alas, halitosis was a possible symptom of his illness, and whilst he didn't think he suffered from it in particular, he was too fastidious to chance it. 'He doesn't hire any of the better-known bands, however – probably because he'd have to pay them a decent fee. Instead he lets youngsters wanting to get a break and perform in front of a live audience have a "spot" on the stage during the evening.'

'And doesn't pay them a penny,' Vincent suggested, his voice grudgingly impressed.

'Right. In fact, I wouldn't be surprised if we don't find out that some backhanders have been going on, and some of these exploited youngsters actually pay *him* for the privilege,' Clement agreed.

'I'm surprised they put up with it,' Trudy muttered.

'Ah, but here's the rub. It sometimes works, and they know it. And the dead man's band, the Rainbirds, are a good case in point,' Clement explained. 'According to Martin Cuthbertson (he's the member of the Rainbirds I mentioned earlier who testified in court – the other one I think was being very careful about what he said) his band owe their growing success to performing regularly at the club. The "fans" began to recognise them, which, apparently, is the first big step.'

'Doesn't sound as if it's any big deal to me,' Vincent argued. Unlike his father he did enjoy pop music and listened to it often, but he would be the first to admit that he didn't have any idea of how the industry actually worked.

'I agree,' Clement said dryly. 'But let's stick to what we *do* know. The Rainbirds is a group of five, of which Ray Reason and Martin Cuthbertson are the leading members. They've been formed for nearly a year, and were unknown until they got a "gig" at the Bootleggers. The teenagers liked them and their songs, and began demanding to hear them. This meant they were able to climb the greasy ladder to getting a spot every Saturday, and at the best time too – the nine-to-ten spot.'

'Hardly world-shattering, even so,' Vincent continued to argue.

Clement nodded. 'Perhaps. But it was getting them noticed, which I think is the point Mr Cuthbertson was making. I imagine the Rainbirds saw themselves attracting the attention of a radio station and getting some airtime, perhaps? Which in turn could lead them towards attracting the attention of a record company? I don't know how these things work, so I may not have that quite right. In any event, the Rainbirds were the star attraction for their teenage fans.'

He paused to pour himself a second cup of nearly cold tea and took a sip.

'The night Mr Reason died, as far as I can tell, wasn't in any way unusual,' he continued. 'The band members began to arrive individually at the club around seven, and went down to the basement common room to set up their equipment and drink beer. Both Mr Reason's and Mr Cuthbertson's girlfriends arrived a little later in order to listen to them perform and dance.

'During the evening – again according to the testimony of the witnesses – Mr Reason was behaving perfectly normally. He didn't seem agitated or particularly excited about anything. He split his time between watching the earlier bands perform so that he could assess if they might be serious competition, having a drink at the bar, talking to his fellow performers and various hangers-on in the common room, and taking the odd trip or two to the gentlemen's lavatories.'

Clement swirled his teacup thoughtfully. 'At around a quarter

41

to nine, four members of the Rainbirds were in the common room and were getting themselves ready for their star turn. At that point, Raymond Reason wasn't there, and it was generally assumed that he was still upstairs in the dance room, probably canoodling with his girlfriend. The first they knew that something was wrong was when a member of the previous star turn, now resting in the common room, left to go upstairs, but couldn't because of a commotion around the spiral stairs. Someone above was shouting down at him to keep the area clear, and that an ambulance had been called.'

'The barman had just found the body at that point?' Trudy put in.

'Yes. Again, according to the statements, Martin Cuthbertson and the rest of the Rainbirds began to hear rumours circulating in the common room that someone had found a dead body on the stairs, and that it was Ray. The girlfriends of both Ray and Martin Cuthbertson – Linda Kempson and a Miss Jennifer Renfrew – were both upstairs at this time, listening to the eight-to-nine band finishing up. But pretty soon they too began to hear rumours that something bad had happened, and gradually got to hear that it was Raymond Reason who had come to some sort of grief.'

'What happened then?' Vincent asked.

'Felix Simpkins at least had the sense to keep everyone away from the stairs, which was a blessing for Mr Reason's girlfriend. The ambulance came, the attendants established that he was dead and the police were called. It wasn't until they were able to move the body that those effectively trapped downstairs were able to get out.'

'And nobody saw him fall down the stairs?' Vincent said.

'No. Or at least, nobody admitted to seeing it happen.'

'But the club must have been packed,' Trudy put in sceptically.

'True. But don't forget, the vast majority of people there were actually in the main dance hall, either to listen to the band, drink or dance. The majority of the staff were either at the bar or working the door. Only a few people would have any reason to be backstage or working back-of-house. The barman who found the body only did so because the bar was running low on gin, and he'd gone back to the furthest storeroom to get some more – and noticed feet lying at an odd angle on the fifth step of the stairs. Because of the tight angle of the spiral, he couldn't actually see the rest of the body clearly. But even so, the sight must have looked odd.'

For a moment all three were silent and solemn as they pictured this.

'Presumably, then, we can rule out anyone down in the basement.' Trudy broke the silence tentatively. 'I mean, if they were trapped down there, then there can't have been any way out except up the stairs? There wasn't a tiny window, or a back door or anything?'

'No, the stairs were the only exit,' Clement confirmed. 'I studied the blueprints of the building.'

'If he was pushed down the stairs, it had to have been someone who'd been in the main room or come through the front door?' she mused.

'Unless,' Vincent said, 'someone lay in wait from him on the stairs below and grabbed him by the lapels or something and yanked him forward?'

Clement gave his son an approving glance. 'Yes. We know Mr Reason came down the stairs very violently, face forward. Which means he was either pushed from behind or impelled from the front. The head wounds would have been in the same place, either way it was done.'

'We can't rule out anyone at all?' Trudy sighed.

'No, I'm afraid we can't,' Clement said quietly.

Almost as one, the three of them sighed slightly and leaned back in their chairs. 'So that's what we're up against,' Vincent said at last, nodding his head.

Trudy began to contemplate the task in front of them. One thing instantly became very clear. This was not a case that could be solved by technical evidence, because there would be very little. Even if she could persuade her Inspector to launch a full-scale investigation, which was extremely doubtful, what would they find? The staircase would be alive with fingerprints – and even if they did find the prints of some of the major players in the case, so what? Felix Simpkins, the band members and their girlfriends, all of them must have gone down those stairs many times in the past.

There was no murder weapon to find and process.

And no witnesses had come forward.

'If we're going to get to the bottom of this,' she said thoughtfully, 'we're going to have to find out who wanted Ray Reason dead. Motive is going to be key. We have no other way in, or starting point.'

'I agree,' Clement said, who'd been thinking along much the same lines.

Vincent, although slightly surprised by their quick agreement, was willing to go along. He knew they had far more experience at this sort of thing than he had, and he was desperate that he be allowed to help. Which meant following their lead and not making waves.

'So how do we go about that?' he asked.

Trudy slowly looked across at Dr Ryder. 'We need to get *inside* their world,' she said simply.

She knew that the coroner wouldn't like what she was going to propose next, because he was very protective of her, but she knew she would have to ignore, for once, his objections.

'No!' Clement said, almost at once.

Vincent stared at him, but his father was too busy scowling at Trudy to notice. 'It's too dangerous,' Clement added firmly.

'What?' Vincent yelped.

'It's the only way, Dr Ryder. I'm the only one who could fit in, and get people talking to me.'

'What?' Vincent said again, beginning to feel annoyed and worried in equal measure.

'She wants to go "under cover" at that bloody club.' Clement scowled at his son.

'It makes sense,' Trudy objected firmly before Vincent could respond. 'I can pass as a music fan, and out of uniform I can make myself look a few years younger. I can mingle and chat with the girl fans, and get to know the singers and players.'

'Yes, and you know what they think of girls who do that,' Clement said bitingly.

It made Trudy blush, because, of course, she did know that everyone would get the impression she was … well … no better than she ought to be.

Vincent finally caught on, and not surprisingly, immediately agreed with his father. 'Trudy, you can't! What if some guitar-playing, drunken gorilla gets you into a dark corner and tries it on?'

'I can handle myself,' Trudy said flatly. 'I'm not totally defence-less!' Although she had no idea if she could hide her police truncheon in a handbag. 'And I have my police training. I can throw a man on the floor faster than you can say Jack Robinson.'

'Which won't help you if there are more than one of them,' Vincent said, before his father could. 'The thing about bands is, they come in groups, remember?'

Trudy, facing two set faces, stubbornly dug her heels in. 'And exactly how far will we get, do you suppose, if Dr Ryder goes to the club this Saturday night and starts asking leading questions? Do you think the likes of Felix Simpkins will answer him? Or young girls who've probably sneaked out of the house, telling their unsuspecting parents they were going to a friend's house? Can you see them chatting happily to a man who's got "authority" practically stamped on his forehead? Or the band members, who'll take one look at him and think he's nothing but an old duffer beneath their notice?'

Clement knew she had a point, and for a moment couldn't think of a counter-argument.

Taking advantage of it, Trudy ploughed on relentlessly. 'But a young fan, who looks like they do, dresses like they do and fawns over the bands and the music like they do – I'll just become invisible. The majority of the people who were there when Ray Reason died will be there again this Saturday. I can mingle and chat to people – they'll be only too happy to gossip,' she swept on eagerly. 'After all, being at the spot where someone "famous" died just yards away from them will be the hot topic of the night. Everyone will be talking about it, and anyone who might have seen something, or knows something that they'd never let on to the proper authorities, would talk to me about it without a qualm.'

Seeing that she was serious, Vincent glared at his father. 'Do something! Talk her out of it!' he demanded.

But Clement was already shaking his head. He could see that she was going to go ahead with it, with or without them. And without them, she would be doubly vulnerable.

Suddenly, Clement turned and looked at his son, assessing him minutely. 'You'll just have to go with her,' he said flatly.

'What?' Trudy said, startled.

'What?' Vincent said, at the same time.

'You can dress down. Get a trendy haircut. You could pass for five years younger,' his father said succinctly.

Vincent was about to deny that vociferously. For a man of thirty, being told that he could pass for a pop-loving near-teenage boy was utterly demeaning. Then he caught the hard glare in his father's eye, and saw him jerk his chin slightly in Trudy's direction, and he finally cottoned on.

It was not his pride that mattered. It was protecting Trudy Loveday from potential harm.

'Oh, er, yeah, I can do that,' he muttered. Then he looked across at Trudy and smiled.

'Fancy a date this Saturday night then, darlin'?' he said, in an atrocious wide-boy manner. 'I know this smashing little club in Walton Street where they sell bootleg booze and smuggled smokes an' everyfink!'

Trudy, looking between the two men, knew when it was time to accept a compromise. She was not silly, after all, and having someone watching her back *would* be safer.

And if some part of her was rather actually looking forward to dancing close to Vincent Ryder on a dark and cramped nightclub dance floor, then so what?

'Fine,' she said, less than graciously.

'That's settled then,' Clement said. 'At the weekend, you two can go and see what you can find out from the regulars at the club. In the meantime, we need to make a plan of action.'

Chapter 6

Ray Reason's parents lived on the far outskirts of Banbury, a market town in the north of Oxfordshire. The town's two main claims to fame were its mention in an old English nursery rhyme, exhorting you to *'ride a cock horse to Banbury Cross, to see a fine lady upon a white horse'* and Banbury cakes, a delicious and long-standing recipe that was still sold in bakeries today.

Neither Clement nor Trudy, however, were tempted to stop at a shop and buy any of the goodies, and neither did more than cast a quick look at the Banbury Cross itself, a statue of horse and lady, as they drove by.

Trudy, who had now passed her driving test (thanks to Dr Ryder teaching her to drive in his Rover) was nevertheless surprised when he'd allowed her to do the driving today. Although he'd taken her side when she'd told him that the police only sponsored young male PCs to pass their driving test, he still always preferred to take the wheel himself whenever they went anywhere.

She was wise enough to know that this was not a reflection on his assessment of her abilities, but because the coroner liked to feel in control at all times and in all circumstances. So when he'd tossed her the keys outside his house and asked if she'd like to do the driving, she'd been a little disconcerted.

It had been a while since she'd been behind the wheel (at work, she still had to use a police-issue bicycle more often than not) so she drove very carefully and a little bit slowly – and wondered why Dr Ryder was now content to be a passenger in his own car.

Over the three years or so since they'd been working together, she had wondered sometimes about some of the things that she noticed, every now and then, about her mentor. The way his hand shook at odd little moments. The strong breath mints he always chewed. His tendency to shuffle his feet when he became tired. In the early days, she did wonder if the great man might have drunk a little more than was good for him, but she'd quickly come to realise that she'd been traducing him. The coroner might be a social drinker, but he never drank whilst at work. She'd simply dismissed the signs as things that happened to people as they grew older.

Now, though, she began to wonder all over again. Was he looking just a little more frail than before? He might have lost a bit of weight too. Although he was still his bluff, no-nonsense self, was he just a little less forceful than usual? Or was she imagining things now?

'Watch out for the signpost for Cropredy,' Clement said, breaking into her fretful musings and forcing her mind back onto the task in hand. 'They don't live in the village, but the road where their house is situated should be in the same direction.'

'I see it,' Trudy said, and after glancing in the mirrors, made the correct signal and turned.

Back at Clement's house, they'd agreed that they needed to start with the dead boy's parents – and that all three of them turning up at once might be overwhelming for the grieving couple. Since the Reasons would already be familiar with the coroner from their appearance in his court (giving evidence of the deceased's identity) and with Trudy wearing her police uniform to lend officialdom to the meeting, it was, naturally, Vincent who had to stay behind.

To stop him feeling left out, they'd asked him to go to the

library and read all the press articles he could find on the story so far, and take any notes that he found interesting. Trudy could tell by the look he gave her that he knew he was being fobbed off, but he'd taken it in good part.

As she thought about Dr Ryder's son, she felt a warm feeling steal over her, and tried to ignore it. After all, he was thirty! And Dr Ryder's son. And wasn't he a professional man in his own right? If she remembered correctly – and she knew she did – he was a junior partner in a firm of architects. Such a man was way out of a humble, working-class girl's league.

'I think this is their house just here on the left.' Clement's voice once again dragged her wandering thoughts back to reality, and she carefully pulled over, parking the big car almost perfectly. She turned off the ignition, feeling ridiculously pleased with herself.

Clement, noticing it, bit back a small smile. 'A very smooth drive, and excellent parking if I may say so,' he complimented her. It wasn't her fault, after all, if he was being forced to take every opportunity these days to be driven, rather than drive himself. Although he still felt safe behind the wheel, it tired him more than he liked to admit and, as a coroner, he knew all about the fatal consequences that could result from driver fatigue.

It was, of course, yet another reminder of why he was going to write his letter of resignation within the next few days.

When he'd had to confess to Vincent at the beginning of the year about his incurable illness, he'd promised his son that this year, 1963, would be his last working year.

But, Clement reminded himself firmly, he still had these last few months to enjoy and make the most of. And he was not going to let depression or gloom deprive him of his last hoorah!

'Thank you, Doctor.' Trudy beamed at him.

Clement looked at her face, pretty and proud, and wondered if she realised just how smitten his son was with her. He thought, on the whole, probably not. For such a pretty girl, Trudy Loveday lacked a certain amount of self-confidence.

But that would change soon enough, he thought, given human nature and the changes that time always wrought. And then, with a pang, he thought that it was a pity that he probably wouldn't be there to see it all happen.

He took a deep breath and got out of the car. He didn't know that his face looked grim and bleak at that moment, or that Trudy had seen it.

Her own smile wiped out, she climbed out of the car after him and swallowed hard. Something *was* wrong. She knew it. At his home, as they'd eagerly discussed the case with Vincent, she'd sensed something unspoken going on between father and son. Some tacit, unhappy thing that hovered, just out of sight, unwanted, unacknowledged, but nevertheless there between them.

She'd tried to pretend she was mistaken, and for a while, had even managed to believe it. Especially when they'd been going over the details of their latest case, and they'd all been so caught up and interested in what might have happened the night Ray Reason died. Dr Ryder's old familiar excitement and determination had been there, the same as it always was, and it had been reassuring.

But now that sense of something bad, of something looming, was back. Just one look at her friend and mentor's face had reinforced it. And it left her feeling a little scared and a little cold.

As if someone had just walked over her grave.

'We'll have to be gentle with them,' Clement said, looking up at the semi-detached council house with its grey render and red-tiled front porch roof. 'Their loss is still raw.'

Trudy saw him turn to look at her, and forced herself to get a grip and stop being silly. She put a slight, sombre smile on her face and stiffened her backbone. 'Yes,' she agreed simply.

Whatever was wrong, she knew Dr Ryder would tell her in his own time. Until then – they had a job to do. A very important job, which the Reasons, whether they knew it or not, were relying on them to do well.

Chapter 7

Larry Reason worked as a dustman for the local council so was out at work, but Rosie Reason answered the door promptly at their knock. The housewife looked tired and drawn, with dark rings under her eyes and a blank gaze that seemed to take them in, but somehow not care who they were, or what they wanted.

It wasn't until Clement introduced himself that she visibly took herself in hand. 'Oh, yes, you're the man who was at our Ray's inquest. Come on in,' she exhorted them, glancing quickly left and right as she did so, to see if any of the neighbours' curtains were twitching. But Trudy got the feeling she did it out of habit, rather than because of any real sense of worry as to what her peers might be gossiping about her.

In Rosie Reason's world nowadays, being respectable could hardly matter, Trudy thought sadly. She hoped that Ray wasn't the bereaved mother's only child, and as Rosie ushered them into a cool, dusted and rarely used front room, she was relieved to see photographs of two other children – both girls – displayed on a sideboard, along with other family mementos.

'Please, sit down. Would you like tea?' Rosie asked, vaguely looking around, as if she'd forgotten in which direction the kitchen lay. She was a tall, thin woman, wearing a flowered apron over a dark blue skirt, and a white V-necked jumper that looked hand-knitted.

'No thank you, Mrs Reason. We're here because we want to conduct some follow-up investigations into what happened the night Raymond died,' Clement said gently, keeping his explanations deliberately vague. He didn't think Mrs Reason was the sort to demand to know any particulars – such as why the police were still looking into things about her son's death after an accidental verdict had been given – and in this he proved to be right. She simply nodded and sat down obediently, patiently awaiting what was to happen next. Hers was the generation that respected authority and obeyed it without making a fuss.

'Ray still lived here at home with you, didn't he?' Trudy began. Before leaving the house, they'd agreed that she would lead the questioning, thinking that Mrs Reason would be happier and feel easier talking to another woman, rather than Clement, who could seem somewhat intimidating.

Instantly, Rosie Reason turned to look at her. She had long dark hair going grey, which she kept swept up in a bun on the back of her neck, and a rather pointy nose and chin. But for all that, she was still a handsome woman. 'Yes, that's right, love,' she said quietly. Her accent was soft with a country burr that wasn't Oxonian. Maybe she'd been born in Devon or Dorset, Trudy guessed.

'And when he left to go and sing that night, did he seem any different from his usual self?' she asked.

'Oh no, love – he seemed much the same as usual. Cheerful, and looking forward to singing, like. He always loved to sing, even as a lad.'

She surprised Trudy by getting up suddenly, but it was only so that she could walk to the sideboard and pick up a photograph. When she brought it back and handed it to Trudy, she could see that it depicted a boy of about twelve or so. No doubt it had been taken at school, by one of those photographers who did the rounds and produced likenesses for their proud parents to buy at a discount.

Trudy could see, even at his young age in the photo, that Ray Reason was going to grow up to be a handsome man. With black hair and dark blue eyes (Black Irish, her granny would have said), he had a foxy-shaped face, and looked as if he'd shoot up like a bean sprout in a few years' time to become a tall and lean adult, like his mother.

'Sang in the choir, he did, and entered talent shows when he was old enough,' Rosie said proudly. 'He always had a good, strong voice, he did. I wish we could have afforded lessons for him, but …' She shrugged her thin shoulders philosophically. 'And then all this modern bang-bang-bang music came along, and he used to laugh and twirl me around and say it was going to change the world. That we could forget old fogeys like Glenn Miller and the big band music that me and Dad like to listen to. That rock'n'roll had swept away all the old ways, and now the new wave of music would lead the way into a brave new world. I couldn't see it myself—' she gave a small, sad smile '—but Ray lived for that band of his. He was convinced he was going to be more famous than Frank Sinatra, bless him. Dad used to laugh at him, but we liked to see that he had a big dream.'

Dad, Trudy knew in this case, didn't refer to Rosie's own father, but to her husband.

'And did Mr Reason approve of his son wanting to get into the world of pop music?' Trudy asked with a curious smile.

Rosie actually managed a sad laugh. 'Well, he didn't take it serious, I don't think. Besides, Dad likes his jazz. But he was happy enough that Ray was doing what made him happy. I think in the back of his mind – well, my mind too if I'm honest – he was sure that eventually all this pop star thing would fizzle out and Ray would settle down to a proper job. He was working in a shoe shop you know, and he could have risen to be a floor manager or something.' She sighed a little, then shook her head. 'Mind you, his band *were* becoming popular – even we knew that, so who knows what might have been if only ...' Aware of straying into dangerous waters, she abruptly stopped speaking for a moment, then straightened her shoulders and forced a smile back onto her face. 'Some of the neighbours who have children a bit younger than Ray told us that some of them were always going on about Ray's band and how good they were.'

'The Rainbirds?' Trudy put in softly.

'Yes. Silly name, isn't it?' Rosie said, looking at her with a smile that was both sad and proud. 'Ray was going to change it to Ray Reason and the Rainbirds. Said it sounded better, and would get them noticed more. He was always thinking of ways like that to try and help them make it to the big time. He wanted to be like them lads from Liverpool everyone's going on about now. I can't remember what they call themselves.'

'The Beatles?' Trudy proffered.

'See! Another silly name,' Rosie said indulgently. 'Fancy calling yourselves after an insect.'

Trudy didn't bother to mention the difference in spelling. 'So he was happy that night then?'

'Oh yes. I can see him now, dressed up in his best suit, carrying that funny-looking guitar of his. Heading out the door, waving goodbye ...'

Her voice petered out, as she remembered that that was the last time she'd seen her son alive.

Quickly, Trudy dragged her back from that precipice. 'Did you know the other lads in the band?'

'Some of them,' Rosie said, with a wavering smile. 'In the early days, Frankie used to come over and practise in the garage. He was the drummer. But the Wilkinsons on the other side—' she nodded her head at the wall to her right '—used to complain, so he didn't come often.'

'And as far as you know, there wasn't any trouble in the band? They all got on well together?'

'Oh yes,' Rosie said, then frowned. 'Well, Ray did like to mutter sometimes about Marty ... Martin, that is. They clashed heads sometimes, but that's just teenage lads, isn't it?'

Trudy mentally filed away that little nugget and cast her net a bit wider. 'And did he have a girlfriend?' she asked artlessly. She already knew that he had, of course, but she was interested to see how the dead boy's mother would react to the mention of her. In Trudy's experience, you could often tell a lot about a boy by the way that his mother reacted to his girlfriend. Usually, they didn't approve, and would tell you why in no uncertain terms!

But Rosie Reason immediately smiled and nodded. 'Oh yes, Linda.'

As she said the name, a slight frown tugged at her brows, as if saying it made her recall some vague, half-remembered thing. But whatever it was, Trudy got the distinct feeling that it wasn't sufficiently important to Rosie for her to try and summon up enough energy to track it down.

Instead, she smiled, a vague, hopeless sort of smile. 'A lovely girl, Linda. Dad and me were so happy when he started seeing her. Her father manages a large warehouse, you know, and her mother works too, for a firm of solicitors. *Her* father was something to do with conveyancing. Lovely people. I often told our Ray he was lucky to have Linda. She's so pretty and quite a catch. I was hoping they'd make a match of it, and ...' But again her voice faltered into a dreadful silence.

Trudy instantly caught on. Linda's family was a cut above that of a dustman and his wife, and this poor woman had no doubt had fond visions of them marrying and settling down in some nice neighbourhood.

'So you know Linda well?' Trudy said gently.

Mrs Reason gave a little start, then nodded slowly. 'Oh yes. Ray used to bring her to tea often. Lovely manners, she had,' Rosie said vaguely, and for a moment seemed to cock her head a little to one side, as if considering something about Linda took her far away. Again, Trudy wondered what it might be. But Rosie had seemed quite genuine in her praise of the girl, so Trudy didn't think it was anything bad.

'Did Linda approve of his singing in a pop band?' Trudy asked curiously.

'Oh well, love, girls have to stand by their menfolk don't they,' Rosie said drearily. The faraway look was coming back into her eyes now, and Trudy could sense she was losing her.

'Had Ray been arguing with anyone that you know of?'

'Arguing? No, love, not that I know of.'

'And he and Linda were still happy together?'

'Oh yes, love, I'm sure they were.'

Trudy cast Clement a quick glance, to see if she'd missed anything, but he just gave a quick shake of his head.

'Well, thank you for seeing us, Mrs Reason. If you think of anything – if some little incident comes back to you about Ray that you think we should know about, you can always contact me.' She hastily wrote the police station number on a page of her notebook and tore it off and handed it over. 'We can see ourselves out,' Trudy added quietly.

But of course, the older woman insisted on showing them to the door. And this time, as they stepped out onto the door-step, she didn't even bother to look left or right, to see what the neighbours thought about her receiving a visit from a policewoman.

*

'That bit always breaks my heart,' Trudy said, once she was back behind the wheel.

Clement said nothing, but she could see he wasn't unaffected by their interview with the dead boy's mother.

'Well, I'd better get back to the station,' Trudy said, glancing at her watch. The day was now well advanced, and she had other duties to do, as well as helping the coroner. And she knew that Inspector Jennings wouldn't let her get away with any slacking.

'Yes, all right,' Clement agreed. 'We'll pick this up again first thing in the morning. I've cleared my diary.' The uncompromising way in which he said it made her wonder what other appointments he'd swept aside in order to do so.

Trudy gave a little sigh as she turned the key in the Rover's ignition. She wished she had the power to just dictate her own working conditions like that.

But she'd probably see a squadron of pigs flying overhead before that happened.

Chapter 8

The next day, Vincent, Clement and Trudy met at the coroner's house, and decided that before they went any further, they really needed to see the scene of the crime for themselves.

Naturally, first thing in the morning, the Bootleggers Club was tightly closed. At night, the colourful lights that spelled out its name plus the street lighting surrounding it might have lent it at least a semblance of glamour, but in the unforgiving bright daylight of a late-summer's day, the building looked dingy, forlorn and ugly.

The windows were badly in need of cleaning, and something green and vigorous was growing in the lower section of guttering that showed on its frontage and probably leaked like a mini-waterfall in wet weather.

As they approached it, posters advertising various acts gave the noticeboards either side of the door a certain gaiety, but even so, none of them were much impressed.

'I had a word with Sergeant O'Grady yesterday,' Trudy told them, as Clement rapped his stick against the door and waited for some sign of life. 'He reckons the club regularly plays host to some serious villains, and that Felix Simpkins is probably the front man for them. Gambling, loan-sharking, smuggled alcohol and cigarettes, that kind of thing. I get the feeling the Sergeant would give his eye teeth to lay Simpkins by the heels.'

'Wouldn't surprise me,' Vincent muttered, eyeing the place with disfavour. 'It looks like a right dive to me.'

The door opened abruptly, and a large man somewhere in his early forties, with a flattened nose and surprisingly friendly-looking big brown eyes looked out at them. 'We're closed,' he said mildly. In one hand was a half-eaten bacon sandwich.

'Yes, we assumed as much,' Clement said laconically. 'We'd like to have a word with the manager, Mr Simpkins. Is he in?'

The man thought about this for a moment, and Trudy supposed he was wondering if they should be admitted. She could almost hear his thought processes out loud. On the one hand, she was in uniform, and it was probably his job to protect his boss from unwanted visitors if possible – especially the law! But then there was also Clement, who had the unmistakable stamp of someone of importance. Also Vincent, who didn't seem to fit into any category, and was probably causing the doorman the most bafflement, since his gaze kept coming back to the coroner's son time and time again, as if he was an enigma that needed solving.

'Hold on a mo and I'll go and see,' the man eventually decided, and quickly withdrew.

Vincent's lips twisted in a vague smile as they all waited to see whether the manager of the Bootleggers Club would deign to see them. A few minutes later – which felt a lot longer than that to all three of them – the door opened again. 'This way then,' the guardian of the gate said amiably.

Trudy noticed, amused, that he'd had time to finish off the rest of his sandwich.

He led them into a small vestibule, where punters no doubt checked in their coats and hats in the evening, and past a set of big double doors to their immediate right, which Trudy assumed was the entrance to the main dance floor and stage.

Their guide took them down a short corridor and knocked ponderously on a door marked, rather grandly, 'Office.'

A vague rumble came from beyond, which their companion took for a summons, as their escort opened the door and stood to one side.

The office turned out to be a perfect square, with one small, barred window overlooking a back alley, and unevenly plastered walls painted a heavy cream. The linoleum on the floor was brown, as were the few pieces of furniture and furnishings.

Behind an untidy-looking desk, a man glowered at them. Trudy guessed his age to be nearing fifty, and he'd once had fair hair that was now turning rapidly grey. He was running to fat now, but had probably once been handsome enough.

'You're the bloke from the court,' Felix Simpkins said accusingly, looking at Clement.

'That's right, Mr Simpkins. I'm a city coroner. You appeared at Ray Reason's inquest to give evidence.'

'There's nothing wrong with them stairs,' Felix Simpkins said at once. 'No bugger else has ever fallen down them. I reckon that was just Ray being his usual clumsy self.'

Clement nodded. 'I'd just like to take a look for myself if you don't mind.'

'I do mind, then,' Felix said belligerently. 'I thought that was all done and dusted. Didn't you lot sign off on an accidental death?' he added, his eyes moving suspiciously from Vincent to Clement, but lingering longest on Trudy in her police uniform.

'The jury brought in that verdict, yes,' Clement agreed mildly. 'We won't be long. Just a quick look around. You have no objection, do you?'

'What if I do then?' Felix asked, chin thrust out.

'Well then, Mr Simpkins, I might just begin to wonder why you're being so defensive,' Clement said, smiling like a shark. 'I might even begin to suspect that you've got something to hide.'

Immediately the club owner began to shift about on his chair.

'Now don't go putting words in me mouth,' Felix complained. 'I ain't got nothing to get in a lather about. You wanna go and look see, go and see. Dave!' he yelled suddenly and without warning, making Vincent jump. The door behind them quickly opened, and their previous companion looked in.

'Show these people the stairs where poor ol' Ray copped it. Then see them out,' he added flatly.

'We'd like a few words with you first, Mr Simpkins,' Trudy said quickly, but only got another glower for her trouble.

'Well, that's hard cheese then, ain't it, 'cause I'm busy. Dave, show these good people the way,' Felix said, leaning back in his chair, his face flat and hard.

'This way then.' The now-named Dave stood back. He looked perfectly capable of reaching out and grabbing them by the arms and yanking them physically out of the room if need be, so Clement took the initiative, inclined his head regally and turned and walked out of the room.

Once outside they were all silent as Dave led them further down the corridor and turned a sharp dog-leg. And there, in front of them, was the opening to a set of spiral stairs.

They spent a few minutes going up and down them, each trying to picture the scene that night, whilst Dave waited, massive and benignly implacable at the head of the stairs.

They quickly checked out the large common area and desultorily explored the darker corners of the basement, but it was all just as Clement's witnesses had described it.

'I think we've seen enough don't you?' Clement finally said, and after they all trooped back up the tight stairs, Trudy thanked Dave politely, and followed him in silence back to the front entrance.

But once there, Trudy paused. She hadn't liked the way the club manager had been able to send them on their way so cavalierly, and she was determined to get something more out of the excursion.

'Did you know Mr Reason, Dave?' she asked sweetly.

The big man looked at her, seemingly surprised that she was

speaking to him, then registered her question, thought about it and – after a pause – nodded. 'Yeah, I knew Ray. An annoying little toad, but he could sing all right, I'll give him that. I likes to listen to the bands – the good ones – sometimes. The best ones come up with some real toe-tappers.'

'Why was he annoying?' Trudy asked curiously.

'Too big for his boots,' was Dave's considered opinion.

'But you said he was a good singer,' Trudy pointed out, careful to keep her voice sweet and merely curious. 'Weren't the Rainbirds doing well? I heard they were getting quite a following amongst the fans, and Mr Simpkins had given them the prime spot, hadn't he?'

'Yeah, but that was because ...' Dave began, then abruptly stopped, as if aware that he was about to say something that he shouldn't. He heaved a big breath and changed course ponderously. 'The Rainbirds are a good little group, right enough. I mean, that fancy toff from the Smoke wanted to become their manager, so they must be good, right?'

Trudy, intrigued by both the bouncer's slip of the tongue and this mention of some new player on the scene, chose to follow up on the latter option. She knew it would be a waste of time, at this point, trying to get Dave to talk about something that he didn't want to talk about.

'Who was that then? This man from London, I mean?' she asked, trying hard to sound more like a nosy girl out for a gossip about showbiz, rather than a police officer investigating a death.

'Dunno.' Dave shrugged his meaty shoulders and rubbed the side of his nose placidly. 'He was some big-time swell who manages stars and stuff – that's what I heard. You know, finds new acts and bigs 'em up and gets 'em good publicity and good places to sing and whatnot. He was interested in signing them on, or so I heard, but Ray weren't quite so keen as the others.'

Trudy frowned. That didn't sound right. 'But surely he'd have been over the moon? Didn't he want the band to be famous?'

But this seemed to be too complicated for Dave who merely

shrugged again. 'Dunno. I might've heard it wrong,' he said vaguely and without worry, as if this was such a common occurrence it had long since lost the ability to mean anything to him.

And with a vague grin goodbye, the door of the Bootleggers Club was shut in their faces.

Vincent drew in a deep breath. 'Well that was … different,' he said, with a slow smile at his father. 'I got the distinct impression that we haven't made it onto Mr Simpkins's Christmas card list.'

'No. He's obviously going to be as difficult as possible,' Trudy agreed flatly. 'Pity, we could have done with him being a bit more helpful. Especially if you and I are going to hang out at his club for a bit,' she said to Vincent. 'I hope he doesn't try to stop us getting in on Saturday. Or even worse, warn everybody that I'm a police officer. Nobody will be seen dead talking to me then,' she wailed.

'Oh, don't worry about our Mr Simpkins,' Clement told her, his eyes glinting. 'I'll make a few phone calls and I think you'll find he'll soon have a change of heart and become more cooperative.'

Vincent looked at his father curiously, but Trudy thought she understood what Clement intended to do. Dr Ryder knew everyone who was anyone in the county, and she didn't think it would take him long to call in a few favours. And once Felix Simpkins started getting phone calls from the fire marshal demanding to make inspections, and calls from the council warning him that he could expect someone from the sanitation department to check out the state of his kitchens, and maybe even a call from the tax man warning him he could expect a spot-check audit …

Oh yes, Mr Simpkins would get the message all right.

'What?' Vincent said, seeing his father and Trudy Loveday exchange conspiratorial, amused glances.

'Oh, nothing you need to worry about, son,' Clement said, only aggravating his offspring even more.

Chapter 9

Back in the car, they decided they should talk to Linda Kempson next, the dead man's girlfriend. This time, Clement agreed that he should be the one to sit out the interview, since the young girl would be far more likely to feel comfortable and forthcoming talking to people nearer her own age.

Besides, Clement pointed out, after testifying at the inquest, she would be bound to associate him with bad memories, and they needed her to feel as relaxed and open as possible.

According to the research on her that Trudy had made time to do yesterday, Linda Kempson worked part-time at a small library in Summertown, and so they split up: Clement, to go back to his office to work on some of his more pressing business for a few hours, whilst Vincent and Trudy took the bus to Summertown.

Trudy's father had been a bus driver for nearly twenty years, but the bus route from St Aldates to Summertown wasn't one that he regularly drove. So as she paid the conductor for a return ticket, she was rather relieved that she wouldn't have to explain Vincent's presence to him at the family dinner table that night.

'I wonder why a presumably pretty young girl would want to work in a library of all places,' Vincent said conversationally as they alighted at the most convenient stop and made their way to the small branch where their witness worked. 'It's hardly a hive of excitement and activity, is it?'

'Oh, I think it'll turn out to be more of a stop gap for her, rather than that she has any real desire to make a career out of it,' Trudy predicted, as they walked down the leafy lanes in the Oxford suburb. A gorgeous and enormously fluffy ginger-and-tabby cat mewed at them from a garden wall, and Trudy stopped to pet it, much enamoured of its inches-thick luxurious fur.

As it purred and pushed against her hand, Trudy filled Vincent in on all she had learned about the girl they were about to see.

'Linda's just turned eighteen, and she has just one older sister, who's now married and living away from home,' she began.

'So she's the baby of the family?' Vincent mumbled, watching Trudy's hand caressing the cat and experiencing a definite hint of jealousy of the feline – which amused him. 'Probably spoilt rotten, in that case,' he added thoughtfully.

'She grew up in Torquay until she was about nine or ten, then her parents moved here. Her parents are well off – not exactly rich, but they could afford to send her to a good local school. She's got some secretarial qualifications, but I think that was just for form's sake. She has no real need to work, you see,' Trudy continued, without envy, 'and I daresay she's just filling in time until she settles down and gets married.'

Reluctantly, she gave the friendly moggy a last ear-scratch and moved on, Vincent happily following. It was a warm day, and he was suddenly enjoying his makeshift summer holiday more than he'd thought possible.

'It's just up here by the look of it,' Trudy said, spotting the council signage on the front of a smallish, one-storey building that looked fairly new.

Inside, they stood amongst the stacks of books, looking around. A middle-aged woman was manning the small desk and chatting happily with another slightly older woman who had selected a huge pile of romance books and was getting them stamped out.

Vincent touched Trudy's arm, then nodded his chin towards a side wall, where a young girl was busy loading books from a trolley and placing them with care (probably in alphabetical order of author) onto some shelves.

Trudy judged her to be shorter than herself by several inches, so around five feet six or so, and she had long brown hair worn loose. As they approached, she seemed to sense their presence, because she turned and looked around, revealing a pair of large brown eyes in a very pretty face. Her eyes flickered apprehensively as she noted Trudy's uniform.

'Hello. Miss Kempson, isn't it?' Trudy said quietly.

'Yes,' the other girl responded nervously.

'I'm working with the coroner, Dr Clement Ryder, on Mr Raymond Reason's, er, case,' she said, deliberately choosing the kindest word she could think of. 'We just have a few follow-up inquiries. There's nothing to worry about, I assure you,' she added quickly, as a look of alarm quickly settled over the younger girl's features. 'Perhaps we could just step outside for a moment?' she added, realising that she was all but whispering now.

Although there weren't many people in the library, she'd always had a fear of being chucked out of one for making too much noise – no doubt as a legacy of some forgotten misdemeanour in her childhood.

'Oh, yes, all right,' Linda agreed with obvious reluctance.

She followed them as they went back outdoors and onto the quiet side street. Spotting a comfortable-looking garden wall of just the right size (which had been kindly concreted over into a nice smooth arch), Trudy indicated it and took the initiative by sitting down first.

'This is Mr Vincent Ryder,' Trudy said. 'He's taking notes for his father,' she added, her eyes twinkling at Vincent as she craftily handed the chore that should rightly be hers, over to him.

He didn't mind, however, and quickly taking the hint, took the notepad and pen Trudy offered to him and settled down to be as quiet and unobtrusive as possible.

Linda nodded vaguely at this, jumped back and sat down a little distance away from them. Trudy noticed that she immediately dropped her hands into her lap and began twisting them. They looked slender and pale, and for some reason Trudy was convinced they'd have felt cold to the touch. Clearly their visit had thrown the other girl for a loop, but she knew she shouldn't read anything particularly sinister in that.

'I'm so sorry about your friend, Miss Kempson,' Trudy began gently. 'You must miss him dreadfully.'

Linda swallowed and nodded, but kept her eyes on her feet, which didn't quite reach the pavement. 'Yes, I can't believe he's really gone,' she said. Her voice was just a little breathless, as if she couldn't quite get the right amount of air into her lungs to enable her to speak, and Trudy suddenly had the feeling that this girl was very frightened indeed. Even close to panic, maybe?

But what, exactly, was she scared of?

If she'd had something to do with the death of her boyfriend, then it might well be that she was afraid she would reveal it to her unwanted visitors. Or did she know something less shocking about what had happened to Ray Reason, but was for some reason covering up for someone else? Yet again, it was possible that Ray had been mixed up in something unsavoury (say to do with the Bootleggers Club, which they all knew wasn't very respectable) and Linda was afraid that she might be the next one to have a nasty accident.

'Tell me about Ray,' Trudy said gently, trying to get a feel for what she was dealing with here. In her experience, asking direct and specific questions only got you direct and specific answers, and what she wanted to do was to get this girl to open up. A broad and general query gave far more scope for that.

But Linda wasn't going to make it easy for her. 'What do you mean?' she said unhelpfully.

'How did you meet?' Trudy tried first.

'I saw him singing at the Carfax Assembly Rooms one night. Afterwards, we got talking and that was it.'

'He must have seemed very glamorous,' Trudy said encouragingly.

'Oh he was.'

'And handsome too?'

'Yes.'

Trudy bit back a sigh. So, direct and specific questions it was. 'Had you known him long?'

'Not quite a year,' Linda said, after a moment's hesitation.

Had she been mentally adding up the timeframe, Trudy wondered, or did something about the question throw her for some reason? But Trudy couldn't think what it might be. It was, on the face of it, an innocuous enough question.

'So you were serious then?'

'Oh yes. We were going to be married,' Linda blurted out, raising her voice slightly. There was something so determined and defiant about it that Trudy instantly got the impression that it was a lie. Or maybe the girl was only guilty of wishful thinking?

But Trudy had to wonder. Would a young man determined to be a pop star really become engaged so young? Wouldn't it put off his adoring young female fans? Surely part of the allure for girl fans was the fantasy that their idol was available and might spot them in the crowd and decide she was the one for him. (Trudy had done her own amount of hero worshipping when she was younger and much sillier than she was now, so she knew what daft ideas young girls could get!)

And from what they were learning about the victim so far, she was getting the feeling that Ray Reason had been a very savvy young man indeed, and would have known all about things like that.

'I see you're not wearing an engagement ring,' Trudy probed very gently.

'It wasn't official, but Ray had promised me one. He said he was looking for just the right one. He thought I should have pearls or an opal,' Linda insisted, biting her lip.

The fact that she had embellished her answer far too much,

left Trudy fairly convinced that Linda wasn't trying to convince her, Trudy, of this, but rather herself.

'Sounds like he was a thoughtful young man,' Trudy lied.

'Yes, he was. Oh, it shouldn't have happened to him,' Linda suddenly burst out wildly. 'It wasn't *fair!* Why should *he* have to die so young? And right now, of all times! There were far worse people who could have fallen down those damned stairs and died,' she added passionately, her eyes beginning to fill with tears. 'That awful Mr Simpkins for one. Ray never liked him. He said he ripped off the bands as well as the punters. But Ray sorted him out,' she added with a sudden spurt of satisfaction.

Trudy ruthlessly suppressed showing any signs of excitement, and shot Vincent a warning look as she felt him stiffen beside her. The last thing they needed to do was spook her now that she was finally giving them new information.

'Oh? Do you know how Ray did that?' she asked, sounding admiring. 'He must have been clever to get the better of someone like Mr Simpkins.'

Linda sighed. 'No, not really. I only know that suddenly, a few months ago, the Rainbirds began to get and keep the best time spots, and got to keep more of the takings than the other bands did.'

Trudy nodded. Now that was very interesting. It sounded as if the dead man had got some sort of a hold over the murky night-club manager. Which gave them, at last, the sniff of a possible motive.

'Ray sounds like the kind of man who didn't take things lying down. We hear he had big plans for the band?' she asked next.

Linda's head drooped a little as she nodded. 'Yes. The Rainbirds meant everything to him. He was so sure it was going to be his ticket to the big time. He said if the likes of Jet Harris and Tony Meehan could make it, then so could he. And he said the band had every bit as good a sound as the Searchers.'

'I'm sure he was right,' Trudy said again, although she wasn't sure at all. She'd heard 'Sweets for My Sweet' a lot of times on the radio a month or so ago, and had thought they were very good. But then, she hadn't ever heard the Rainbirds sing, so who was to say?

'Can you tell me again what happened that night?' Trudy said, and Linda sagged visibly.

'I don't know what I can tell you. I don't know anything. I didn't see anything. I went to the club – the Bootleggers – about half an hour or so before Ray was due to sing. I was dressed in my best skirt suit, one just like Jackie Kennedy wears, and I went down to the common room to wish him luck. I wanted to talk to him on his own, but it was always so crowded and noisy in there. He came up to the bar and got me a drink, and we watched the Undergrads who were on stage for a bit, but then he left again to get ready for their stint. And then, just before they were due to go on, I could tell something weird was happening.'

She paused, swallowed hard and shrugged forlornly. 'There was an atmosphere, you know. People were getting together in groups and talking and looking sort of … excited.' She swallowed hard. 'It makes me feel sick to think of it now.'

Trudy nodded. Not wanting to take her as far as the moment when she learned her boyfriend was dead, she drew her back a little. 'Did he drink much at the bar?' she asked casually.

'Only a shandy,' Linda said, instantly defensive. 'Ray would never go on stage the worse for drink.'

'No, I'm sure he wouldn't. It sounds like he was really professional. You say he didn't get on with Mr Simpkins though. Was there anyone else he was, shall we say, unhappy with?'

Linda sighed. 'He didn't like that Titus Crowther-Beauley man much. The agent who wanted to sign them up.'

'Oh?' Trudy frowned, genuinely surprised. Now that the would-be agent had been given a name, she recognised it immediately. And was impressed. 'But I understand that he manages a lot of famous people,' she said. 'And he was interested in signing up the Rainbirds?'

'Yes he was,' Linda confirmed listlessly.

The band must have been really good. 'That must have been exciting?' Trudy nudged. 'To have such a first-class agent interested in signing them up?'

Linda shrugged. 'The rest of the band certainly thought so. Marty was all for it, and so was Jenny Wren.'

'*Jenny Wren?*'

'Sorry, Jennifer Renfrew, Marty's girlfriend. We all call her Jenny Wren.'

Trudy smiled and nodded. 'Yes, rather neat, that.'

'They call me Lindy-Lou,' Linda said with a shrug. 'To tease me, you know, because I used to love all the American rock'n'roll songs before I heard the Rainbirds, and it fits with all the American songs. Peggy-Sue and whatnot.'

'Lindy-Lou. I take it your second name is Louise?' Trudy asked, trying to sound more like a friend now than a police officer.

'Yes,' Linda confirmed shortly. Her hands, Trudy noted, still looked white and cold. And for all she was talking cooperatively enough, Trudy knew she was no closer to penetrating Linda Kempson's shell now than she had been when she'd first started.

'Linda, is there something you want to tell me?' she asked gently. Sometimes, a direct appeal could work where everything else failed.

But all that happened was that Linda went paler than ever, and her body went rigid. 'No! I've told you all I know. I have to get back to work now,' she added, then hopped off the wall and walked very quickly back to the library.

It happened so unexpectedly that neither Vincent nor Trudy made any move to follow her.

'Well, what do you think?' Trudy asked, once the other girl was out of sight.

'I don't know,' Vincent said, shutting up the notebook and

handing it, and her pen, back to her. 'She was obviously upset, poor kid.'

'Yes,' Trudy agreed. But she thought, more than anything else, that Linda Kempson was a girl who not only was in mourning for her lost love, but seemed to have the weight of the whole world on her shoulders as well.

The question was – why?

Chapter 10

Patty Nesbitt heard a sharp rap coming up through her floor. The girl in the bedsit below her used a broom to bang on the ceiling whenever she wanted to get her attention, and with a sigh, she rolled off her bed, where she'd been painting her nails, and trudged to the door of her tiny quarters.

There she opened the door to a dim and cramped landing, and yelled over the stair rail. 'What?'

'Phone!' the answering voice wafted up, and Patty sighed. Wrapping her pale pink nylon housecoat around her, she trudged down the uncarpeted stairs to the phone that hung on the wall in the tiny hall, and which all the residents of the converted Edwardian house used.

She picked up the receiver somewhat cautiously and said warily, 'Yes?'

Patty usually had good reason to be careful. At twenty-eight, she'd been knocked around by life enough to know it paid to look after number one at all times.

'Patty?'

At the sound of the gruff voice, Patty put her hand into her housecoat pocket, feeling nervously for the packet of cigarettes and the small lighter that she kept there. Her first instinct was to hang up the phone and light one desperately, but she knew she shouldn't.

'Yeah? Who is this?' she said, but she knew who it was, right enough.

'It's me, Felix,' the voice said impatiently. 'Now listen, girlie.' Her caller went from gruffness to a downright snarl, and Patty felt a distinct chill creep into the back of her neck. 'You're gonna keep your mouth shut, yeah?'

'Course, Felix,' she said automatically. 'I told you before. And you know me.'

'I *do* know you, girlie. I'm trusting you to be smart enough to know that you can suffer some serious damage if you act stupid.'

Patty's fingers clasped around the packet of cigarettes compulsively, almost crushing it. 'No need to act all heavy with me, Felix sweetie,' she said, putting a little-girl wistfulness into her voice. Most men, Patty had learned, responded well to a little feminine helplessness.

'Cut that out! That stuff don't work on me. I'm not one of your punters,' Felix Simpkins warned her savagely. 'Just shut that pretty mouth of yours and listen. I've had a visit from a couple of nosy parkers about that Ray Reason business.'

'But I thought that was all done and dusted!' Patty burst out impulsively. She wouldn't normally interrupt someone like Felix Simpkins when he was talking, but she hadn't been able to help it.

'It is, and it isn't,' Felix grunted. 'The inquest's all done and dusted, but the bloody coroner and the cops are still tying up loose ends. So just you remember. If anyone ever asks you, you saw nothing, did nothing, know nothing. Got it?'

Patty brought out the lighter and stared at it longingly. A near chain-smoker since the age of twelve, she longed to be dragging some soothing smoke into her lungs right now. She was not normally a panicky sort, but having the likes of Felix Simpkins breathing down your neck was enough to make any girl shiver a bit.

75

'Saw what, sweetie? Know what? I was just at the club having a little dance and a little drinkie,' she said blandly.

There was a mollified silence for a moment, and then: 'Right. And make damned sure that's all you say in future.'

'Of course, Felix. You know I don't blab.'

There came a vague grunt over the phone, and then: 'I'm serious, girlie. That little favour I asked you to do? You ever talk about that, and it'll be last thing you ever *do* talk about. Understand?'

Patty understood all right. 'What favour, sweetie? I have no idea what you're talking about,' Patty said, forcing a gaiety into her voice that she definitely wasn't feeling.

There was another moment of silence, then a slight sigh. 'Good girl,' Felix said abruptly, and hung up.

Instantly, Patty fumbled the phone back onto its cradle, then lit up a cigarette. She took three long drags, her fingers trembling, then made her way shakily back upstairs. Her first gentleman caller was due in a while, and she needed to get ready. She hoped the nurse's uniform he liked to see her in was clean. She couldn't remember the last time she'd washed it.

She returned to her bedsit and went straight to the washbasin plumbed into one corner of her brightly sunlit but shabby room to begin her toilette, but her mind wasn't on her work but on a dark smoky room, and the steady beat of insistent pop music.

In the mirror above the basin, Patty met her troubled reflection. She was a strawberry blonde (alas, only with the aid of chemicals) with big blue eyes that had always been her best feature. Tall and thin, she was more gawky than elegant, but she got along all right. With the help of a few men here and there who liked to 'look after her', the odd legitimate job (usually waitresses or bar work) and a touch of shoplifting if things were really tough, she was content enough.

Despite skirting with the law ever since she'd hit puberty, she'd never thought she would ever get mixed up in anything serious – nothing really *bad*.

And yet, here she was, wondering if she should pack her bags and flee town. The trouble was, she liked Oxford well enough, and had been here for a few years now, and didn't really fancy starting somewhere new. On the other hand, what if Felix Simpkins started to worry about her?

She'd first gone to the Bootleggers whilst in the company of one of her gentlemen friends who turned out to have a small stake in various betting shops in town. He'd had to flee to Spain quite suddenly last spring, but luckily by then he'd 'introduced' her to several of his friends who also had financial interests here and there in various not quite legitimate enterprises.

She'd begun doing quite a nice bit of business at the club, so when Felix Simpkins had taken her aside that Saturday night and told her that he needed a favour doing, she'd been in no position to say no. She'd been worried that whatever it was he wanted from her might turn out to be really shady, so she'd felt nothing but relief when he'd told her what it actually was.

For a girl like Patty, there was nothing much to it, so she'd agreed to do it at once – especially when Felix had slipped her five one-pound notes for her trouble.

And it had all gone well at first – at least, from her point of view. Ray had seen her around the club a few times, so he'd seen nothing suspicious in her getting rather close to him at the bar.

It was only later on in the evening that it all went belly-up.

Patty had been dancing on the floor with some young fat businessman-type she'd picked up at the bar. He'd been trying to look a part of the young scene with his outfit and flashy gear, but in fact he'd stood out like a sore thumb – which made him perfect prey for her.

She was sure he'd be taking her home that night, and had already let him know that she was available, but before leaving with him and negotiating a price, she'd needed a pee. So she'd gone off to the ladies' …

But Patty didn't want to remember what had happened next.

And in her small sunny bedsit, she pushed the memories firmly away. What did it really matter, after all? Life was never fair, was it? Everyone except little kids soon found that out. And what was done was done – you couldn't go back and do things over, could you? You just had to get on with things and be happy, right?

So instead of brooding, she reached determinedly for her lipstick – Baby Pink – and with a hand that trembled just slightly, painted her mouth.

She was just slipping on her stockings and attaching them to her suspenders, when a knock came on the door.

Quickly smoothing down her white mini-skirt (that no nurse would be caught dead wearing) and straightening her tunic, she put the nurse's cap on her fluffy blonde head. Then, putting on a welcoming smile, Patty went to the door.

But even as she greeted her 'poorly patient' and set about curing what ailed him, her mind kept slipping back to that Saturday night.

She tried to convince herself that she had nothing to worry about. That what had happened to Ray Reason at the Bootleggers Club that night couldn't possibly come back and give her grief. Who but Felix knew she was in any way mixed up in it anyway? And he was hardly likely to tell anyone, was he? With all that he had to hide.

And yet …

And yet, Patty Nesbitt was very much afraid.

Chapter 11

Martin Cuthbertson lived in Cowley, where he rented a bedroom in a semi-detached council house near a large car-manufacturing plant. His landlord worked at the car plant, whilst his landlord's wife worked part-time at the local co-op.

No doubt it was a far cry from the sort of place he could see himself living in should the Rainbirds make it big, Trudy mused wryly as they approached it.

'He's from Witney, originally,' Trudy informed Clement as she carefully drove his Rover to a smooth stop at the kerb outside the house.

After leaving Linda at the library, she'd dropped Vincent off at his father's house, and reported back at the station to do some of her regular work. Luckily the station had been quiet though, and Inspector Jennings let her leave without too much grumbling after she'd put in a few hours and worked through her lunch hour, allowing her to meet the coroner once more at Floyds Row, where he had his office next to the mortuary.

'His father and mother are still there,' she continued her biography of their next witness. 'The father works for the council, in the parks department I think, and his mum works part-time in a sweetshop. He's an only child. He left home last year and now works odd hours at a petrol station, on the pumps. But he seems to drift from job to job every few months or so. Too busy trying to become a pop star to bother settling down to a proper job, I suppose.'

Clement gave a brief smile. 'I wonder what his parents think of that?'

Trudy grinned. 'I doubt they're thrilled. But maybe they are, who knows?'

They got out of the car and stood on the pavement, looking around. It was a narrow street, crowded with council houses set within well-maintained front gardens, all of which had been built just after the war. The council had been careful to plant a tree – either a flowering cherry or a flowering almond – in each front garden, giving the street a leafy look. They looked as if they had all been built with indoor toilets and probably with a pantry in the kitchen. 'Nice,' Trudy said appreciatively.

Clement looked at her, surprised, then at the rows of square, roughly plastered grey walls and uniform red-tiled roofs and felt vaguely depressed. His own Victorian terrace house overlooking the park, with its white gingerbread trim, tall chimneys and decorative white and black brickwork had at least some semblance of elegance to it. It made him feel a little guilty – and uncomfortable – that his young friend should be impressed by the (to him) soulless surroundings.

'Well, let's see how Mr Cuthbertson is taking the death of the band's lead singer,' Trudy said jauntily, unaware of her companion's sudden silent gloom, and after pushing open the gate of a house almost squarely in the middle of the street, walked briskly up to the front door. There she lifted the simple iron doorknocker built in around the letterbox and rapped it hard.

Clement, walking behind her and using his walking cane, followed more slowly and carefully.

At this time of the day Trudy expected that only the lodger – Martin himself – was likely to be in, and she was right. After a short delay the door opened, and a young man stood there, looking at them.

He seemed slightly taken aback by their appearance, and his opening words quickly explained why.

'Oh. You're not the reporter.'

Trudy, in her police uniform, was clearly not a reporter, and she smiled amiably. 'No, sir. Expecting one, are you?'

Trudy knew from reading the coroner's notes that Cuthbertson was the same age as Ray Reason had been, which put him at nineteen, nearly twenty. He was about six feet tall, with darkish blond hair and darkish blue eyes. His nose was a little too big and his fair skin was still prey to the occasional bout of acne. When he spoke, she'd noticed that his teeth were visibly misaligned, otherwise she'd have called him handsome enough. But not as good-looking as the dead man had been by quite some margin – and she wondered if that had that rankled.

'Yes, I was as a matter of a fact,' Martin responded to her question with a slight shrug. 'I'm doing a piece with one of the local papers to try and reassure our fans that the Rainbirds are going to carry on. I'm a musician, and that's the name of the band I'm in,' he explained. As he talked, he looked at her with a slight, puzzled frown on his face.

He was dressed in a cheap pair of brown trousers and wore a white shirt, slightly frayed at the cuffs. He pushed one of those cuffs back now to glance at his watch.

When he looked back up, his eyes focused suddenly on Clement. 'I've seen you before,' he said, almost as an accusation.

'Indeed you have, in the coroner's court, Mr Cuthbertson,' Clement said mildly. 'You testified at my inquiry into your friend's recent death.'

Martin paled slightly. 'This is about Ray then? Of course it is, sorry. You'd better come in then. I'm due at the petrol station later, so I don't have that much time right now.'

In the tiny hallway, he hesitated visibly. 'Er … I can't show you into the rooms down here – they're not mine. I've only got the bedroom upstairs.' His gaze went to Trudy and away again, and he flushed slightly. 'I don't have much room up there, I'm afraid – only the bed and a chair, like.'

'That will be fine, sir,' Trudy reassured him. 'You can sit on the bed, Dr Ryder can have the chair, and I'll be happy to stand,' she added cheerfully.

With visible reluctance, he turned and headed up the stairs, his shoulders looking rather stiff and tight.

Trudy noted as she climbed that the runner in the centre of the stairs had been recently swept and, though old and slightly worn, was perfectly clean. She guessed that Martin's landlady was the no-nonsense and hard-working sort, the kind who would provide him with a good evening meal, and make sure he had clean sheets every fortnight, but wouldn't stand for any noisy band practices or young ladies in his room.

She could tell that the council house was very similar to the one she lived in with her own parents, and would probably have two double bedrooms and a smaller single. Martin, it turned out, had the spare double room, which looked out the back of the house onto a large garden. Pushing aside the lace curtains at the window, she could see that he had a nice view of the back garden, and beyond that, the back garden of the house in the next street along. It seemed the road curved around, giving a view of several properties.

On a warm September day, a lot of the housewives had their washing out, and toddlers too young to go to school played out on various lawns.

Turning her back on the charming domestic scene, Trudy settled herself with one shoulder comfortably against a wall, and took out her notebook. On the way over, they'd decided that Clement should handle the interview this time, as a young man would be more likely to respond to an older male authority figure, than to a girl in a uniform.

'I'm just tying up a few loose ends in your friend's case,' Clement began, reaching out and pulling towards him a plain wooden chair that had been pushed up against one wall. Thankfully sinking into it, he left his stick propped up against the wall, and the moment the weight was off his legs, he felt his left knee begin to tremble.

He hoped it was obvious to neither of the young people in the room.

Martin nodded without enthusiasm and sank onto the edge of his bed – which had been neatly made that morning – and sighed.

'Poor Ray. It was a real shock, that,' he said, somewhat perfunctorily Trudy thought.

Apparently Clement thought so too. 'You were good friends?' he asked amiably enough, but his watery grey eyes were sharp as they scanned his face.

Martin hesitated, then shrugged. 'Not really no. I mean, we'd only known each other for a year, just about, when we formed the Rainbirds. It's not as if we went to school together, you know?'

'I see. So you were more … what, colleagues, shall we say?' Clement said.

'Yes, that's right.'

Clement nodded. 'And Ray was the lead singer? How are you—'

'What? No, he wasn't the lead singer,' Martin interrupted quickly and forcefully. 'Who told you that?' he demanded.

Clement looked mildly puzzled. 'Oh, it's just the impression people gave me. Was he not the leader of the band then?'

'No he bloody wasn't,' Martin said flatly. 'We shared the singing between us, and the songwriting.'

'Oh I see. But wasn't the band going to change its name to Ray Reason and the Rainbirds? Which seems to imply he would get top billing,' he said innocently. 'That's what somebody told me anyway.'

Martin's spotty face flushed a deeper red. 'Oh that! No, that was just one of Ray's daft ideas. He'd get them now and then, but we just ignored him. No way we'd have changed the name of the group. The Rainbirds is the name we're getting known under, and that's how it's going to stay,' he said firmly.

Trudy's eyebrows rose slightly.

'It must be hard, losing a major member of the band though,' Clement mused. 'Are you going to go on without him, or …'

'We might get in another singer who can play guitar,' Martin said. 'I've already started asking around. If I find enough people good enough, I'll do some auditioning.'

Again Trudy made a brisk note in her book. Although Linda was clearly mourning the loss of her boyfriend, it didn't look as if his fellow band member was shedding many tears for him. And she noticed that, for all Martin had tried to make it sound as if the Rainbirds was a democratic band, he'd said *I'll* do the auditioning. Not we. Would the other band members get a say in who he picked? Somehow, she didn't think so.

'That seems rather quick off the mark,' Clement said, careful to keep any censure out of his voice.

Martin shrugged and tried to look contrite. 'I know, I know, but the trouble is, you can't hang around. We've got to keep playing the clubs, otherwise we'll soon get forgotten. And right now, we've got a big agent from London looking as if he wants to sign us up and we can't afford to wait or muck about. We have to show him we're still a good band, and losing Ray isn't a problem.'

He looked at Clement with a mixture of aggression and guilt, but Clement merely nodded. 'Yes, I can see it's awkward for you. On the night Ray died, did you think Mr Reason was acting like his normal self?'

Martin sighed and bit a thumbnail, seemingly unaware that he was doing so. 'Yeah, I think so. I mean, yeah he was.'

'He didn't seem depressed or have anything on his mind?' the coroner pressed.

'Ray? Nah, he wasn't the sort to let anything worry him,'

Martin said with a brief smile. 'Ray was always sure he had the world by the tail.'

'And he hadn't been drinking more than usual?'

'No, Ray never drank much before playing,' Martin said, unknowingly echoing Linda's evidence. 'Afterwards, mind, he could knock the beer back a bit.'

'And you didn't see him arguing with anyone?' Clement persisted.

'Nah.'

'You don't know if was on the outs with anyone at all? Somebody at the club maybe, or on the music scene in general? No trouble with zealous fans, or other bands who were maybe getting jealous of your growing success?'

'Well, no not really. I mean some geezer in the Washboards used to have a pop at us now and then, but that's only because we've got a better sound than them and they know it.'

'So you can't think of anyone who might have had a grudge against him?'

Clement's eyes sharpened as Martin hesitated a bare fraction of a second before answering. 'Nah, nothing like that.'

'Are you sure?' Clement said briskly.

'Yeah, course I'm sure,' Martin said at once. But he didn't meet the coroner's gaze and he began to chew on his thumbnail with a bit more vigour. Then, realising what he was doing, he abruptly lowered his hand to his side.

'Where were you when you first realised that something was wrong that night?' Clement asked next.

'In the common room with the rest of the band,' Martin said quickly. 'We were making sure the instruments were all right, and the gear was all working properly. Pinky – sorry, Pete – our keyboard player was cracking his knuckles, just like always, before we went on stage; I remember that. It always gives Ian Scraggs, our bass guitar player, the willies when he does that, and I remember him telling Pinky to cut it out.'

'And the last time you saw Ray alive?'

'In the bar,' Martin said at once. 'Having a drink with his bird. I was with my bird, so I left them to it and went downstairs. Five, ten minutes later, I heard the stairs was blocked and we couldn't get up because somebody had fallen down 'em and was still lying there. It filtered back to us that it was Ray ... Well, you know the rest,' he said levelly, looking the coroner straight in the eye.

'Yes.'

'Look, I really am sorry about Ray, but ...' He looked at his watch again and stood up. 'I really have got things I need to do. Honest. Is there anything else?' It wasn't so much a question as a demand for them to leave.

'Not right now, Mr Cuthbertson,' Clement said, deciding that it wouldn't accomplish anything – at this point – to antagonise his witness, when he heard Trudy speak.

'If you could just give us the contact details of the London agent who's interested in signing you up, that would save us some time, sir.'

Clement knew he should have thought of that (and a year ago, he knew he would have) but tried not to look annoyed with himself as Trudy jotted down the answer.

'Look, you ain't going to go bothering him, are you?' Martin said anxiously as they moved past him in the small room. 'He's a very important man, and I don't want him to be put off us. The Rainbirds, I mean. This is our big chance, and I don't want him ... well ...'

'We'll be very discreet sir,' Trudy promised, but this was clearly not the answer he'd been hoping to hear, for as he stood in the doorway downstairs a minute later, watching them walk away, he looked both unhappy and anxious.

Back in the Rover once more, Trudy watched him finally shut the door, and sighed.

'An ambitious man, that,' Clement said quietly beside her.

'Yes. And I don't think there was too much love lost between him and the dead man, do you?'

'No. Sounds to me as if they were two cockerels wrestling it out between them as to who was going to be top of the dung heap, I reckon,' Clement said with a grim smile. And after a moment's thought, he added, 'And we all know how vicious cockfights can be, don't we?'

Chapter 12

Trudy made doubly sure that the traffic was clear for her to pull out (and thus not endanger the paintwork on the coroner's lovely car) before manoeuvring away from the kerb. This was probably why she failed to notice the identity of the man who had just pulled up a little way behind her now vacant parking space.

But the man noticed them all right.

Duncan Gillingham recognised the coroner's car at once, and could just make out the outline of Dr Ryder's trilby hat in the passenger seat, and the neat police cap of the young woman driving.

Instantly he felt his heart rate accelerate a little. Partly because his reporter's nose had just scented the possible whiff of a story, but mostly, he acknowledged grimly, because any glimpse of WPC Trudy Loveday tended to make him just a little breathless.

It was not, he knew, something that a recently married man should admit to. A tall, dark-haired and good-looking young man, he'd been working on the local paper owned by Sir Basil Fletcher for most of his career, when he'd met Glenda, Sir Basil's only child, at a staff party one Christmas. Much to her father's dismay, Glenda had been much taken with the young man, impressed by his humble working-class origins, good looks and ambition. Sir

Basil, Duncan knew, didn't rate him very highly, thinking him cocky and less than respectful of his elders, and wilfully oblivious of his so-called 'place' in society. But even he had had to admit that he'd provided his newspaper with several solid and good scoops over the years, making it very hard to fire him!

For his part, Duncan had been at first merely amused and flattered by Glenda's interest (mainly because he could see how much her dear daddy disapproved!) but hadn't taken it all that seriously. However, when the heir to her father's fortune proved to be rather stubborn in her choice of man, he'd quickly come to see the practical advantages of marrying the heir to the paper he was working on.

Also, Glenda was pretty enough, shared and encouraged his ambition to make it to Fleet Street one day, and seemed amenable to most of his suggestions, and so they had become engaged.

Since he was in no hurry to get married and tied down, though, he'd managed to convince her that a long engagement was for the best. In this, he was ably backed up by Glenda's father, who took the opinion that the longer the marriage could be put off, the more likely it would be that Duncan would blot his copybook and Glenda would give him the elbow.

Alas, Duncan had been far too wily for that.

And then he'd covered a story that had brought him into the orbit of one very attractive, young, naïve but feisty woman police constable, and he'd been severely tempted. At first, he'd thought he could hide a dalliance from Glenda, and had been somewhat surprised – and peeved – to discover that Trudy Loveday seemed immune to his charms.

Oh, she'd been attracted to him at first, of that he had no doubt. A young man as good-looking as himself had learned enough about the fairer sex to know when he'd made an impression. But the instant that interfering old man, Clement Ryder, had told her about his engagement, Trudy had started giving him the cold shoulder and rebuffed his every advance.

And even though he'd now reported on several of the suspicious death cases that the coroner and Trudy had unearthed in the last few years, even managing to help save her life on one occasion, he'd never been able to win her over again or gain her trust. His refusal to break off the engagement to Glenda had seen to that!

Now, as he watched the coroner's car disappear down the road, he felt the old familiar thrill of the chase creep over him – both the professional and the personal kind.

He turned and looked at the house he was about to visit, his green eyes alight with speculation. Ostensibly, he'd arrived here thinking that he was going to be doing a run-of-the-mill 'filler' story for his editor about a rising young pop band, and the tragic death of their young lead singer. The kind of sob story to pull at the heartstrings of their readers over their morning marmalade and toast, but one they'd quickly forget as they got on with their daily lives.

But now, he was hoping that he had stumbled onto something far more interesting. For where there was Trudy and Dr Ryder, so too was there was a story. A *real* story?

For some reason that nobody in the news office could quite find out, the city coroner, Dr Clement Ryder, and a lowly WPC had been allowed to investigate several cases that had turned out to be red hot. So the fact that the dynamic pair had just been talking to the man he'd come to interview was definitely making him wonder. Was there more to the death of Ray Reason of Rainbirds' fame than met the eye?

He hoped so, if only because it would give him a good excuse to see more of a certain pretty WPC. He would need to get some quotes from her, wouldn't he? And nobody, not even Glenda or her eagle-eyed father, could say anything about it, because he was only doing his job, wasn't he?

With a definite spring in his step now, Duncan Gillingham walked up to the house where Martin Cuthbertson was expecting him and rattled the letterbox doorknocker. In his head he was already abandoning the mild questions he'd scheduled and was trying to think up ones that would get him started sniffing in the right direction.

*

Unaware that they'd been observed leaving Martin's house – and by whom – Trudy and Clement chatted as she drove him back to Floyds Row.

'What do you want to do tomorrow?' Trudy asked him, as a Foden lorry nearly cut her up at a T-junction.

Clement, who had a hand on his still-trembling knee, didn't even react to the near-miss and gave it some thought. 'We should talk to Martin's girlfriend ...' He searched for her name, but to his horror, couldn't think of it. To cover his lapse, he said quickly, 'The one with the amusing nickname.' At least he remembered that much.

Trudy nodded. 'Jenny Wren? Yes, they have a thing about names, don't they? Linda being called Lindy-Lou, and now Jennifer Renfrew. All right, I'll make sure I know her details, then pick you up tomorrow,' she promised.

She parked the Rover in his reserved parking spot, said goodbye and trotted off on the short walk back to the station. If she knew Inspector Jennings, he'd have a load of jobs for her to do. Probably cataloguing the evidence locker, or something equally gripping!

She sighed, but was cheerful enough, as she wove her way through the busy streets, her eye, as always, routinely on the lookout for traffic violations, pickpockets or drunk and disorderly men weaving in and out of the pubs.

Back at the entrance to the mortuary, Clement watched her walk away and felt his heart sink. Soon he was going to have to tell her that this would be their last investigation together, and he wasn't looking forward to it.

But that could wait until they'd finished the case, he told himself firmly. Why spoil it for her? He wanted her to enjoy their last case without a pall hanging over her, as it was him.

With a grim expression he turned and made his way to his office.

At least his knee had stopped feeling so weak. For now.

Chapter 13

The next day, Friday, dawned warm and fine.

Fifteen-year-old Delia Pinney trudged through the gates of her school, her satchel hanging loose from her hand and almost dragging on the playground's tarmac. She was a small, very thin, dark-haired girl with glasses, and wore her uniform resentfully, as if they were pieces of rag.

Normally she didn't mind going to school so much – she was quite bright really, and enjoyed most of her lessons – well, except maybe for maths. But now she was finding it harder and harder to just to get through the days, doing all the usual things she had done before, all the while desperately pretending to both herself and everyone else that everything was all right.

As she headed across the playground, her English teacher noted her drooping shoulders and downcast gaze and frowned. In the past week or so, he'd noticed that Delia wasn't herself. Her essays, which he usually enjoyed reading, were now distinctly lacklustre and sometimes even late, a hitherto unknown occurrence. She looked constantly tired in class too, as if she wasn't sleeping right. He wondered if there were problems at home.

Delia, unaware of adult scrutiny, made her way wearily to assembly, standing at the back of the hall and barely singing the hymn or listening to the headmaster's daily exhortations to do her best. As she trooped out behind the others filing away to get to their first class of the day, she felt her best friend, Hilda Bainbridge, fall in beside her. Like Delia she was also dark-haired and needed glasses, (a common bond that had probably first drawn them together) but she was taller than Delia and, being plumper, had a much better bosom. A fact that Delia secretly but fiercely resented.

'Hello, you look a right misery guts today. What's up?' Hilda asked jauntily.

'Nothing,' Delia said instantly and sharply.

'Sorry I asked,' Hilda shot back, but the look she cast her friend wasn't so much hurt as speculative. She too was very aware that something was upsetting her friend, but so far she hadn't been able to winkle out of her what it was. Which was very annoying. Hilda liked to be in the know about things.

'Fancy coming over to my place tonight?' Hilda said, as they negotiated their way through the busy corridors to room 12B where their geography lesson was about to start with old 'Chewed-Up Bones', known to his face as Mr Tudor-Jones. 'You remember those patterns for those shift dresses that I sent away for? Well they've come, and Mum's bought some lovely flowery material so we can make our dresses at last! We'll look great in them.'

Delia shrugged. 'Sure, why not,' she agreed listlessly. It was easier to just comply than to try and think up an excuse to stay away.

Hilda huffed an exaggerated sigh. Now she *knew* something was definitely up with her friend. Usually Delia would be cock-a-hoop at the thought of a new dress. Although Hilda had a better figure for fashion, it was Delia who was really into that sort of thing. Fashion, pop music, the cinema – all that sort of stuff.

'Well, don't sound so excited,' Hilda complained. 'I can always make a dress for just me, on my own. I don't have to let you make one for yourself, you know.'

Delia tried to look contrite. 'Sorry, Hills. Of course I'll come.' She didn't say more as they were now trooping into the classroom and everybody knew old Chewed-Up Bones didn't like his class talking too much when they came in and got themselves settled down.

Delia and Hilda went to 'their' desks, which they'd picked on the first day of school because they were side by side with an aisle gap either side, and, lifting up the wooden top, Hilda reached inside for the textbooks that were kept there. Today was Norwegian fjords. Hilda rolled her eyes and sighed with anticipated boredom, picking up her pencil and seeing if the tip was sharp.

Delia simply sat staring down at her desk, and Hilda was obliged to give her a quick dig in the ribs with her elbow to get her cracking before old Chewed-Up spotted her slacking.

Delia jumped, then belatedly retrieved her own books. Hilda watched her, feeling a mixture of anger and worry. If Delia didn't pull her socks up soon, she was going to get in serious trouble.

As their teacher began to talk about ice ages and how they formed rock formations, glaciers and fjords, Hilda wondered what had her best friend in such a state of gloom. It couldn't be a boy, because Delia always told her straight away who she had a crush on. And she had got over that silly toad Jeremy Collingsworth ages ago. Anyway, nowadays all she could talk about was some drummer in a local band.

She might have had a fight with her mum or dad, Hilda supposed, since they could be a bit strict, but again, usually Delia came straight to her to air her grievances after a family row.

It wasn't anything to do with school. Hilda knew that Delia was a bit cleverer than herself, though she was doing all right, getting mostly B's to Delia's A's.

Catching the geography teacher's eagle eye on her, and fearing that she wasn't looking attentive enough, Hilda straightened her spine and tried to look intelligent. But once the old man's eye had passed her over, Hilda let her thoughts wander again.

One thing was for certain – whatever was bothering Delia, she was going to get it out of her one way or another. But how? That was the thing. It was no use just demanding that Delia spill the beans, when it was obvious that she wasn't going to. She'd had plenty of time to confess the source of her woes by now, and she hadn't done so. And it was no use trying to trick her into confessing what the problem was, since, well, Delia was too clever for her.

No, if she was going to get to the bottom of things, Hilda knew she would have to try another angle. Come at the problem with a fresh approach. Hilda let the teacher's geological gems float over her head and put her thinking cap on.

So, what did she actually *know*? When did it all start, first off? Maybe that would give her a clue. She'd been all right a week Friday, because she was all of a giggle about going to see that pop band she was so obsessed with.

Of course, her parents didn't know that she went out on Saturdays to see pop singers; they thought she was going to another friend's house to play Monopoly. That's what Delia told them. Could they have found out somehow and banned her from sneaking into the nightclubs? That would certainly give her the glooms.

Hilda shot her friend a quick look and saw that she was once again staring blankly at her desk – not even taking notes. And for the first time, she felt almost afraid.

Delia looked awful! Something was definitely wrong with her, and Hilda needed to find out what it was so that she could help her.

They were best friends, after all.

And if she was also madly curious to know what was up, well, that was only human, wasn't it?

Chapter 14

Jennifer Renfrew had worked in Oxford's Woolworths shop for over a year now, and didn't like it much better now than the day she'd started.

Having just recently celebrated her twentieth birthday, she'd been in Oxford since running away from home when she'd been sixteen, and she was getting impatient for her life to get started.

She was born in the poor but respectable back streets of London's southern fringes, where her father William had died when she was just ten. Her mother, Doris, had remarried two years later, and Jenny couldn't stand the man who had tried to take her father's place. He was too free with his fists for one thing, and wanted to have far too much say in how she was supposed to live her life for another.

After two years of putting up with it, she had left, choosing Oxford on a whim. She'd seen a poster advertising the charms of the beautiful university city on a railway poster and liked the look of it.

After the size, dirt, noise and grime of London, it had seemed like a bit of a rural backwater at first, but Jenny had quickly found consolation and like-minded free spirits in the ever-shifting student population of bright young things who regularly came and went. These students, she'd quickly found, could always be relied upon for a laugh. More importantly than that, they shared her excitement at the way the times were changing, and like her, believed that in this brave new decade of the 1960s, anybody could achieve anything they wanted.

In their ranks she felt as if she'd found her tribe. So much so, that she'd found digs for herself in an Edwardian house in St Ebbes, which was rented out almost exclusively to students. Lying to the landlady by claiming that she was reading Jurisprudence at St Hilda's College, Jenny quickly settled down to enjoy her newfound freedoms, with her pick of young male students.

It thrilled her that she could find herself sitting next to a posh peer of the realm in some café one day, and then listen to the Marxist rants of some working-class male who was going to destroy the system from within the next.

In the end, it was one of the more cosmopolitan and irreverent Hooray Henries who'd introduced her to the delights of the Bootleggers Club one evening, where she'd drunk dodgy champagne and danced to a variety of bands, some good, some bad, some indifferent.

She'd always enjoyed modern music, but her allegiance to the more American-style rock'n'roll quickly changed to pop when it became clear that Britain was beginning to lead the world in this new wave of music, along with the fashion that came with it.

That first night at the notorious nightclub, it had been the Rainbirds who'd caught her eye – and Martin Cuthbertson in particular. Although Ray Reason had been better-looking, she knew she had a good ear, and thought Martin was marginally the better singer and guitar player.

Martin was also much easier prey for her than the smug, sure-of-himself Ray, suffering as he did from a distinct lack of confidence, which had been engendered in him by his bandmate's obvious popularity with the female fans.

But Jenny had big plans for Martin, primarily as her meal ticket into the jet-set lifestyle she saw being dangled in front of her in the glossy magazines. And it hadn't taken her long to court, dazzle and ensnare him.

Now, at just gone nine-thirty in the morning, she was dressed in her smart Woolworths shopgirl uniform, which ironically enough suited her lean angular figure, and made the most of her short blonde hair and large grey eyes. She knew she was striking-looking rather than being actually pretty, but she was happy enough with the deal nature had dealt her. Prettiness could be insipid – striking could never be anything less than eye-catching.

Working at Woolworths was a total chore, obviously, but Jenny knew she wouldn't have to stick it for much longer. Martin and the band were on the verge of making it big-time – she could just smell it. The fact that that shark Titus Crowther-Beauley was sniffing around was proof enough of that.

In the meantime, she made good use of her employee discount at the shop's make-up counter and clothes section.

She was currently helping stock up the sweet counter, and was just emptying a big bag of sherbet lemons into the nearly empty clear plastic 'bin' when she sensed a presence beside her.

She looked around, surprised to see a woman police officer looking at her with a polite smile. Beside her was a tall, good-looking man in his late twenties with dark blond hair and a foxy-shaped face.

'Hello. Miss Renfrew?' the policewoman asked pleasantly.

Instantly, Jenny felt a moment of panic sweep over her. Like most of those born working-class and poor in London, she didn't like it when the police took notice of her. And although she hadn't been – technically – on the run from a *police* point of view, she'd nevertheless cultivated a very private and wary outlook since having been forced to fend for herself. For the first two years of her life in her new home town, she'd lived in fear that her stepfather might locate her and drag her back by the scruff of her neck. Which made her wary of anything out of the ordinary – like a visit by these two.

Realising her unwanted visitors were waiting for a reply, she forced a puzzled smile onto her face. 'Yes, that's me,' she agreed cautiously.

'I'm Police Constable Loveday.' The woman held out her police identification card. 'I'm helping the city coroner, Dr Clement Ryder, close the inquest of Raymond Reason.'

Jenny let her already slightly puzzled look deepen. 'Oh? I thought that was all over with? Wasn't it ruled an accident?' she said, letting her gaze drift to the handsome young man, then back to the policewoman.

'Yes, it was, we're just tying up some loose ends,' Constable Loveday said casually.

Jenny didn't like the sound of this. 'I didn't know there *were* any loose ends that needed tying,' she said, but made sure that she kept a small smile on her face as she said it. 'So, how can I be of help?'

'We just wondered if you noticed anything different about Ray that night. His behaviour, I mean.'

Again, Jenny's eyes went from the policewoman – who was rather young and attractive underneath that ridiculous cap – to the young man beside her. Who was he exactly? Jenny fretted. He wasn't in uniform, so if he was police too, he had to be in plain clothes. Did plain-clothes police investigate deaths that had already been ruled an accident? Somehow, she didn't think so.

'I'm sorry, this is Vincent Ryder, Dr Ryder's son,' the police-woman said.

Jenny noticed that she spoke reluctantly, as if she'd rather been hoping not to have to explain his presence at all. Then she caught the look in his eyes as Vincent Ryder glanced at his companion, and instantly she felt a little better about things.

He was her boyfriend! The crafty mare was combining her work with a little pleasure. Well, good on her, Jenny thought sourly. But why couldn't they go pick on someone else?

She didn't need this right now!

'I see,' Jenny said. 'And no, to answer your question: Ray seemed much the same as usual that night.'

'You didn't see him arguing with anyone, say?'

Jenny pretended to think about it, her mind racing. Why were they asking things like that, if they were convinced it had been an accident? And if they *weren't* sure, then she needed to throw somebody under the bus! Jenny hadn't looked after herself for years without learning that you always looked after number one first.

Right now, the Rainbirds didn't need any bad publicity. They were riding high with their fans, having their sympathy vote because of Ray's shocking demise. And it had even brought them to the notice of some of the industry's minor movers and shakers. But the local radio stations wouldn't give airtime to an unknown band that had the whiff of something dodgy about them. And as for being signed up by a record company, they could forget about it.

Damn Ray! The big-headed sod was still causing everyone problems even now he was dead!

'Miss Renfrew? I asked if you knew anybody that Mr Reason might have been having issues with?' the policewoman repeated, shaking Jenny out of her inner grumbling.

'Only that slimy toad who runs the club,' she said casually.

'Felix Simpkins?' the policewoman asked sharply.

Jenny made sure she didn't look smug. So, somebody else had also noticed that Ray must have had something on good old Felix and had already said something to the coppers. Good.

'Yes, Felix. For some reason, he and Ray never got on,' she said mildly. 'They often had little digs at each other,' she added vaguely. It didn't do to be *too* keen. She just needed to do enough to keep their attention away from the band, that was all.

'Do you know why?'

Jenny could make a good guess – but the sooner this disconcerting pair left her alone, the better she'd like it. Besides, only a fool volunteered information to the authorities – everyone knew that. Let them do their own dirty work! She simply shrugged. 'No idea, sorry.' She even managed to sound genuinely regretful.

'And you were in the bar with Linda Kempson when you heard that there'd been an accident?' The policewoman kept at it.

Jenny bit back a sigh and forced herself to be patient. And careful. 'Lindy-Lou? No, not *with* her, exactly. I mean, we were both having a drink and listening to the band that was up, but we weren't together, together.'

'You're not friends?' the policewoman asked, looking interested.

Jenny shrugged again. 'She's all right, but we don't really have that much in common. And I haven't known her that long, you see. Look, I don't want to sound hard or anything, but if I don't get on with this—' she indicated the bags of sweets on the floor around her '—my supervisor will have my guts for garters, so …?'

The handsome young man and the policewoman both gave understanding smiles, and WPC Loveday thanked her politely for her time, and then they both left.

Jennifer Renfrew watched them disappear past the stuffed toy aisle and all the way on until they were out of sight, then slowly reached for the giant bag of gobstoppers nearest to her and began to pile them into the correct 'bin'. She made sure the little scoop was in place before closing the lid and reaching for the liquorice dolly mixture.

Yet her mind was not on confectionery but on her visitors.

They were a complication she really didn't need right now.

She checked her watch (bought at a discount at the shop) and counted down the time until her lunch break, when she could meet Martin at his place. He was due to see Titus Crowther-Beauley to discuss life after Ray and what any contracts between them would entail, and Jenny had made him promise not to start without her.

Marty was a bit of an innocent really – well, all the boys in the band were, being only local country bumpkins. But she knew that people like the showbiz agent didn't get to be as big-time and as rich as they were by being generous, and she was determined to read and fully understand what every word and line meant before she let the band sign up with him. Even if she had to spend some of her hard-won wages paying a solicitor to explain it all to her.

As ever, Marty had agreed with her reasoning (she was getting him trained just right) even though he was almost bursting with excitement at having the Londoner for their manager.

Soon they would have to choose a new guitar player to replace Ray as well, and she was going to be there for that too. It was vital that they made the right choice and found someone who'd be happy to just play guitar and to sing back-up vocals. And not someone too good-looking either.

The last thing she needed was to be saddled with another Ray Reason!

It was Martin's turn now to take on the role as lead – and sole – singer of the Rainbirds.

Once she'd badgered him into getting his teeth seen to by a good dentist, and got some proper treatment for that skin of his, he'd brush up well. With proper clothes and the right haircut, he would be every bit as charismatic as the dead man had been.

She wouldn't let him be anything else.

Chapter 15

Linda Kempson glanced nervously around the quiet library as she approached the shelf dedicated to botany. It was her local branch (not the place where she worked) and was seldom packed, but she still felt oddly exposed as she made her way through the bookshelves.

She knew it was only her guilty conscience that was making her feel as if accusing eyes were watching her every move, and she told herself not to be so stupid. Nobody could possibly know why she was there, or what she was looking for.

She selected several books, all dedicated to British wild flowers and their habits and habitats, and took them to a deserted table in a far corner. Once she was seated, she reached into her bag and pulled out a notebook and pencil.

Another quick glance around told her that absolutely nobody was paying her any attention whatsoever. Nevertheless, she felt her hands shake a little as she reached for the first book and opened it up to the index. She felt vaguely nauseous too, and could feel the beginnings of a nervous headache.

She hadn't slept more than a few hours at a time since her world had imploded and now she was beginning to feel distinctly unwell. Not eating properly hadn't helped either. Before, she'd always felt as healthy and as fit as a horse, and it was coming as a bit of a shock to her now, to feel her body betraying her in this way. She'd always taken youth and strength for granted, and now she felt weak, both mentally and physically, and it was beginning to truly frighten her.

She'd lain awake for hours last night, trying to see any other way out of her predicament, just as she had lain awake for hours every night since Ray had died, hoping that something would occur to her. That the answer on how she could return her world to normal without having to resort to dire measures, would somehow magically appear from the ether.

But it never did.

Now she had finally faced the fact that she needed to act, before it all became too late.

Trying to summon up a clear head and a cold heart, she started work, reading assiduously, making notes occasionally and going back to the shelves for more books on herbs, old folklore and medicine, as and when needed.

Eventually, after a few hours of diligent work, she was satisfied that she had made the right choice. It seemed that the flower pennyroyal was her best bet. A member of the mint family – *Lamiaceae* – its crushed leaves tasted a bit like peppermint, so it wouldn't even taste nasty to swallow. Better still, it was a common wild plant, so she should have no trouble finding it growing somewhere nearby in the fields and hedgerows; it was distinctive-looking enough for her to be sure she could spot it with confidence and not mistake it for something else.

Best of all – it was an acknowledged abortifacient.

Now feeling more sick and shaky than ever, she slipped her notebook full of research back into her bag, then put all the books back neatly on the shelf. Another hasty look around reassured her, yet again, that no accusing or knowing eyes were watching her, and she walked quickly from the library.

Outside, she paused against a nearby lamp post and took

several deep, calming breaths. She still half expected the housewives in the street, doing their daily shopping, to stop and stare at her, as if she had some kind of bright scarlet or black-as-night brand on her somewhere, advertising her sin and the greater sin she was about to commit.

She watched one woman, a middle-aged, comfortable old biddy, walk past, checking her shopping list, probably on the way to the butcher's down the street. How many children did she have? Linda wondered bleakly. Three, four? More? And how quickly would the pleasant expression on her bland, amiable face change to condemnation if she could have read Linda's thoughts?

If only Ray had been pleased to hear about the baby! If only he'd said he would stand by her and marry her right away. They might have had to marry in haste, and people would inevitably have talked, but it wouldn't have mattered – not really. Times were changing and, besides, people could be surprisingly pragmatical about things like that – just so long as the couple married.

Instead he'd been horrified when she'd told him she was pregnant.

For weeks she'd put it off, thinking she might just be late, or maybe there was another reason for missing her periods. But last Saturday night, she'd taken the plunge and told him.

She could still see the expression of disbelief on his face, and then the dawning panic grow in his eyes as she'd explained to him her condition.

She could remember it as if it had happened only a moment ago. Standing in the dingy back corridor, the sound of the Undergrads belting out a song in the background, the smell of cigarette smoke and beer wafting from the main dance room.

And Ray, dressed in his best suit, excited about the new song they were going to sing and hopeful that the fans would go wild over it. And then all of that joie de vivre just seeping out of him as he'd understood what she was telling him, as the stark reality of life intruded so rudely into his dreams.

He'd tried to make a joke of it at first, to make her admit that she was just pulling his leg and giving him a scare. But then, when he realised that it was all only too real, and she explained the need for a quick wedding, his face had darkened and become set.

They'd argued.

He'd tried to persuade her that they simply couldn't marry – that it would ruin the band's chances of fame. That the teenage girls wouldn't come and listen to a boring married man with a baby singing about teenage love and conquering the world!

She'd tried to make him see the good things about it – that he would be a daddy, with his own little son or daughter to love, and that they could be so happy. But even as she spoke, she could see that the idea of domesticity only filled him with dread.

He'd offered to help her get rid of it – to pay for the procedure and drive her to wherever she needed to go and back again. And it was then that something in her heart began to crack and leak, spreading a cold, seeping poison into her blood that made her vision blur and her mind fill with fear.

And when, not long after that moment, in a last desperate bid for freedom he'd said that he couldn't even be sure that the baby was his anyway, it had been the final straw. The accusation of infidelity had shocked her to the core, and sent her into a blind, overwhelming rage …

Linda took a deep breath, and pushed the ugly memories aside. It was no good thinking of all that now.

She had other, even more ugly things to think about.

And do.

Chapter 16

As Linda walked away from the library, her thoughts as black and bleak as midwinter, Jenny Renfrew all but skipped along the street to Martin's place, her thoughts on her bright new future.

As she walked towards Martin's lodgings, Titus Crowther-Beauley drove past her in his ostentatious Bentley. Spotting her, he let rip with a nasty curse. He'd thought that he would be seeing Martin Cuthbertson on his own, giving him plenty of time and scope to work his magic on the gullible new leader of the band.

He was already confident that the other members of the Rainbirds would follow where he led, only too willing, like the brainless sheep they were, to be dazzled by the promise of fame and money. Poorly educated teenage lads could always be easily manipulated, in Titus's experience. The Rainbirds weren't the only pop band he was currently wooing, and he'd already landed a number of such groups for his stable. Several of which were beginning to do quite well for him in this new emerging pop culture. He didn't know how long this latest fad would last, but he was looking forward to reaping the benefits of the nice little sideline they represented in his business for at least the next couple of years.

Unlike some of his more seasoned and cynical actors, young

lads dreaming of pop stardom were easy to please. Make sure they got good venues, had access to plenty of booze and pretty girls, and most of them could be gulled into thinking that the money he paid out to them was a good portion of what they actually made. With almost no exceptions, most of the new pop groups that were emerging nowadays consisted of working-class lads who'd grown up living on the wages that their labourer fathers earned. So they already knew that the most they could expect from life was the pittance that the factories paid them, or the mines, or shops. To them, the amount that Titus paid felt like luxury indeed.

Of course, it was nothing compared to his own bite of the cherry!

Very rarely, he came across a lad with a bit more about him – like Ray Reason – who, either through above-average intelligence or because of a natural innate guile figured it out when an expert was trying to bilk them.

But Titus knew how to deal with the likes of them.

With Ray now out of the picture, he had no worries that he wouldn't be able to get Martin Cuthbertson just where he wanted him. Although he was no dope, he *was* hungry for success and that alone would be enough to blind him to the harsh conditions set out in Titus's standard contracts.

But his bloody girlfriend was a different matter. Although he was still in the early stages of wooing the Rainbirds, he was a fast and accurate judge of character, and the amusingly named 'Jenny Wren' wasn't the least bit as charming as her nickname suggested. In fact, it hadn't taken him very long at all to come to the conclusion that she was as hard as nails.

Somewhere, somehow, that young woman had learned some hard lessons in life, and would be very unlikely to sign a contract without studying it first. Worse, she had her claws very firmly into the Rainbirds' new leading man, and she might just have enough power and influence over him to queer Titus's pitch.

If there was one thing that could turn a teenage lad's mind from money and fame, it was sex! It was obvious to Titus that Jennifer Renfrew had selected Martin to be her ticket to fame and fortune. And a girl like that would be no pushover.

Seeing her striking blonde head and lean figure heading towards Martin's house came as a distinct and nasty shock.

Cursing her fluently and prolifically under his breath (public school had been an education in more ways than one) he pulled the car to the pavement and got out. So much for his plans to get the Rainbirds all sewn up and in his pocket today.

He had been hoping to get Marty to sign on the dotted line without delay, buoyed up and reassured by the fact that one of Titus's other bands had currently made it into the hit parade with some awful racket called 'Love Shoots Me Down'.

Now he sighed and forced a smile onto his face once he'd parked and climbed out of his car, because Jenny Renfrew, spotting him, had speeded up quickly to intercept him.

'Miss Renfrew, lovely to see you again,' Titus lied blithely as she reached his side, panting just slightly. He couldn't help but run his eyes over her quickly. She wasn't beautiful, but she certainly had something. And the minx knew it.

'Hello, Titus,' she said coolly. 'When Marty said he was seeing you today, I couldn't wait to hear what it was all about. Congratulations on "Love Shoots Me Down" by the way. Of course, the song's not much, but it's got a catchy beat. The lead singer can't sing as well as Marty, though, can he?'

Titus smiled, knowing that the dratted little chit was quite right – on both counts. The song currently catching the hearts – and loins – of the teenage population of the nation wasn't a particularly good song, but it was making him a lot of money. And Martin Cuthbertson *was* a better singer.

As he met her slightly mocking big grey eyes, he could cheerfully have strangled her. 'Oh, Marty is going to be a big star, I have no doubt,' he said blandly.

Jenny Renfrew's smile grew wider. 'Nice to see we agree on that,' she said amiably. 'Now, why don't we go on up to Marty's room and see what else we can agree on?'

Titus smiled even more widely. 'Yes, why don't we?' he agreed pleasantly, already mentally rearranging his strategy, and trying to think of a way to make sure that the next time he met with the Rainbirds front man, this annoying little fly-in-the-ointment would be excluded. And, ultimately, how to prise her out of Marty's orbit.

Mentally, he began making a list of potential nubile young women who owed him a favour, or would be willing to do him a favour, in exchange for a helping hand up the greasy ladder of stardom. It shouldn't be hard for one of them to seduce a relative innocent like Marty. Pretty soon, his current girlfriend would be nothing more than a memory.

He bit back a smile as he followed Jenny up the garden path, to where Martin was eagerly waiting for them.

Martin might not know it, but he was about to become very popular with the ladies!

*

Whilst Martin Cuthbertson eagerly listened to Titus's promises of wealth and fame, Dr Clement Ryder sat in his office wondering what day it was. He was due in court later and had reached for his desk diary to check something. After pulling it to him and opening it up, however, he suddenly realised that not only did he have no idea of the date, he didn't even know what day of the week it was.

For a moment, he sat frozen in panic, his mind scrambling for something to seize on. Something, some event, to give him a clue. Had he seen the morning paper? Did that help? Had he read about an event due to take place at a set time that would help him work it all out?

Just as he was about to go over his activities of that morning in an effort to find some other clue, his mind suddenly and easily supplied the answer.

It was Friday.

Of course it was Friday. Tomorrow was Saturday, when his son and Trudy were going to visit the Bootleggers Club and mix with the crowd and listen to what everyone was saying about Ray Reason, and see if they could pick up anything that would help their case.

He remembered now, he and Trudy had agreed that they were going to see that oily character Felix Simpkins tomorrow morning to squeeze him some more for general information. Also to make sure that he didn't 'out' Vincent and Trudy to his regular club-goers when they showed up at the club later that night.

By now, they'd reasoned, Clement's influence would have made itself more than apparent to the nightclub manager, and he should be in a more cooperative frame of mind.

The coroner leaned back in his chair and let out a tense sigh. Although it had felt as if it had lasted for minutes, his total lapse of memory had probably only lasted a second or two – maybe even not that long. Thought processes often acted quicker than people realised. But the fact that it had happened at all frightened him.

It wasn't often Clement admitted to feeling fear, but neither was he a man to duck ugly facts. For a moment there, he had not known what day it was.

True, this was the first time that this had happened to him in any significant way. But how long would it be before it would take him more than a moment or two to remember things? And how long would it be before the episodes of confusion became more frequent?

Not much was known about Parkinson's disease compared to other conditions, but what little research had been done was enough to confirm his own conclusions that his time was slowly running out.

And his moment of disorientation was a warning bell that he heard loud and clear. He could no longer – totally – rely on his own faculties.

He'd been putting off this moment for a while now, even after making the mental decision to retire, and promising his concerned son that he was going to do so. Now, sitting at his desk, and holding on firmly to the fact that it was Friday and he was due in court soon, Dr Clement Ryder knew he could put it off no longer.

Reaching into his desk, he withdrew a sheet of paper. It was of good quality, of course, and bore the shield and legend of Coroner of the City of Oxford at the top, with his office address rendered in embossed black italics underneath.

He glanced at his diary, confirmed the date and neatly inscribed it in the top right-hand corner, as was his habit.

Then he calmly and resolutely wrote out his letter of resignation.

He kept his reasons for leaving vague, and a wry smile crossed his lips as he realised that there were probably a few people who wouldn't care why he was leaving, just so long as he did!

He wondered who they would have in mind to replace him. He had his own candidate in mind, of course, and would make damn sure that the man of his choice got appointed. Just as a final reminder that, whilst he might be going, he was still the old vulture and they'd best not forget it.

For a moment, with the short but implacable missive now written, he found his fountain pen hesitating at the bottom of the page. And his hand began to shake.

With a curse, and before the tell-tale shakes could get any worse, he signed his name with a determined flourish.

He blotted it, put it in an envelope and then locked it in the top drawer of his desk, where his secretary couldn't accidentally stumble across it.

She would be sad to see him go, of that Clement was sure. They'd understood each other and worked together well during

113

his tenure. And he wanted to tell her that she'd have to start working for a new boss soon.

That done, he stood up and walked across to where his short black robe hung on a stand, and began to get ready for his court appearance.

When he swept through his outer office, his face was bland and he smiled briefly at his secretary before leaving.

Chapter 17

Saturday morning dawned relatively bright and sunny, and it was, unusually, Trudy's day off! It wasn't often she got a whole Saturday to herself, as junior members of the police force tended to find themselves on duty, leaving the weekend free for their superiors to enjoy. But sometimes not even the powers that be could interfere with the fates and the police roster, and this time, miraculously, Trudy didn't have to report to the station before heading off to Dr Ryder's house.

Vincent answered the door, a smile of welcome crossing his face as he saw her. Trudy felt a warm glow at his obvious pleasure, and she was glad that, for once, she wasn't dressed in her uniform, but a pretty floral skirt and white blouse, with a one-colour cardigan over it that matched one of the flower colours. She'd left her hair unencumbered for once and, curly and long, it fell well past her shoulders in a dark mass. She didn't miss the admiring look the coroner's son gave it as she passed him in the hallway, and she felt her heart skip a little.

Vincent ushered her through to the kitchen, where Clement was sitting at the generous oak kitchen table, reading the newspapers. He quickly put them aside as she walked in and nodded a greeting.

The breakfast dishes were already washed and stacked neatly in the dish rack by the sink, Trudy noted, and the scent of toast and Oxford marmalade lingered faintly in the air.

'Tea?' Vincent asked, and she nodded, taking a seat opposite her mentor and resting her folded hands neatly on top of the table. Dr Ryder looked rather tired, she thought, as if he hadn't slept well.

'Me and Dad have just been discussing the best strategy for tonight,' Vincent said cheerfully as he filled the kettle and set it to boil. 'We thought it would make sense to arrive at the club as a couple, but then split up after a bit and see what we can learn. I'll talk to the girls, you to the boys, and between us we should pick up on any gossip worth having.'

'Makes sense,' Trudy agreed. Having Vincent constantly by her side would prevent lone males from chatting freely with her, and vice versa.

'You'll also need to try and talk to the rest of the Rainbirds,' Clement put in, eyeing Trudy's pretty outfit with a small smile. He'd noticed his son notice it too. 'See what they can remember about the night Ray died.'

'What do we do if Linda and Jennifer are there? Won't they recognise Trudy?' Vincent asked, spooning tea leaves into the brown crockery teapot and shooting the young policewoman a questioning look.

'Maybe not, out of uniform and with my hair long. I'll be sure to put on plenty of make-up too. And it's sure to be pretty dark in the main dance hall,' Trudy said. 'I doubt Linda will be there anyway – she can't be in the mood for singing and dancing right now. And if Jenny Wren *is* there, I'll just have to do my best to avoid her.'

'Sounds like a plan,' Vincent said with a grin. 'Let's hope we strike gold somewhere.'

116

Chapter 18

As Vincent, Trudy and Clement discussed their strategy for the coming night, Delia Pinney was busy sewing the hem of her new shift dress. In her friend's small box bedroom at the top of the house, they felt safe from the prying big ears of the grown-ups and were chatting freely.

Hilda, the better seamstress, had already finished her garment and was trying it on, and was now observing herself in the mirror hanging on the inside door of her wardrobe. 'It needs to be tighter round the bust, don't you think?' she asked idly.

Her friend looked up and scowled. Hilda's bust looked quite big enough to her! 'Which boy are you trying to impress?' she asked sarcastically.

Hilda grinned, good-naturedly not taking offence. 'None of your beeswax! Actually, I was thinking of wearing it to that club you're always on about.' She could see her friend in the reflection, sitting on the edge of the bed, her head bent over her dress.

As expected, she saw Delia's head shoot up at this remark. 'What? What do you mean? You *can't* go to the Bootleggers Club!' she squeaked.

'Why not?' Hilda asked defiantly. 'You do. You keep telling me it's easy to get past the doorman. You just dress up and put on a lot of make-up and tell them you're eighteen. Or have you been telling fibs all this time, and you're really not as daring as you pretend?' she mocked tauntingly.

But Delia only bit her lip and returned her attention to her dress.

'I was right!' Hilda crowed. 'I'll bet you haven't even seen or listened to that great pop group you've been bragging about. "Oh, the Rainbirds are fab, Hilly, you should hear them. They're even better than the Beatles." Phooey!' Hilda said. 'Admit it. You've never even seen them play.'

'That's not true,' Delia denied hotly, looking up from her dogged stitching. 'I've seen them play plenty of times.'

'Well then. If you can do it, so can I,' her friend shot back with quick satisfaction. 'Tonight, why don't we go together? If you're so well known to the man on the door you can get me in too,' Hilda added implacably.

In truth, she had always been a little jealous of her more daring friend's exploits, and when Delia had first started boasting about sneaking off to nightclubs, Hilda had been intrigued but also a little scared. Nice girls like them didn't sneak out to go and watch pop groups and drink alcohol and lie to their parents.

Did they?

But as Delia's tales grew more and more impressive over the weeks, culminating in how she had developed a crush on the Rainbirds' drummer and was determined to find a way to speak to him in person, Hilda's fear grew less and her envy grew greater.

Now, as she watched her friend's tight, white face reflected back in the mirror, she didn't know whether to feel disappointed that she'd been right all along. Delia had been making it all up! Otherwise, why wasn't she jumping up and down at the idea of a night out on the town together? With a sigh, Hilda closed the wardrobe door and flopped down hard on the bed beside her friend, making Delia bounce a little on the edge of the mattress.

'All right, just confess,' Hilda said with a grin. 'You made it all up. But *I'm* still going to go the club tonight anyway!' She was looking at her friend out of the corner of her eyes as she made this daring boast, and felt a little shaft of alarm flicker through her at her friend's frightened expression.

'You can't!' Delia said at once. 'It's not safe there!'

Hilda sat up straight on the bed, her eyes fixed to Delia's face. 'What do you mean? Why not?' she demanded.

Delia looked quickly away, bending her head so far over her stitching that her hair fell forward and all but hid her face from view. 'A man died there. Remember?' she said, all but whispering now.

Hilda, who'd read all about it in the papers, reached out and put a gentle hand on her friend's shoulder. 'He was a member of that band you like, wasn't he?'

'Yes. The lead singer.'

'Not the drummer though? Not the one you really like?'

'No, it wasn't Frankie Everett,' Delia admitted.

'So you really *have* been watching them play?' Hilda said wonderingly.

Mutely, Delia nodded.

'But it was an accident, wasn't it? He fell down the stairs,' Hilda pointed out, not quite understanding why her friend was acting so weirdly.

Delia said nothing.

'We can still go tonight then,' she insisted. Now that she'd got the idea in her head that she might do something exciting and forbidden, like dance at a nightclub, she didn't want to let it go. Especially if she had a more experienced friend to go with her to give her moral courage. 'Oh, come on, Del, it'll be fun,' she insisted.

Delia continued stitching the hem, her needlework getting progressively more ragged and untidy as she worked. 'I don't want to,' she finally muttered stubbornly.

'Because your favourite band won't be playing, I suppose? But there'll be other bands there, right?' Hilda reasoned. 'We can still have a dance and a good time.'

Delia shrugged.

'Oh come on. I dare you! Double-dare you!' Hilda said, using the one thing that she knew her friend couldn't back away from. Ever since they were tots, they'd played 'dare' and neither one of them refused a double dare! Hilda had even raced through a patch of stinging nettles once because Delia had double-dared her. Hilda could still remember it vividly – so could her mother, who'd had to lather her in calamine lotion!

To her astonishment, Delia sighed heavily. 'We're not six anymore. I don't want to go, all right?'

'But why not?' Hilda asked, genuinely bemused now. Then she frowned. 'Hang on – the last I heard, you said you'd found a way to get to meet this drummer boy of yours in person. Did he give you the brush-off? Is that it?'

'No!' Delia said hotly, stung to the core. 'I never even …' Abruptly, she cut off what she was saying, then forced a shrug. 'It just didn't work out how I thought, that's all,' she said instead, careful not to meet her friend's eye. Seeing that Hilda was waiting for more, she sought out another lie and quickly came up with one. 'I thought I'd found a way to get to the basement, where the bands all hang out but it went wrong. I … I was nearly caught,' she added on a rush.

'Oh, I get it. And now you're being a scaredy-pants!' Hilda crowed.

'Am not,' Delia flashed back.

'Are too! You're too scared to go back to the Bootleggers in case you've blotted your copybook there.'

'No – no one saw me. I was … it was dark …'

'Then there's no problem,' Hilda pointed out in satisfaction. Then, seeing Delia was still wavering, she turned and lay on her stomach, propped her chin on her folded arms and wheedled, 'Come on, Del, be a sport. Hanging out at the city hotspots might be old hat to you, but I'm dying to see what it's like. Let's go. *Please!* We don't have to stay long. I daren't anyway. If I tell Mum and Dad I'm going to your house, they'll expect me back by ten o'clock. Come on, be a sport. You can show me how to do my make-up so that I'll look just like Audrey Hepburn.'

Delia sighed. 'In your dreams,' she said, her lips finally twitching. 'Oh, all right.' She finally gave in. She knew Hilda would just nag and nag until she got her way. Or worse – she might really go to the club without her as she threatened. And Delia couldn't let her do that.

She, better than anyone, knew it really wasn't safe to be in that place.

And as much as the thought of going back to the Bootleggers Club made her feel sick and panicky, what kind of a friend would she be if she let Hilda get into trouble? Besides, a quick visit – in and out in half an hour … that wouldn't be so bad, would it? Nothing bad could happen to them if they stuck together. Besides, nobody had seen what she'd done – she was sure of that – so they'd be OK.

Wouldn't they?

Chapter 19

As Delia and Hilda put the finishing touches to their new dresses, Trudy and Clement made their way back to the Bootleggers Club.

Once again, the mammoth doorman was persuaded to show them to the manager's office, and once again Felix Simpkins watched them sourly as they came in and each took a seat in a chair opposite his desk.

His eyes lingered a little on the young woman, who was proving herself to be quite a looker out of her copper's uniform. Not that *that* was fooling him – now he knew her to be a bluebottle, she could look like Gina Lollobrigida and he wouldn't look at her twice.

'You've been having a high old time, haven't you, getting your cronies to gang up on me,' he said bitterly to Clement. 'I take it I do have *you* to thank for a visit from the city ratcatcher?'

Clement smiled politely, and mockingly doffed his trilby hat. 'I take it her majesty's sanitary inspector has been calling?' he asked innocently.

Simpkins grunted, then sighed. 'All right, all right, enough of the Laurel and Hardy routine. What d'yah want?'

Clement smiled. 'That's a much better attitude, Mr Simpkins. Now, what do we want, Trudy?' He turned and looked at his companion, who obligingly got out her notebook and a pencil.

'We understand you were in the habit of giving the Rainbirds top billing here, so to speak,' she began. 'Any particular reason for that? It wasn't due to Mr Reason, was it – no pun intended?'

The club manager shifted a little on his chair. 'Dunno what you're implying. The Rainbirds were popular—' he shrugged elaborately '—so they got a good spot.'

'We've heard they got to keep more of the takings,' Trudy remarked casually. 'Not like some of the others, who have to pay *you* for the privilege of singing here. Why was that, do you suppose?'

'I don't take bribes, officer,' Felix said, po-faced.

'Of course you don't,' Trudy said dryly. 'Did Mr Reason have something on you, Felix?'

'Mr Simpkins to the likes of you,' Felix shot back, going red-faced. 'And again, I dunno what you're implying,' he said innocently.

'If Ray Reason had caught you out doing something naughty,' Trudy continued thoughtfully, 'and was indulging in a little bit of blackmail, you're probably not sorry to see him gone. Right?'

'Wrong,' Felix shot back, almost before she'd finished speaking. 'The Rainbirds pulled in the punters, and one of the main reasons the little darlings come here and pay their entry fee is so that they can moon over the likes of Ray. Now he's gone my takings will probably be down,' he whined.

'You don't kill the goose that lays the golden egg – is that it?' Trudy said.

'Who says he was killed?' Felix said. 'He fell down the stairs and hit his bonce, poor sod.'

Trudy sighed and gave it up as a bad job. Although they'd been picking up titbits here and there that indicated Ray Reason and the nightclub owner had their issues, Felix was never going to admit to it. 'Tonight, myself and a friend are going to enjoy the hospitality of your club,' she informed him. 'And we'd much prefer it if you didn't broadcast my profession about to all and sundry.'

Felix sneered. 'Ashamed of the job, huh? Not surprised.'

Trudy felt herself flush in anger.

Clement, seeing it, put in icily, 'Don't forget, Simpkins, it won't do *your* reputation any good if your punters learn there are plain-clothes police officers in the place. So just keep your mouth shut, and everyone's happy. Yes?'

Simpkins opened his mouth to argue, but then shut it again without saying a word as he realised the accuracy of the old man's sentiments. 'Oh all right, fine, fine,' he mumbled. 'Just don't go around asking too many of your flat-foot questions and upsetting the teenyboppers, all right?'

Trudy smiled grimly. 'I'll do my best not to let my flat feet show, Mr Simpkins,' she promised him through gritted teeth.

They left his office with all three of them bristling with mutual antipathy, and once back on the doorstep outside the club, Trudy let out a long shuddering breath.

'One of these days, I hope I have the pleasure of arresting that man for something,' she said feelingly.

'Can I quote you on that?' an amused voice asked, and both Trudy and Clement swung around to see Duncan Gillingham, lounging against some railings and watching them with a speculative smile on his handsome face.

Her heart sank, and her face must have reflected her feelings, for she saw the newspaper reporter's mouth tighten into a grim line. Not wanting to antagonise him, she sighed, forced a smile and said mildly, 'Hello, Duncan. What brings you here?'

Clement regarded the reporter with a look of distinct disfavour. He'd never liked the way this young man had hung around Trudy when he'd been engaged to another woman, and he still didn't like it now. A while ago, he'd noticed the announcement of this man's marriage in his father-in-law's newspaper, and he hoped that Trudy had done the same. Just in case she hadn't, he stirred himself to smile.

'Mr Gillingham. My congratulations on your recent nuptials,' he said dryly.

Duncan shot him a dirty look. 'Dr Ryder. Still up to your old tricks then?' he gritted. Then he let a distinct beat of time pass, before adding just as dryly, 'Investigating things that should be left to the police, I mean?'

Trudy bridled at this. 'I seem to recall that you nosing in on our business hasn't exactly done *you* any harm in the past,' she pointed out coldly. 'Haven't you had any number of scoops handed out to you because of us?'

Duncan sighed and held out his hands in a dramatic gesture of defeat. 'All right, all right – pax! We seem to have got off on the wrong foot. Can we start again?' he pleaded.

Trudy smiled and felt some of the tension in her shoulders relax. She didn't like being at loggerheads with people and was more than willing to meet him halfway. Noticing her body language, Duncan too felt some of his angst leach out of him.

'So, am I right in thinking there's more to the death of the lead singer of the Rainbirds than meets the eye?' he teased. 'I have to say, I'd been wondering the same thing.' This, of course, was a lie. Until he'd seen Trudy and the old vulture sniffing around Martin Cuthbertson's place, he'd thought the verdict of accidental death was pretty much all there was to it. After all, it wasn't exactly remarkable, was it? A dark, twisting staircase and a young man in too much of a hurry perhaps. Moreover, one who'd maybe had a little too much to drink – these things happened all too often.

But he liked to give the impression that he was smarter than his fellow reporters, so he nodded at the dingy building behind them and smiled. 'This place has always been a dive. You know the manager's a front man for some proper villains, don't you?'

Trudy, wisely not rising to the bait, said nothing.

Duncan grinned. 'Bit of a sore point, that, is it? What's the matter – can't her majesty's constabulary prove it? Well, don't feel too bad – none of us members of the fourth estate can prove it either. My editor would whoop for joy if I could bring anything home to our Mr Simpkins here. Any chance he's to blame for Ray Reason's spectacular tumble down the stairs?'

'We're just tying up some loose ends, Gillingham,' Clement said curtly. 'There's nothing here to get your nose twitching.' The last thing he wanted was this pest hanging around, getting in their way.

Duncan grinned. 'No? So why is it twitching like a veritable rabbit's then?'

Trudy laughed at the image, and Duncan's gaze softened on her. She really did have a lovely laugh. If only she—

'We have to be going Trudy,' Clement put in quickly, careful to keep his voice neutral. 'Mr Gillingham. No doubt we'll be seeing you around,' he said stiffly.

'No doubt you will,' Duncan shot back rapidly. Now, more than ever, he was sure that there was a story to be had at this nasty little nightclub.

'Bye,' Trudy said uncertainly, and by way of reconciliation gave him a brief wave. She didn't know why the coroner disliked Duncan so much. To her, he had always been a mild irritant, but she could sense that Dr Ryder had far more serious misgivings about him. Even though he had helped them out significantly on their last case.

Duncan nodded back at her, but to her eyes, he wasn't looking particularly mollified. In fact, she could feel his stare boring into her back as they walked away.

Duncan watched them out of sight, admiring Trudy's slightly swaying figure as she moved. Out of that prim uniform of hers, she looked even more sensational than in it. He still couldn't quite believe that he'd never managed to seduce her.

He was happy enough, he supposed, with his new wife, and his assured future within her father's newspaper empire. He'd be an idiot to throw that all away on a fling with a silly little police girl who thought she was something special, and he knew it. Even his trusting wife would have trouble forgiving him for getting caught out in something like that.

Even so …

Reluctantly, he dragged his thoughts away from Trudy Loveday, and turned to look at the nightclub's shabby exterior with speculative eyes. So, the lead songster of the Rainbirds hadn't fallen down the stairs accidentally. It those two were sniffing around, they must think – at the very least – that he'd had a helping hand tumbling down those hard, unforgiving iron stairs.

So who had been involved?

A fellow member of the band?

Simpkins?

A woman? A handsome and single lad like Ray, so popular with his teenage female fans, must have been able to take his pick of the young ladies. Had he been too free with his favours, perhaps? Had some young girl become obsessed with him and taken exception to him being too free and easy with her competition? Or the relative of a debauched young lady, perhaps?

One thing was for certain: tonight, when the Bootleggers opened its doors to the usual Saturday night crowd, he'd be amongst them. And he didn't think he was flattering himself unduly to believe that he had a way with the ladies. If any of the Rainbirds' fans had been hearing whispers about Ray Reason, he was going to know all about it before the night was through.

And if he could solve the case before Trudy and her pet vulture … well, all the better. It would do that pair good to be taken down a peg or two.

Whistling slightly, Duncan turned away from the club and ambled back along the pavement. He had gone there to try and get an interview with the manager, but now that he'd seen Trudy and the coroner, he thought that that could wait until he had more to go on.

Chapter 20

By six o'clock that evening, the city of Oxford was buzzing. The working week was over and the big night was here. Saturday, when old married couples ventured out to the cinema for their weekly treat. Saturday, when children were allowed to stay up an extra hour and watch more telly. Saturday, when the old folks had their knees-up at their local pub, having a sing-song or battling it out at the darts board.

Saturday night, when the bright and young streamed out into the city, seeking fun, adventure, music, romance and dancing.

And that Saturday night was no exception.

In their respective bedrooms, Delia and Hilda donned their new dresses and put on as much make-up as they thought they could get away with, unchallenged. Precious bottles of perfume and hairbrushes and hairspray were buried deep into handbags that were then nonchalantly slung over their shoulders. Then, hiding their finery under their coats, they sauntered past their parents, each saying they were going to the house of the other to play cards and listen to records.

Duncan Gillingham dressed in his latest trendy clothes and kissed his wife goodbye, taking pains to explain where he was going and why. He didn't trust his father-in-law not to check up on him, and in this case, he really did have a legitimate excuse for being absent on such an important night, so why not make the most of it?

And at Clement Ryder's house, Vincent Ryder nervously paced, waiting for his 'date' to arrive. Like Duncan, he too was dressed in the most fashionable clothes he had, and he'd even been to the barber's that afternoon to get an up-to-date haircut.

His father watched him pace, lips twitching in unspoken amusement.

And in her house, Trudy descended the stairs, not surprised to see that both her parents were waiting for her in the hall.

Barbara and Frank Loveday both smiled widely as she appeared, determinedly putting on bright faces. They worried about her on a regular basis, of course, and though they were proud of her and her unusual choice of career, Trudy was well aware that both of them would have cheered and celebrated had she come home one day and said that she was resigning her job to take up something else instead. Anything else. A job in a knitting shop. Sheep farming. Anything.

To try and put their minds at rest, Trudy had got into the habit of telling them – probably more than she should – about her job and what she was doing. Normally her duties were so boring, like filing, taking witness statements or searching female shoplifters, that it made them feel much better about what she did.

But sometimes, like now, not so much.

So they knew that she was going to go to a nightclub for the first time in her life, and why she needed to. But she had been quick to add that Dr Ryder's son, Vincent, would be going with her to 'look after her'. She'd been so careful to hide her resentment that she'd felt compelled to add this for their sakes behind a wide smile of her own.

'So, how do I look?' she asked now, giving them a twirl.

She was wearing a knee-length dark blue dress with sparkling sequins at the neck, waist and wrists. Her hair was up – not in a fashionable beehive, but in a mass of curly brown rings, two of which had been allowed to escape her bun and dangle down strategically either side of her ears.

She had on lipstick, but not much else by way of make-up, and she wore a pair of clip-on diamante earrings that would sparkle and catch whatever light there was to be had in a dark room. She wore black shoes with a modest heel.

'You look smashing, love,' Barbara said bravely.

'Like a picture,' her father echoed.

Trudy dutifully kissed them both, admonished them not to wait up for her and left the house feeling a mixture of guilt, defiance and remorse.

She knew they would wait up for her no matter what she said.

A neighbour had offered to give her a lift to Dr Ryder's house, as he was on his way to a meeting of some club or other that he belonged to, and it was on his way. She'd been glad she'd arranged her own transport to the coroner's house, as she hadn't wanted to ask Vincent to come to her house to pick her up.

If pressed, she couldn't have said quite why this was. Perhaps she didn't want to reinforce the feeling that this was in any way a proper date. Because it wasn't, she reminded herself firmly. Vincent was *not* actually her boyfriend, picking her up for a night out on the town.

Perhaps she just hadn't wanted to introduce Vincent to her parents. Even knowing their night out wasn't real, was she worried that they might actually begin to have hopes, nevertheless, that Vincent Ryder might actually … what?

But at this point, Trudy shook the thought away and settled down beside Mr Greenslade and chatted with him about his wife's lumbago and where they'd been on their summer holidays that year. It would only take them ten minutes or so to get to the Ryder residence.

*

At the Bootleggers Club, the doors were opened and the place was ready for another Saturday night of brisk, profitable business. The bars were stocked, the bands were getting ready and eager to play, and the young people who'd come to hear them were more than ready to meet up, dance and maybe find themselves an exciting new boyfriend or girlfriend for a few weeks or so.

Ray Reason, though hardly forgotten just yet, already seemed to belong to the past.

Or so quite a number of people fervently hoped.

Chapter 21

Duncan Gillingham was trying not to feel old and was almost succeeding. Dressed in the latest fashions he could find in the High Street, he was enjoying the music all right, and the booze at the Bootleggers Club had always been top notch, but being surrounded by noisy teenagers felt a little bit bizarre. He was more used to having a pint down the local with his contemporaries.

He was having no trouble getting people to talk to him, but he just wasn't learning much of use. So far, he'd heard nothing that he could use in an article about the demise of the Rainbirds' lead singer, nor anything that gave him any hint as to what might have tipped off the old vulture of a coroner that something was amiss with an accidental death verdict. Apart from the fact that quite a number of the pretty girls that were now dancing happily around him had claimed to be in deep mourning, nothing remarkable had come to light.

Some of the boys had muttered darkly about Ray maybe being drunk – or worse – when he toppled down the stairs. But Duncan had already checked the inquest records, and knew that the medics thought it unlikely that the dead man had been taking drugs, and that Ray had only imbibed a reasonable amount of alcohol on the night of his death.

Rumours abounded that his girlfriend was distraught, but scattered amid the commiseration and sympathy were plenty of sly comments that Lindy-Lou hadn't been the only girl in the dead singer's life. Several claimed to have seen Ray 'snogging' other girls in darkened rooms and corners throughout the club, but when pressed for details, Duncan could get no corroboration.

Not that he wasn't willing to believe that a man like Ray – the object of so much female teenage desire – hadn't been saint enough to resist temptation. But he did find it hard to believe that the young man would have been stupid enough to kiss other women in the Bootleggers when his girlfriend was actually present.

He was listening half-heartedly to the first band of the night – a bunch of young lads who were singing Buddy-Holly-type ditties with varying success – when he saw Trudy Loveday walking through the door, her hand looped over the arm of Vincent Ryder.

At this cosy sight, he cursed under his breath. How much longer was the coroner's son going to hang around her like a puppy dog begging for treats? It was pathetic.

He watched as they made their way further into the crowded room and onto the dance floor. Trudy's dark blue dress clung to her like a glove, emphasising her small waist, and the modest (by today's standards) skirt swished appealingly around her bare legs as she moved. There must have been something sparkly on the dress because every now and then it caught the light and glittered as she moved. Its randomness fascinated him for some reason.

She looked both sexy and refined, and once again he wished that she wasn't so standoffish.

He wanted to go across and break them up, demanding a dance himself, just to see the look on the handsome Vincent Ryder's face as he was cut out, but his professional curiosity made him stay put.

He didn't think it was a coincidence that the pair had decided to go out dancing at this particular club. And sure enough, after ten minutes or so, Trudy leaned close to Vincent so that he could hear her, and said something in his ear. The blond-haired man nodded and moved off, and Duncan tracked him, watching as he asked a girl to dance, took her onto the floor and began to chat to her.

Trudy, he noticed, had also given some lucky sod the nod, and was currently dancing with a boy who couldn't have been more than seventeen, with a bad rash of spots on his forehead. She was listening intently to what he had to say.

He smiled in the semi-darkness. Just as he'd thought. They were doing exactly what he'd been doing – trying to pick up on any gossip or inside knowledge about the life and death of Ray Reason.

It would put a dent in her night if he started letting everyone know that she was actually a copper, he thought vindictively, but though he was tempted, he knew it would be folly to get on her bad side. She would be very unlikely to even talk to him again if she found out what he'd done, and he still had hopes that he might sweet-talk at least a few titbits out of her before the night was out.

Eventually, Duncan was forced to drag his eyes away from the circulating, scintillating Trudy Loveday when he noticed the arrival of a very big fish indeed.

Titus Crowther-Beauley, Duncan knew, was just one year off forty, but he looked and dressed much younger. That his slim figure was clad in the latest couture came as no surprise to Duncan. The 'agent to the stars' was known for being dapper. What did surprise him slightly was that his companion was not a young and lovely girl (as he was usually photographed with on the showbiz pages of the country's newspapers) but a rather young and lovely lad. About twenty or so and traditionally tall, dark and handsome, he looked far too self-assured for Duncan's liking.

Since Titus was known for his many love affairs – all with the opposite sex – Duncan dismissed his first thought about why they were together, and watched with interest as Titus made his way to the bar, his companion dogging his steps closely.

*

Near the bar, Hilda and Delia were propping up a wall, Hilda in particular looking around wide-eyed and breathless. 'Isn't that the man who made Perry Hillman famous?' Hilda shouted loudly into her friend's ear. She was an avid reader of the 'star-maker' type of magazines. The rise of the young English actor had been well documented, and she was sure that she'd seen his picture taken with the man now only a few feet away from her. 'I'm sure it is! Perry said he owed all his success to his agent, and I'm sure it's the same man.'

Delia, whose eyes also kept darting around the room, couldn't resist showing off a bit to her friend, and shrugged casually. 'Probably. Sometimes you can spot a lot of celebrities here,' she lied glibly.

Hilda took a drink of her orange juice, trying to pretend it was a swanky cocktail and stared at Titus openly. 'Who do you think that is with him? He's rather gorgeous, isn't he?'

Delia nodded, but didn't really look. She was sweating uncomfortably and feeling a little sick. Ever since they'd arrived, she'd felt a tension headache building, and was longing to leave. She didn't feel safe here. Although she knew it was her imagination, she was sure that she could feel accusing and hostile eyes staring at her. She took a sip of her own drink – a lemonade – and wished she'd had the audacity to ask the barman to put a little vodka in it. Not that she'd ever tasted vodka …

The young group on the stage sang their last song, and then Felix Simpkins stepped out onto the stage.

'And now, ladies and gentlemen – a slight change in your line-up tonight!'

There were a few groans as the fans of the group due to go on made their displeasure known, but Felix was defiantly beaming and holding out his hands in appeasement. 'I'm sure you'll all welcome a surprise turn by our very own Rainbirds, who are bravely going to do their set after losing their great friend Ray Reason in such tragic circumstances.'

There was a distinct buzz at this, and Trudy, who'd been talking to a loquacious girl who'd been pretending to have an 'in' with several of the local bands, looked around to see where Vincent was.

She spotted him not far away, looking as surprised as she was by this announcement.

Surely, she thought, it was in very bad taste for the Rainbirds to be performing again so soon? But then, when she thought about it further for a moment or two, she supposed that Martin Cuthbertson had probably been afraid that their fickle fans might quickly forget them if they didn't get back on public display.

As Felix slipped out of the spotlight, the Rainbirds came on stage to tremendous cheers and applause and Trudy was able to see them for the first time. The four of them looked the part, at least, in matching smart suits and similar haircuts. The drummer started up with an undeniably catchy beat, and the bass guitarist joined in. Then it was the turn of the man on the piano. From her notes, she knew the keyboard player's nickname was Pinky for some reason, but that his given name was Peter Rossiter. He was probably the best-looking one of the group now that Ray was no longer on stage, she mused, having seen the publicity photos of Ray and his band in Clement's case file.

But when Marty stepped forward and began to sing, Trudy quickly realised that his voice was quite distinctive, strong with a good range and immediately demanded that you listen to it. What's more, the song he was singing was both mournful and catchy, and she wasn't the only female in the room listening with close attention.

Couples came quickly together and began to sway in a more intimate way than they had been before, and she jumped a little as a hand touched her elbow. When she turned, she found Duncan Gillingham grinning down at her.

'Dance? And I promise not to blow your cover,' he promised.

Trudy scowled, but had no choice but to let him put his arms around her as they began to sway to the slow but catching song of lost love. Making a fuss would only draw attention to herself, and she couldn't risk that. As he well knew!

'What are you doing here?' she asked, but she already knew the answer to that. Duncan could smell a story a mile off.

'Now, don't be like that,' he said with his best charming smile.

As they moved around the floor, with Duncan trying to worm his way into Trudy's good books, Delia Pinney was watching the drummer intently. Her friend, noticing, poked her in the ribs. 'He's not bad, Del, but I still think the boy on the piano is better-looking.'

Delia ignored her.

At the back of the room, Titus listened to the band, feeling more and more happy with his latest choice of signing. Even without the good-looking Ray Reason fronting the band, they were doing all right. Marty had a great voice, right enough, and this latest song was a new one that he hadn't heard from them before. Marty must have been working on it like a Trojan to get it finished in time for its debut tonight.

Which meant that Titus was reasonably confident that Cuthbertson could be relied upon to continue being the musical talent and force behind the band, providing them with much-needed hits. But the Rainbirds still needed a pretty boy to bring in the necessary female interest and spending power. When it came to the time when he needed their records to fly out of the nation's Woolworths stores, it would be the besotted female fans who would be spending the most money.

Turning to the young man beside him, he smiled. 'So – what do you think. Are they as good as I promised, or what?'

Beside him, Ewan Treadwell nodded. Titus had found him in Wales, of all places, busking outside a cinema. Tall, dark, handsome, he could sing well enough and play – almost well enough – an acoustic guitar. For a while now, he'd been looking for the right placement for him, and as a 'back-up singer' for Marty, he was sure that Ewan would look the part front and centre on stage. Titus already knew that the camera loved Ewan, for he'd had some photo shoots done as a matter of course. Soon all of the teen mags would be begging to feature his bankable looks on their front covers. It would give the Rainbirds that added edge they'd almost certainly need to push them into the big time.

'They're great,' Ewan said enthusiastically. 'Good song too. I just hope they like me.'

Titus Simpkins smiled. 'Oh, don't worry. They will. You'll walk the audition,' he said reassuringly. The Rainbirds didn't know it yet, but he planned to introduce Ewan to them later, down in the basement when they'd finished their stint, and he'd ask them to give the young Welshman a hearing. And once he'd made it clear to Marty that signing Ewan on with the band would be a condition of him, Titus, taking over their careers, he was sure there'd be no problems.

He smiled contentedly and drank his whisky.

Chapter 22

The Rainbirds were on stage for not quite an hour. They went off to enthusiastic calls, and Titus and Ewan made their way through the crowd, heading for the door leading into the back, interior corridor.

If Titus felt any frisson of unease making his way down the steep, narrow spiral staircase where Ray Reason had died so recently, he made no sign of it, and luckily for him, the young Welshman was oblivious to being in the vicinity of tragedy.

When Ray had died, Ewan had been in Tregaron pulling pints behind the bar of a working men's club.

In the sweaty-smelling, dimly lit basement, Titus ignored the grime and decay of the room, and put a big smile on his face as he approached the young men sitting on one of the larger sofas. The drummer was sitting on the floor and leaning back against the legs of the bass player, busily smoking, and all of them were holding beer bottles or glasses. The first band on stage had decided to get changed out of their gear behind some makeshift screens, and could be heard rowdily dissecting their various performances.

'You were great,' Titus said at once to the group on the sofa. 'And I loved the new song. One of yours, Marty? I think it's got the makings of a big hit.'

He saw the look of relief pass over Marty's face as he nodded, and Titus felt a smug glow of satisfaction. The lad had been anxious to please him, which meant his fish was almost landed. Taking advantage of this psychological position of power, he said, 'This is Ewan Treadwell, by the way,' and indicated Ewan to come front and centre. 'I discovered him busking. He's good on acoustic guitar, and I promised him an audition with this great new band I want to sign on. So here we are.'

He saw Martin look at the young Welshman without much enthusiasm as it dawned on him that Titus had been speaking about the Rainbirds.

'He'll be great as a back-up singer too, as he's good at harmonising,' Titus added smoothly.

'I don't think the band needs another member,' a cold female voice cut in, and Titus felt his hackles rise as Jenny Wren, who'd come down to be with her man and join in the celebration of the Rainbirds' return, slipped around them and settled down in Martin's lap.

The bass player gave her a happy leer and said something slightly ribald to Martin, who merely smiled abstractedly. He was still looking at Ewan thoughtfully. 'Jenny's right, you know. You heard us up there tonight – the four of us sounded good.'

'Yes, you did,' Titus said at once, far to wily to contradict him openly in front of the other members of the band. 'But five is a better fit for you, I think. Gives you more range and scope. And like I said, I think Ewan is going to be good for you guys. Trust me, I know how to make you more marketable.'

Jennifer Renfrew looked daggers at Titus, who shrugged elaborately. She knew his game all right. As if she was going to let this good-looking young interloper into the band now! 'The fans seem to like the band just as it is. Didn't you hear them cheering?' she challenged.

'Sure,' Titus said, determinedly holding on to his smile. 'But they're just a small bunch, in a small club, in a small town. If you want to make it big – in London, hell, maybe even in America, you need to widen your appeal.'

Jenny's hand curled around Martin's forearm protectively, but the truth was, she was in something of a quandary. She knew this man had the contacts to give the Rainbirds their best shot at fame. But she also knew he was a shark who would fleece them for all they had, if they weren't careful.

'If you want my help, you need to take my advice,' Titus said more firmly now, ignoring Jenny's hard stare, and looking Martin in the eye. Soft-soaping his stars was all part and parcel of his business, but he knew that sometimes you had to remind them who was boss. Who the brains was and who wielded the power behind the scenes. And it was time Martin understood that he would need to toe the line. 'I know what I'm talking about. I know what the movers and shakers in the music world are looking for. I know what image I can sell. You've got the voice and you can write the songs, but that's not enough. There are hundreds of bands out there who can say the same. If you want me to take you on and push you to the top, I gotta know you're gonna be smart and work with me. Otherwise, what's the point?'

Unspoken in the air lay the threat that Titus could always find another band with just a click of his powerful fingers.

Marty sighed and backed down – just as Titus had known he would. 'Fine, we'll give him an audition,' he said casually. He winced as Jenny's fingernails dug deeply into his arm, but wisely, she said nothing.

But as Titus smiled and accepted a glass of unwanted beer from the keyboard player, he knew that Jenny Wren was maybe going to be even more of a problem than he'd originally hoped. Her long, level, hard gaze told him as much.

She wasn't going to want a rival in the band who might steal Marty's limelight – as, if all went to plan, Ewan was sure to do. He understood it, could even admire it, in a way. She was protecting her man, and her meal ticket.

141

But he wasn't about to let the little schemer get in his way. She might think she could wrap Martin Cuthbertson around her little finger – and maybe she could, in one way. Beautiful women had always been able to lead men around like a bull with a ring through its nose. Hadn't history taught them that? But he'd seen another kind of hunger in the lead singer's eyes just now, when Titus had mentioned helping them make it to the big time. And that was a hunger for fame. Riches. Success. A hunger to get away from being a nobody and become a somebody.

And he had the feeling that pretty Jenny Wren wasn't going to find it as easy to control her man as she thought. Once Ewan was ensconced in the band, and the contracts were all signed, he'd make sure that Ewan kept him apprised of everything that went on in the band. He'd owe him, after all, and Titus would make it clear that he expected his loyalty. And if, as usually became inevitable, the band eventually cottoned on to the fact that he was raking in most of the profits, and started to become troublesome, he wanted to know all about it well in advance.

And if anybody became really annoying and started making too much fuss, they could always be 'voted' out of the band. Nobody was indispensable, after all.

And nobody got in the way of Titus and his profits.

*

On the dance floor, the next act was belting out more noise than melody, and Trudy had managed to shake off Duncan, who'd gone off in search of other prey.

He'd noticed two young-looking girls, who were nervously staying close to a wall and chatting only to each other. One of them – a thin, small little thing – looked as nervous as a cat at a dog show and the other, bigger girl looked distinctly star-struck. Duncan guessed it was probably her first time at a club.

He made his way to them without any real hopes of success,

142

but something incongruous – and slightly touching – about their obvious innocence intrigued him. They were not the usual kind of rebellious teenager he associated with places like this. He saw them look at him nervously as he approached, as if unable to believe he'd noticed them at all and unsure what to do. Simultaneously, they abruptly stopped speaking to each other and watched him with wide, nervous eyes. Both were wearing glasses, and a look of mixed alarm and repressed excitement passed between them as he came to a halt in front of them.

'Hello, ladies,' he said, amused to think of himself as the big bad wolf – which was clearly how they'd tagged him. Not wanting to disappoint them, he smiled widely. 'You two haven't danced all evening. Can't have that – if the rest of the young men in here are blind as well as stupid, I'm neither.'

Both blushed to the roots of their hair. 'Now, which of you can I persuade to give me a dance first?'

Delia gulped and without hesitation, pushed her friend under the bus. 'My friend, here. Hilda. She said she's been wanting to dance all night long.'

'Have not!' Hilda squeaked, but looked thrilled and terrified in equal measure as the handsome, older man held out his hand.

In a daze, she allowed the vaguely amused man to lead her out into the writhing mass that was 'dancing' to the wail of electric guitars.

Delia watched them go, not sure whether to be relieved or jealous, and wished that her headache would go away. She was really beginning to feel unwell now. She should never have let Hilda persuade her to come back here. She knew it was a mistake.

She made up her mind then and there that it was time to leave. She'd finish her drink and then go. Hilda would be all right on her own. The last bus home wasn't for an hour yet, and she probably wouldn't want to leave early anyway. Besides, Delia reasoned spitefully, now that her friend had her handsome dance partner to distract her, Hilda probably wouldn't even notice that she had left.

Out on the dance floor, Duncan watched his companion with detached amusement. 'Your first time here?' he asked.

Hilda immediately looked horrified. 'Oh no! Can you tell? Is it that obvious?' She looked so appalled that Duncan had to laugh.

'Only a little! But it doesn't matter. So what made you decide to come tonight?'

'Oh, Delia, my friend. She comes here all the time, and I just wondered what it was like, that's all, so I decided to come with her this time.'

Duncan cast a look in Delia's direction. 'For someone who's come out to have a good time, she doesn't look very happy, does she?' he said thoughtfully, taking in the girl's drooping posture and the quick, nervous glances she kept darting around.

Hilda frowned. 'No. I know. I don't know what's up with her. She's been moping a lot just lately.'

Duncan didn't think that particularly surprising or noteworthy. He remembered his own teenage years, when his moods were all over the place.

'So who's your favourite band?' he asked.

'Oh, the Rainbirds. Well, I mean they're Delia's,' Hilda amended. 'She's in love with the drummer. I don't really know that many groups, but I liked their songs tonight …'

Hilda suspected she was blathering, but couldn't seem to stop herself. It was like a fantasy come true – go to the club and have this gorgeous older man pick her out and dance with her. She could see, now that they were being forced to dance close together and all but shout in each other's ears, that he had green eyes. She'd never met anyone with green eyes before. And he was so *handsome*.

She felt a little bit breathless just looking at him. 'What's your name?' she asked daringly.

'Rudolph, like the red-nosed reindeer,' Duncan teased her with a grin. 'So, if your friend's a Rainbirds fan, she must be pretty cut up about their lead singer dying.' Even though his dance partner seemed a non-starter as a source of information, it wasn't in his nature not to try out even the least little lead to see if it might lead him somewhere.

'Oh, she is. She was actually here … you know … the night he died.'

Clearly Hilda found this fact thrilling, but to Duncan it meant nothing. Most of the people in the room could say the same thing. He nodded. 'Don't suppose she ever got to speak to him?' he persisted half-heartedly.

'I don't think so,' Hilda said, frowning thoughtfully. 'But she did say, once, that she had this plan all made up, where she could get close enough to talk to that drummer she fancies on his own.'

Duncan perked up a little at this. 'Oh? What sort of plan?'

'Oh, I dunno.' Hilda shrugged. 'Something about sneaking in the back way or something.'

Duncan turned to look at the now far more interesting Delia, and with a start, saw that her space by the wall was empty. 'Where's she gone?' he said out loud.

Hilda's head swivelled in the same direction, and she felt a lance of alarm shoot through her to see that Delia had gone. 'She's probably just gone to the loo,' she said hopefully. It was one thing to be here with a friend, but it was another thing to be here all alone.

Duncan nodded. But throughout the dance, and then the next one, he kept his eye on the vacant spot near the wall. And so did Hilda.

But Delia didn't return.

It wasn't much, but Duncan thought it odd enough to make a note. It was easy enough to charm Delia's full name out of Hilda and get an idea of where both she and her now absent friend lived. And when Hilda grew visibly more restless and worried at being abandoned, the hardened newspaper reporter found himself touched enough to walk the girl from the club and wait with her at the bus stop.

145

Ten minutes later, Hilda was still waving forlornly at him through the window of the departing bus as he turned and made his way back to the club.

With a bit of luck, he thought, he might manage to get another dance out of a certain pretty police constable.

Chapter 23

When the club finally closed that night, Trudy and Vincent briefly compared notes and had to admit defeat. Neither one of them had come up with anything worth writing home about. She told Vincent that she'd have to put her thinking cap on overnight, and then meet up and discuss things with his father to see if they could come up with some new ideas to advance the case. She also let him drive her home, but once at her house, thanked him hastily and hopped out before he could say much more that a startled and quick 'goodnight'.

Duncan Gillingham left the club in a fairly bad mood, not having got his second dance with Trudy Loveday. The club closed up – the doors were locked, the shutters came down and the lights were turned off. Walton Street became quiet once more.

The big doorman, David Deane, said goodnight to his boss, Felix, who was busy greedily counting the night's takings in his office. He left by the back alley. He went straight to his old Norton motorbike, and drove east, making his way through the less salubrious parts of the city of dreaming spires to a small, terraced house, in a dark, narrow street.

There he parked his bike on the pavement and let himself into the small communal hall. The house, even as small as it was, was divided into four so-called flats, and his tread was heavy on the stairs as he shifted his bulk upwards on the uncarpeted stairs.

He paused outside one of the doors off the landing and put his ear to the wood. All was quiet. Good. Patty wasn't 'entertaining'. He knocked softly on the door and a few moments later, it was opened cautiously.

Patty Nesbitt looked at the big man smiling at her and sighed, pulling open the door. 'Come in, Davey,' she said, a shade wearily. She'd had a long but not particularly profitable day, and the last thing she needed was this big lug coming around with that look on his face.

On the other hand, he liked to think of himself as her boyfriend, and amiable though he usually was – in spite of his size – it wouldn't be smart of her to give him any reason to start believing otherwise. In her line of work, having a big and known bruiser for a boyfriend came in very handy. Although Dave's primary job was to keep the peace at the Bootleggers, most of her clients were aware of who he was, and thus were careful to treat her with respect.

It paid to keep him sweet.

With a happy smile, Dave reached inside his leather jacket and withdrew a bottle of gin he'd filched from the bar. He knew that Felix was well aware that he sometimes helped himself to the odd bottle or two, but Dave looked on it as part of his wages, and since he never said anything, so – presumably – did his boss.

Patty perked up a bit at the sight of the booze. 'I'll get some glasses. What a day I've had. How was the club tonight?' she asked chattily. She wasn't about to go back to the Bootleggers any time soon, of course, but she wanted to keep an ear to the ground about what was happening there.

'Not a bad night. The takings were up a little, I'd guess by the numbers that came through the door,' Dave said, taking off his leathers and slouching back on Patty's second-hand sofa. It squeaked a little under his weight, but it had been sturdily built. 'That band that lost their singer, the one who took a header down the stairs, they were up and playing again tonight. From what I could hear, they sounded good as ever. I reckon most of the extra punters only came because they read about the death in the club. Proper lot of ghouls, people, have you noticed?' He opened and took a swig from the bottle, unwilling to wait for a glass, and belched. 'Not that I reckon that bloke dying did them any harm. That bigwig is still sniffing around 'em and still looks keen enough to sign 'em up.'

Patty returned with the glasses and took the bottle from him, pouring them both a healthy dollop, all the while being careful to look casual. 'Sounds like it's all business as usual then?' she murmured, sitting half on his lap, half on the rest of the sofa. She knew he liked it when she snuggled against him.

'Yeah. Mind you, the boss ain't particularly happy,' Dave mused lazily. He was a Birmingham boy, born and bred, but had come to Oxford years ago 'on loan' to Felix from a fellow club owner back in Brum, and had somehow never returned to the country's second biggest city.

Not that he minded. Oxford was a queer place, with too many push-bikes, and at certain times of year, you stumbled across fellas in them fancy colourful gowns that meant they were something big in the university, but Dave didn't mind the eccentricities. The youngest of a huge family, he was used to just getting along. It was smarter that way. Like on the door – he seldom had to get physical, preferring to talk a drunk down, or reason with some obstreperous young student who thought the world owed him a living. Mind, he could get rough if need be, but there was never anything personal in it, with Dave.

'Oh? What's he got to be upset about then?' Patty said bitterly. 'He's sitting in clover. He's got a cushy job, and plenty of hangers-on to do any dirty work that needs doing for him without *him* sticking his neck out. He's got it made.'

Having to do that dodgy favour for Felix still rankled. As if she *liked* touching a dead body!

Dave, oblivious to his companion's angst, merely shrugged. Felix was the boss, and as long as he kept the money coming in, everyone was happy. That's how life worked. Why kick against it? And if Felix fell down on the job, he'd be replaced quickly enough. What did it matter to him who he worked for so long as he could eat good, had a pretty girlfriend like Patty to keep him warm on a winter's night, and had a decent roof over his head. He took a swig of the neat gin – this time from the glass Patty had given him – and sighed contentedly.

'I mean it,' Patty said, seeing from the sleepy look in the big man's eyes that he'd nod off on her if she didn't poke him a bit – and she was unwilling to let her grievances go. Besides, she needed to know what might be going on with the slippery, always dangerous nightclub manager. 'What's he unhappy about?' she demanded.

Ever since she'd had to do Felix that favour on the night Ray Reason died, she'd known that she was going to have to tread carefully for a while. And Felix's unnecessary warning to her to keep her mouth shut had been playing on her mind.

If something was in the air, she needed to know about it.

'Dunno,' Dave roused himself to say, putting a meaty hand on her thigh and squeezing it suggestively. Patty gave it a quasi-affectionate pat. 'I think he don't like having the cops nosing around the place. Don't sit right, does it? Stands to reason.'

Patty almost shot off his lap in alarm at this, but forced herself to relax back against him. 'Cops?' she repeated super-casually. 'What do you mean? Why are there cops at the club? I thought Felix kept everything under the radar?'

'Relax,' Dave said with a grin. 'I don't mean flatfoots in uniform, raiding the place and frightening the fish. Hell, if the club had been raided, I'd be in the nick now, wouldn't I?' he said, trying to reassure her. It was funny what women worried about. 'Nah, it's just some female copper dressed in civvies, sniffing around and asking questions. She's something to do with that man who deals with dead people and stuff. They came to the boss's office before, but he wouldn't play ball. Then they came back earlier today, and next thing I know, he tells me when this female copper turns up at the club tonight, I'm to turn a blind eye.'

Dave didn't like it when the routine changed, but he'd been careful to pass the information on, so his backside was covered. Now he'd just have to wait and see if anything much came of it. 'Not sure what he's playing at, but I reckon he's having to play ball for some reason.' For all he might look like a huge but placid bear, Dave had a far sharper mind than most people gave him credit for.

'So why did he change his mind?' Patty asked sharply. She didn't like the sound of this either – not one bit. What sort of game was Simpkins playing at? Didn't he know the actual owners of the club would cut him off at the knees if they knew he was talking to the law? Or maybe they *did* know? Was that why he was so nervous? In which case … What if Simpkins was getting ready to throw her to the law in order to save his own skin?

She tried to quell her rising panic, but her sense of danger was growing by the second.

'I think the old geezer who deals with dead people put a bit of pressure on him, that's all,' Dave said.

'What? Who do you mean – deals with dead people?' Patty demanded impatiently. She wanted to shake the big dozy lug, but she knew he'd only think it was foreplay.

'You know. Sits in a court, like a proper judge, only he gets to say why and how people died.'

'You mean the coroner?' Patty shuffled off his lap and got up, beginning to pace. 'I don't get it. What's he got to do with Felix of all people?'

Dave watched her curiously. It was clear Patty had her knickers in a twist about something, and suddenly he wanted to know why. What had she been up to that he didn't know about? He'd have to wheedle it out of her, obviously, but he needed to be canny about it. Patty spooked easily.

'Well?' She turned on him now, her voice all but screeching.

Dave sighed, playing dumb. 'I dunno, Pat. It's something to do with that singer who took a header down the stairs, that's all I know.'

It was enough for Patty. Just as she thought – the death of Ray Reason was coming home to roost, and Felix was squirming on the end of some hook, like the worm he was. Her instincts were right.

She was in danger.

She forced herself to smile and climbed back onto her boyfriend's lap. It wouldn't do to let the silly lug know anything was wrong. He'd only get in the way, or start demanding explanations.

But as soon as he left tomorrow, she was going to pack a bag and lie low at a friend's for a while. Just until she could figure out what, exactly, was happening and decide what she needed to do. She didn't really want to relocate and start all over again if she didn't need to. It was such a pain finding digs and building up a new client base – but she would if she decided she had to.

She wanted nothing to do with cops or coroners – and she sure as hell didn't want anything to do with Felix right now. Something had obviously gone wrong over the whole Ray Reason fiasco, and she wouldn't put it past Felix to be planning something very bad for her health.

No. She'd keep her head down and watch and wait and see what happened. She'd have to let Davey know where she was though, once she was safely in hiding. She needed him to be her eyes and ears.

Chapter 24

The next morning, as the city's many church bells rang out for Sunday morning services and Patty Nesbitt fled her tiny flat for safer pastures, Trudy was up and about early. She left the house quietly and waited out on the street. She'd arranged with Vincent last night for him to pick her up and take her to Dr Ryder's house for a morning meeting, and she wanted to be gone before her parents got up. Luckily, Sunday was the day they indulged in a lie-in.

It was nice not to have to report in at the station for once and give the impatient Inspector Jennings a progress report first. Or be sent out to get witness statements, or do the filing, or get him a cup of tea! Or have to do any of the one hundred and one usual boring chores that were habitually assigned to her and to no one else.

The unusual sense of freedom made her smile.

Vincent arrived in his father's Rover and watched her climb in.

'Morning, sunshine,' he said cheerfully. 'You look happy.'

'I feel it. I've almost forgotten what it felt to be free.'

Vincent laughed. 'Ah, that Sunday feeling. If you hate your job so much, why don't you leave it and do something else instead?' he asked curiously.

Trudy sighed. 'I like my job well enough. Well, most of it. Well … bits of it,' she said, then laughed at her own response.

They arrived at the coroner's impressive Victorian house overlooking the park in about ten minutes and found Clement had the tea already brewing. A large brown porcelain teapot, underneath a knitted tea cosy, sat waiting on the kitchen table along with mugs, milk and sugar. The newspaper boy had already delivered the morning papers, and they sat in a neat pile on one side, waiting to be read.

'So, Vincent tells me you didn't have much luck at the club?' Clement began, once they were all seated around the table, sipping tea and delving into a biscuit tin, which the coroner had opened by way of breakfast for them all.

'No,' Trudy sighed. 'And even worse, Duncan was there, chatting the girls up and sniffing around,' she said morosely. 'He can smell a story. You know him – he won't give up until he gets one.'

Vincent shifted in his seat, but wisely said nothing. His father had told him that the reporter had eyes for Trudy, which he'd been able to clearly see for himself. And watching Duncan dancing with Trudy last night had made him want to punch the good-looking so-and-so in the nose.

But he knew Trudy would have been angry if he'd drawn attention to them, and hearing her talk about the reporter without the slightest hint of affection, reassured him that he had nothing to worry about. The attraction was strictly one way.

Clement sighed. 'He can't know anything specific,' he pointed out. But he too frowned a little with worry. Annoying though the man was, Clement didn't underestimate his skills. He'd seen for himself on their last but one case just how dogged he could be – and, if the need arose, to just what lengths he'd go in order to get his damned scoop. Even to the extent of risking his own skin!

'No. But then, neither do we,' Trudy pointed out ruefully with a half-laugh. 'What, exactly, do you think we've learned, if anything, since taking the case on? I think we need to reassess and get self-critical.'

Clement nodded. 'I agree,' he said solemnly. Since this was his last case, he'd be damned if he'd let it end in failure. And his young protégé was quite right. They needed to regroup and discuss things. 'All right. I think his girlfriend – what do they call her, Lindy-Lou? – knows something she's not saying. Agreed?'

Trudy nodded, but slowly. 'But that mightn't necessarily mean anything bad, as you well know.' She spoke now mainly for Vincent's benefit, knowing that (as a man) he didn't like asking for things to be explained to him. 'As we've learned over the years, lots of people keep things back when someone they love dies, and it doesn't mean a thing. Perhaps Linda and Ray had an argument before he died, and now she feels bad that the last words they had were harsh ones. Something like that could make her act guiltily.'

'Yes. But, on the other hand, she *might* have been the one to push him whilst having the argument, which would *also* make her act guilty,' Vincent felt compelled to say.

Trudy nodded. 'Exactly. Detecting isn't easy, is it? Not like it is in the books. Though I do love reading Agatha Christie,' she said in an aside.

'Either way, I think we need to shee her again,' Clement said, refusing to be distracted. Had he slurred one of his words just then? He thought he had, and when he spoke next, he was careful to pronounce carefully. 'If she is keeping something back we need to know what it is, if only to eliminate her as a suspect.'

'OK,' Trudy said, writing neatly in her notebook. 'Reinterview Linda. What else?'

'I think Felix Simpkins is up to shumthing,' Clement said, and could have sworn out loud. This time, he knew he'd slurred his speech. 'I know the man's a criminal, and so he's going to be obstructive as a matter of habit. But I sensed more than the expected animosity in him the other day. He was hiding it well, but I think he was in a muck sweat about something.' He spoke more slowly than usual, and hoped neither of the other two noticed.

'Yes, I agree,' Trudy said. 'From what we *did* hear last night, it seemed the Rainbirds have been the star attraction at the club for some time, but that wasn't always so. And it still makes me wonder why.'

Clement nodded. 'From what we're learning about Ray he was nothing if not ambitious. And driven. It's possible he'd stumbled on something that gave him the upper hand with our Mr Simpkins, and if he had, I believe he was the sort of man who wouldn't have hesitated using it to his ad-ad-advantage.'

He thought he saw his son look at him quickly, then away again, as he stumbled over the last word. He fought back a sense of helplessness and anger, and took long, slow, deep breaths. Getting agitated would only make his speech even worse, he knew. He had to relax.

'Blackmailing someone like Simpkins would be dangerous though,' Vincent put in.

'Perhaps it was,' Trudy said grimly.

Clement sighed. 'The trouble with a man like Simpkins is that it's hard to frighten him, or get to him. He's not like your average petty crook. Some serious people are behind the club – people who are well protected in this town. And that protection, to some extent, covers our Felix as well. If Shhhimpkins is our man, it's going to be hard to bring it home to him.'

For a moment, the three people around the table sat in gloomy silence as they contemplated the truthfulness of this statement.

Trudy sighed. 'When men like him finally go down it's usually because of some internal trouble,' she mused. 'The death of Mr Reason has focused attention on the club and Felix's bosses won't like it. If we continue to put pressure on him and the club, it's possible they might think Simpkins isn't worth it, and …'

But here she petered off uncertainly. Much as she would love to arrest Felix Simpkins for something, she didn't want to find him badly beaten in a back alley somewhere. Or worse.

'Hmmm. Let's shelve the problem of Mr ...' Here Clement paused momentarily to make sure his lips were forming the upcoming sibilant sound properly. '... Simpkins for a minute,' he said, breathing out in relief that he had sounded as clear as a bell. 'What do we think about the rest of the band members? Do we have any reason to suspect them?'

'I don't see why,' Vincent said, beginning to feel tense. He could tell his father was struggling a little with his speech and knew how desperate he must be feeling to keep that fact from them.

But if he'd noticed, how long before Trudy did? If she hadn't already? Feeling for his father, he tried to help him out by taking over the conversation as much as he could.

'As far as we can tell, Ray was doing all right by them,' he said briskly. 'Getting them top billing at the club, for instance. He was popular with the fans too, wasn't he?' He turned deliberately to Trudy, hoping that she'd engage with him from now on, giving his father time to recover his equilibrium.

'I think, from what I could tell from chatting to them last night,' Trudy mused, 'that they're basically good, normal lads, hoping to make it big. As long as things were going OK, I think they'd have been happy to go where Ray led. Everyone except Martin,' she added, looking at the coroner speculatively.

Clement nodded. 'I agree. We know there was tension between the two. That whole thing about Ray wanting to rename the band, for instance.'

'What's this?' Vincent asked curiously, again looking deliberately at Trudy for the reply. Instantly, she obliged him.

'The dead man wanted to call the band Ray Reason and the Rainbirds. Like Billy J. Kramer and the Dakotas. He said that he thought it sounded better,' Trudy explained.

'I'll bet it did. To him!' Vincent grinned. 'But from what I heard last night, the man singing was good – and could play guitar too.

He wouldn't want to suddenly take a back seat to a front man.'

'Right. Of everyone in the case so far, I think Martin had the most to gain by Ray's death,' Trudy said. 'Also, they didn't agree over this agent who wants to manage them,' she added. 'For some reason, Ray didn't seem as keen as the others to sign up with Titus.'

Vincent frowned. 'I can't imagine why. Surely it's every aspiring actor, model or singer's dream to be on *his* books. Everyone knows he's a star-maker.'

'I think you'll find,' Clement put in dryly, 'that Mr Crowther-B-Beauley makes his money by taking more than his fair share of his clients' profits. I've been asking around, and he's known for his sssshtringent contracts. A band making peanuts might think fame and fortune go hand in hand – but fame is one thing, and keeping the money you make from that fame is another thing altogether. Especially if you're tied up with a legally unbreakable contract.'

'And Ray sounds as if he might have been a bit more on the ball than the others.' Trudy nodded.

'Doesn't that give the agent a motive for getting rid of him then?' Vincent asked. 'If Ray Reason was standing in his way? Ray might well have persuaded the rest of the band not to sign with him but look around for a better offer.'

Trudy nodded. 'I think you're right. Men like that get rich and stay rich because they're ruthless about making money. We definitely need to speak to him at some point,' she agreed, writing it down on her to-do list. 'Not that that's going to be easy,' she added morosely, almost to herself. 'People like him think they're untouchable. We'll probably have to make an appointment to see him and then fight our way through ranks of secretaries,' Trudy said glumly. 'And if he even gets a hint he might need a solicitor, he'll probably clam up completely.'

All three contemplated this without much favour.

*

As Clement, Vincent and Trudy discussed their case around Clement's kitchen table, in her bedroom not many miles away, Linda Kempson sat cradling a glass of cloudy liquid.

She was nerving herself up to drink it, but so far couldn't manage to get it down her. Every time she lifted the glass to her lips, her throat seemed to close up, and she knew that if she tried, she might choke.

The trouble was, she was scared. It was one thing reading about herbal medicines and such in the library. It was even easy enough to go out and find the things you needed in the countryside. In some ways, it had also been interesting to boil and distil and watch the chemistry happen for real, just as her notes had said it would.

But it was another thing altogether to then put the fruits of your labours to your lips and drink.

The thing that worried her the most was that she wasn't at all sure how *right* she'd got it. A lot of it had had to be guesswork on her part. It wasn't as if the books she'd read had given her an exact recipe. Do this, add this, boil that, put so many drops of that into this, give it a shake – and there you are. A perfectly safe and guaranteed way of aborting a baby.

What if she'd used too much of one thing? Or too little of another? Or misunderstood something and ground the root instead of boiling leaves?

And so she sat on the side of the bed, staring down into the cloudy liquid in her glass, her heart hammering painfully in her chest as her family went about their business in the house around her.

From the kitchen wafted the aroma of roasting beef. So normal. So everyday. And so meaningless now. All her life, she'd sat down to a roast dinner on a Sunday with her parents. Brushed her teeth, walked to school. Then, after a few years, walked to her job. Listened to records. Read books. All the usual things that everybody did.

Now her life had somehow shimmered away like a mirage and had concentrated down and inwards to this bed, this moment and a single glass of cloudy liquid.

If she drank it, there'd be no going back.

She didn't exactly know what was involved in a miscarriage – but there'd be blood, surely? And pain. Stomach cramps, like a bad period. Sickness? Would she feel faint – or pass out?

And if she'd got it very wrong, it could even kill her.

At the thought, Linda felt her whole world pause, and her mind suddenly became very calm. So what if it *did* kill her? Really, would she care? Ray was dead, and here she was, contemplating the taking of yet another life.

Somehow, her own life didn't seem that important anymore. If she lived, she lived, and if she didn't ... well then.

She took a deep breath. One thing was for sure – she couldn't live with the shame that would face her if she didn't drink this foul concoction. So why was she sitting here, dithering like a silly little nitwit?

Taking a deep breath, Linda put the glass to her mouth, tipped her head slightly back and swallowed it in three gulps. It tasted a bit acrid and caught at the back of her throat a little, and for a while she sat coughing on her bed, her eyes watering as she gasped for air.

But slowly, the coughing fit subsided. And she lay back on the bed, for the moment feeling calm and almost numb, just waiting for whatever was going to happen to happen.

Chapter 25

The sun had decided to come out, so when Hilda called around for Delia, Delia's mother shooed them out into the back garden to keep them out from under her feet as she cooked the Sunday lunch.

The two girls made straight for their usual place, an old wrought-iron bench set up against the garden's back wall, under a plum tree. At this time of the year the wasps would start making their usual raids on the fruit once the day got properly warm, but in the still-cool morning air, they had the place to themselves.

'What happened to you last night then?' Hilda began the attack at once, as soon as they were safely away from the house.

Delia, knowing that she'd been in the wrong by deserting her friend, was feeling guilty and therefore mulish. 'I just got bored, that's all,' she shot back.

'Well, that's nice, that is,' Hilda huffed. 'Leaving me in the lurch. Some friend you are!'

'Didn't know you were such a 'fraidy cat,' Delia mocked. 'Besides, last I saw you were doing all right, dancing with tall, dark and handsome!'

She didn't know it, but the tall, dark and handsome man was at that moment approaching her house from the front street.

Duncan Gillingham, needing an excuse not to have to attend church with his wife, had cited a new lead that he needed to follow up, and watched her leave without regret. Then, finding himself alone and bored in their handsome new house (bought for them by her loving father), he had decided he might as well make good on his lie and follow up on the Ray Reason story.

He wanted to talk to the girl who had left the nightclub so mysteriously last night. He'd easily chatted up and milked little Hilda dry of all she knew, but from what she'd told him, it was her friend who might have more interesting tales to tell. According to Hilda, Delia had been a regular at the club, and had a crush on the Rainbirds' drummer. Even better, she'd been boasting of finding a way to get to talk to him in person. Who knew what she might have seen or heard if she had?

He'd easily been able to read between the lines of Hilda's innocent chat, and realised that Delia had been reluctant to come back to the club last night, and had been acting oddly for the last week or so. It had intrigued him enough to track Delia's address down, and now he approached the house but paused outside, thinking hard.

No doubt Delia's parents wouldn't be any too pleased to have him turn up on the doorstep. Although some people liked reporters and thought (oh how stupidly) that having their names or photos appear in the newspapers made them a minor celebrity, something told him that the Pinneys were probably not of that ilk. To him, this modest house, in its modest cul-de-sac, in a modest part of town just screamed respectability.

So, he eschewed the front entrance and started off seeking a less obvious route. At some point, Delia Pinney was bound to escape the family confines and head off somewhere into town, and to catch her on her own would require patience. Since lurking about in plain sight in front of the house was guaranteed to have the nosy neighbours' curtains twitching, he needed to find a more concealed waiting place.

Oblivious to the man circling the house, in the garden Delia and Hilda were still talking and trying to score points off each other.

Hilda, at the mention of her mysterious dance partner, smirked smugly. 'He was rather dreamy, wasn't he? What's the matter, Del, jealous?' she teased. 'Because he danced with me and not you?'

Delia, who *was* a bit jealous, laughed scornfully. 'You can keep him. I've got Frankie, remember? And *he's* a drummer in a rock band. The bloke you danced with is probably a clerk in a boring office somewhere. Or worse. He could be a … a … a plumber! That's it – I bet he messes about with other people's toilets!'

Duncan, finding the entrance to a narrow back alley that ran behind the houses, heard the chatter of female of voices, but was, at that point, too far away to hear the aspersions being cast about his possible profession.

'No he doesn't,' Hilda said hotly. 'He was dressed too nice.'

'Even plumbers have their best Sunday suit,' Delia derided, but her heart wasn't really in it. Going back to the club had been a mistake, and last night she'd had nightmares that kept waking her up, a silent scream hovering on her lips. She was feeling miserable and a little tearful, and the last thing she wanted to do was argue with her best friend.

Hilda sighed heavily, sensitive as always to her friend's mood. 'Oh well. He had nice eyes anyway. They were green. I've never met someone with green eyes before, have you?'

By now, Duncan had made his way to the sound of voices emanating from behind a garden wall, and was in time to hear the mention of green eyes. And to recognise Hilda's voice. Unable to believe his luck, he came closer and eyed the wall thoughtfully. It was high, a little taller than himself, but was made of rough local stone, and he thought he might be able to get a foothold and lever himself up to peer over the top of it.

He needed to know if the girls were alone, or if Delia Pinney's father was out and about tying up his runner beans or what have you. The last thing he needed was a protective father sticking his nose in.

'I was hoping he'd walk me home, but he only walked me to the bus stop,' Hilda said mournfully, as Duncan quietly leapt up, catching the top of the wall with his hands and scrambling about with both feet, trying to find a toehold in the stonework.

Luckily he did, and using his upper body strength, he pulled himself up to reconnoitre the lay of the land. He saw a standard-sized garden, laid out with fruit trees and a small vegetable patch nearest the house, the almost compulsory lawn, and a few flower beds, now ablaze with asters. Thankfully, it was father-free.

And right below him, the two heads of the two girls from the nightclub. Having just caught Hilda's lament, he couldn't resist it.

'Ah, but if I'd had my car with me, I'd have been happy to take you home,' he said.

Both girls stifled yelps and shot up off the bench. Hilda's eyes widened at the sight of his face, appearing as if by magic over the top of the wall.

'What are you doing here?' she blurted.

Duncan grinned. 'Sorry, didn't mean to frighten you.' He contemplated Delia thoughtfully. Now that he could see her in full daylight, she looked much younger than she had last night, when she'd been done up in all her war paint. So too, did Hilda. They were nothing more than kids really, trying to be women. The thought sobered him a little. He'd need to be careful around these two. Knowing he couldn't maintain his precarious position on the wall for long (already his calf muscles were beginning to strain) he made a quick decision.

Although he might not impress their parents with how he made his living, he thought the chances were fairly good these two would be more easily manipulated. So he grinned, his best goofy, harmless grin. 'Don't worry, I'm perfectly harmless. I just wanted to ask you girls a couple more questions. I'm a reporter. I'm writing a story, and I think you could help me.'

164

At this, Hilda shot a triumphant glance towards her friend. 'See! I told you he wasn't a plumber!'

Duncan blinked, but as unexpected as that comment was, he knew he couldn't afford to take the time now to pursue it. At least, not until he managed to sweet-talk this pair into meeting him somewhere where he wasn't clinging onto a wall like a precarious limpet. 'Hey, how about you girls meeting me out here? We can have a proper chat.'

'Sure,' Hilda said eagerly.

'No,' Delia said abruptly at the same time.

The girls usually agreed on most things and shot each other questioning looks.

Duncan bit back his impatience, whilst trying not to wonder what it was about him that might lead anyone to assume he was a plumber, of all things.

'I just want some background information for my story,' he pleaded. He'd learned very early on in his adolescence that the fairer sex liked it when men asked for their help. It brought out the protective instincts in them. And right now, he needed to get this pair on his side. 'It's all about the Bootleggers Club. I'm writing an article on the city's burgeoning night life,' he lied glibly, 'and about the glamorous and beautiful young ladies who are taking advantage of it.'

Hilda flushed with pleasure at this, as he'd hoped, but Delia, he noticed, only went very pale and looked, if possible, even more appalled.

'Does this mean we'll be in the papers?' Hilda asked breathlessly.

'If you want to be,' he said cautiously, but his eyes were fixed on Delia. Unless he was mistaken (and he seldom was, when it came to reading people) the young girl looked almost ready to faint. Or throw up in her father's asters.

'We can't,' Delia said sharply. 'Sorry, but I don't have anything to say about the Bootleggers. Come on, Hilda, let's go back inside.'

She reached out to grab Hilda's arm, clearly intent on dragging her away, but Hilda, for once, wasn't having any of it. Instead, she shook her friend's hands off angrily. She didn't know what Delia's problem was, but she wanted to stay and talk to the reporter. She'd never met someone who did something so wonderful and exciting. All her father's friends worked in the car factory or drove lorries, or boring stuff like that.

Duncan inwardly cursed, then acted fast. 'No, don't let me run you out of your own garden.' He grinned disarmingly at Delia. 'If you don't want to talk to me that's fine. I can always find lots of other girls who will. I'll be off – see you then, Hilda,' he said and launched himself backwards.

He turned and began to walk away, but his ears were on high alert, listening out for any sound.

In the garden, Delia immediately climbed onto the bench seat, then stood precariously on the back of the bench, which elevated her just enough to allow her to peer over the wall. She watched the newspaper reporter saunter away, turn into the alley at the end and disappear.

With her knees feeling distinctly weak, she climbed back down then slumped onto the bench. Her heart was beating so hard she felt sick. When he'd first popped up over the wall like that, she'd nearly fainted. But when he told them he wanted to talk to them about the nightclub, she thought she'd actually die.

Hilda, about to harangue her for chasing off the most fascinating man she'd ever met, suddenly saw that Delia was literally shaking, and felt her stomach drop. 'Del, what's up?' she wailed.

At the end of the alley, Duncan stuck his head around to risk a quick look back, saw that the coast was clear and crept quickly back along to his previous position. He was sure he'd caught the sound of feet scrambling just behind the wall, and had guessed that one of them – almost certainly Delia – had climbed up to see if he'd actually gone.

Now he pressed close to the wall and listened intently.

Hilda, suddenly feeling almost as afraid as her friend, sat down beside her and put her arms around her shoulders. 'Come on, Del, tell me what's wrong?' she pleaded.

'Nothing,' Delia sobbed.

'But you're shaking. I can feel it! Something's been off with you for ages now. You go around looking like a ghost. Come on, you can tell me. I won't snitch – you know I always keep our secrets.'

Delia nodded. That was true enough. Hilda had never blabbed to anyone whenever they properly wanted to keep something secret. And she had been feeling so lonely, ever since that night she'd sneaked into the back of the club. She'd thought she could forget about what she'd seen, but somehow it only seemed to get more and more into her head. Grow larger and larger until it seemed there was nothing else to think about. Nothing felt right anymore. It was scaring her.

And now she was scared about that reporter, asking questions. What if he found out about what had happened that night?

If only she knew what she should do!

'I'm your best friend, aren't I?' Hilda said, hugging her close. 'I'll help you. Pinkie swear. If you're in trouble you can tell me.'

'Oh, Hill!' Delia wailed and began to sob in earnest, heart-wrenching wails of misery.

Even with a solid wall between them, Duncan could hear that this was no normal teenage girl crisis about a bad haircut or parents who wouldn't let them out after nine o'clock at night. This girl was wailing as if her life was ending.

Hilda too began to cry, even though she didn't know why. She'd never seen her friend so distressed, and for some reason it made her feel properly frightened. For a while, the two girls simply sat, rocked and cried together.

Eventually, though, Delia began to find some release from all her tension and fear, and pulling out the handkerchief she always kept up her sleeve, she wiped her face. Slowly, her heaving shoulders and painful ribs began to still, and her breath came in deep ragged gasps.

'It's about … that night. When that man died in the club,' Delia began, and on the other side of the wall, Duncan felt his heart begin to race. He whipped his notebook out and in his impressive reporter's shorthand, wrote down every word that was being said verbatim.

'I knew it,' Hilda said quietly. 'Did you sneak into the back like you said you would?'

Delia nodded. 'I found this window open. It was really dark and smelly inside – not nice at all. Not glamorous, like I thought the hidden parts of the club would be. I think the toilets were nearby, and I could hardly see anything. But I knew the band met in the basement. It was no secret that they got changed down there and drank and stuff between their stints on stage. I wanted to get down there and talk to Frankie. I knew, if I could just talk to him alone, he'd see we were meant for each other.'

Delia sighed.

'*Did* you talk to him? Did he tell you to get lost? Is that what's hurt you?' Hilda asked and then bit her lip as her friend laughed out loud. But it was not a nice laugh. Not a laugh you used when you found something funny.

Instead it kind of made her stomach lurch all over again.

'Oh, Hilly, if it was only something like that,' Delia said raggedly. 'No. I never even got to see Frankie. I never even made it to the basement. Instead I saw … I saw … It was on the stairs. Those spiral stairs. Like I said, it was dark; the light bulbs were really weak in there and I was in this long, thin corridor. I'd just seen the top of the stairs though and thought I was home free, but when I looked over the railings around the opening …'

'What? What did you see?' Hilda asked, sounding as scared now as her friend looked.

But Delia could only shake her head helplessly.

On the other side of the wall, Duncan Gillingham held his breath.

'Del, did you see … him? The dead man?' Hilda whispered in awe.

'Yes,' Delia burst out, nodding her head emphatically. 'I did! But that's not really … Hill, it wasn't that. That I saw Ray, I mean. There was this girl standing over him … and she was touching his body. Hill, she was *doing* something to him.'

Chapter 26

Trudy looked up as a sharp and peremptory knock sounded on the door. Vincent got up and answered it, scowling the instant he saw who it was.

Duncan Gillingham scowled right back at him. 'I need to talk to Trudy or the old vul … your father. They are here, right?' he asked anxiously.

He knew Trudy wasn't at her own home because he'd just been there, and her mother had told him she was probably with Dr Ryder. He was impatient to get things moving, and he didn't want to meet with another delay now.

'Yeah, they're here,' Vincent admitted reluctantly. Part of him wanted to lie, just to get rid of him, but he could see that the other man was really excited about something. He was almost humming with it in fact, so his curiosity won out. He was beginning to understand more fully why his father had been so keen to work cases by himself – this detecting business was addictive.

Since helping out his father and Trudy on their last case, he was eager to stay involved with this one – even if it meant putting up with the likes of the importunate reporter.

'Follow me.' He sighed and led Duncan through to the kitchen, and as he went through the door, caught Trudy's curious eye. 'We have a visitor,' he announced, unnecessarily.

When he stepped back and Clement and Trudy saw the visitor's identity, Clement's face went set and cold, whilst Trudy looked mostly nonplussed.

'Duncan?' she said.

'Don't all look so pleased to see me,' Duncan said resentfully. 'I'm only here to do you the biggest favour of your life.'

Trudy smiled at the hyperbole. 'That's nice,' she said mildly.

Duncan had the grace to laugh at this. 'Yeah, it is actually. I've just learned something important about the Ray Reason murder.'

'Who says it's murder?' Clement asked at once.

'I do. Or rather, the witness I just found says so,' Duncan said. And he basked with satisfaction in the gratifying reaction this got out of all three of them.

'Really?' Trudy said, eyes brightening and sitting up straighter.

'Who?' Vincent yelped at the same time.

Clement merely grunted. 'You'd better sit down,' he said grudgingly, nodding at the spare chair at the kitchen table, 'and tell us all about it.'

Duncan did. And if he got immense pleasure out of showing them all how clever he'd been, well, why not?

*

When he'd got to the part where Delia had told her friend that she'd seen a woman standing over the body – doing something to it – he paused.

By now, Trudy was frantically taking notes and Clement was watching him with reluctant attention. Even Vincent had temporarily forgotten his antipathy towards him and was listening closely.

'So what happened then?' Vincent prompted impatiently.

'That's what Hilda asked.' Duncan grinned at him, enjoying

171

himself enormously. 'And Delia said that she turned and ran, back the way she came. Slipped back out of the window and ran off down Walton Street all in a tizzy, and has been in one ever since, poor kid. You should have heard her, crying and stuff,' Duncan said, pausing in his narrative. 'She's nothing but a child really. She shouldn't have had to see stuff like that,' he added.

He looked a little shame-faced suddenly, as if admitting to feeling sympathy for someone was a weakness that dented his tough-guy reporter persona, but Trudy found her attitude towards him softening. 'Anyway,' he said sharply, before anyone could make a comment, 'she just went on a bit about having nightmares, and being scared that the killer might have seen her, and wishing that she hadn't gone back last night and stuff like that, whilst her friend tried to reassure her.'

'Why *did* she go back last night?' Trudy asked. If she'd been so traumatised at such a young age, she couldn't imagine wild horses would have dragged her back to the crime scene.

'Her friend double-dared her or something,' Duncan said with a brief, slightly despairing laugh, the simple ridiculousness of it all making him wince. 'Of course, Hilda then went into fits of hysterics over that, saying that she hadn't known and if she had, she'd never have dared her, and they'd never go near the place again. When they went back into the house, Hilda was swearing to stick with Delia everywhere she went and act as her bodyguard.'

Again, the pathos of it made all four of them silent for a while.

'Well, I've got to talk to her and get her statement,' Trudy finally said.

'I know. that's why I came,' Duncan said simply. 'I know there's a story here, but it's got to be done right.'

Vincent sneered. Here was the true reporter back and on form again. 'Oh, I'm sure you'll get your story,' he muttered.

'Damn right I will. I've earned it,' Duncan shot back.

Trudy held up her hand, before the two men could start to bicker properly. 'But you won't print anything until we've got more to go on, right?' she said, fixing Duncan with a gimlet eye. 'Come on, Duncan, we need to know the identity of this woman Delia saw, and what exactly it was that she'd been doing. You said yourself, your witness was a young girl, and it was dark back there on the stairs. Who knows what it was she actually saw? If you publish too early, and then it turns out you've jumped the gun, you'll be a laughingstock.'

Duncan nodded. He knew, of course, that what Trudy was saying made sense. He needed far more facts before he could present something coherent to his editor. It was one of the reasons why he wasn't back at the office writing the minor scoop right now.

Besides, once the information was out there that there might be a murder case getting underway, he'd have every other newspaper reporter sniffing around the breaking story, and he wasn't ready yet to give up his potential for an exclusive front-page exposé. He was hoping for the bigger prize of a more complete story, if he was just a little patient. 'Sure, but I want you to promise me that when you do know more and make an arrest, I get the exclusive.'

Clement nodded. 'Yeshhh, you've earned that right, I think.'

Duncan shot him a quick glance. The old man was slurring his words – had he been hitting the bottle? Although it was now past lunchtime, it was a little early to be drinking, wasn't it? But it was not his business.

Mind you, the idea of the old vulture being a bit of a booze hound on the sly was something he was going to tuck away for future reference. You never knew when it might come in handy. And besides, he felt he owed the old man a black eye. He was sure it was the coroner who'd put Trudy off him.

And the thought of printing a story about the old vulture being the worse for drink at some point in the future was too delicious not to savour. Especially if he could get a photo of the old man looking pie-eyed! That would put a dent in that superior manner of his.

*

After Duncan had left, the three of them got their heads together again.

'Well, if we're looking at the women in the case, there's really only his girlfriend, Linda, isn't there?' Vincent asked.

'She's got to be the prime suspect yes,' Trudy agreed. 'But there's still Jenny Wren.'

'What's her motive though?' Vincent asked.

Trudy shrugged. 'We know she wants Martin to be top man in the band, and Ray Reason was trying to take over the whole show. I know, it's a bit weak. But we can't rule out anyone at this stage.'

'I agree. Including the men,' Clement said. And when both of them looked at him curiously, he smiled. 'Even if this young girl Delia *did* see a woman on the stairs crouching over Ray's body, it doesn't necessarily follow that the mystery woman had anything to do with his death. She might have just found him, and was trying to see if he was hurt. What Delia saw as sinister might have been nothing more than someone trying to assess the situation. What if one of the club-goers that night was a nurse, say, and had found him on the stairs and was checking his vital signs?'

'If so, why didn't she report it?' Vincent asked sceptically. 'Why leave him for someone else to find?'

'She might have panicked,' Trudy said. 'People often do. She might not have wanted anyone to know she'd been at the club, for instance. It does have a risky reputation. And if she'd reported it, maybe her parents or regular boyfriend would have found out. Or she might have been scared at the thought of being pulled into a notorious scandal. I can see why someone might not want to get involved and do the right thing. I come across it all the time in my job.'

'OK,' Vincent concluded. 'What do we do next?'

'We have lunch,' Clement put in dryly. 'I, for one, am hungry. After that, we need to talk to Linda and Jenny, and see if either of them will admit to finding Ray dead. And, of course, we need to get Delia's story down in an official statement. Trudy, you'll have to be the one to do that.'

Trudy nodded. 'Sounds like a plan. And once I've done that, I'll have to report it to Inspector Jennings. If nothing else, the fact that we've got someone on the scene who didn't report a dead body will convince him we need to keep on digging.'

She only hoped that it wouldn't stir him enough to make him take the case away from her altogether and give it to Sergeant O'Grady instead. The thought of being sidelined now was too awful to even contemplate.

'Maybe I'll wait until Monday morning,' she said insouciantly. 'No need to disturb his Sunday.'

Vincent and his father swapped smiling looks.

Chapter 27

After eating together at Clement's house (Vincent, it turned out, cooked a very good roast chicken dinner) they all split up. Clement went to call on Linda Kempson, whilst Vincent was sent to call on Jenny Wren and see what he could get out of her. Trudy set off on the important job of interviewing Delia Pinney.

Vincent was the first one to get to his destination, but was immediately out of luck. Jennifer wasn't answering the door at her digs.

Feeling deflated, he wondered if he dared go to Delia's address and 'help' Trudy, but he was pretty sure she wouldn't want him looking over her shoulder and getting in her way. Loath to go back to his father's empty house and twiddle his thumbs, however, he decided to go on to Linda Kempson's house instead, sure that his father would give him a much better reception.

Clement, unaware that he was shortly to be joined by his son, had just knocked on the Kempsons' front door. There was no immediate response, but he was sure he could hear voices inside. And to his ear, they sounded distinctly agitated.

He knocked again, and after a while the door was suddenly yanked opened by a harassed-looking middle-aged man. Dressed in baggy flannel trousers and a plain white shirt, Clement guessed that he was Linda's father, and that he liked to feel comfortable on his day off and dress accordingly. His face, though, far from looking relaxed, seemed pinched and taunt. 'Yes?' he demanded impatiently. 'Now's not a good time, so if …'

He wasn't allowed to finish the sentence, however, as a woman's voice – presumably his wife's – called from somewhere behind and above him. 'Wally! Wally! Come on up, I think she's passed out now! Oh, Wally, I think we should call an ambulance!'

At that, Clement stiffened. 'Mr Kempson? My name's Ryder, Dr Clement Ryder. I used to practise medicine. Is everything all right?'

As he spoke, the other man's face seemed to sag with relief. 'A doctor, you say? Can you come in? It's our daughter. She's not right,' he said in a rush. As Clement quickly brushed past him into a small hallway, the girl's father pointed at the stairs. 'Up there – first door on the right.'

Clement nodded and went up quickly, Linda's father hard on his heels.

As Clement went into the room indicated, he could smell vomit in the air. It was a nice room, decorated in shades of lilac and cream with accents of mint green. A girl was lying on her side on the bed with a middle-aged woman, obviously her mother, kneeling on the floor beside her, brushing the hair off her daughter's pale and clammy face. She was watching her anxiously, and was clearly feeling fear and helplessness in equal measure.

She sensed Clement approaching, and thinking it was her husband, looked up, her mouth opening as if she was about to say something. Clement saw a look of consternation cross her face as she realised her mistake.

'I'm a doctor, Mrs Kempson,' Clement said, which was not – technically – still true, but he wasn't about to waste time explaining. His eyes were already on the girl he'd seen briefly in his courtroom during Ray Reason's inquest.

'Oh thank the Lord,' the girl's mother said, not questioning his sudden, miracle-like appearance in her hour of need. She

177

scrambled to her feet to make room for him as Clement sat on the side of the bed beside his unexpected patient.

'Linda, can you hear me?' Clement said loudly.

'I don't think she can, Doctor,' the girl's mother said, literally wringing her hands in her distress. 'She stopped speaking to me about five minutes ago. Before that she was moaning and seemed not to know who I was.'

Clement gently moved the girl's head a little further around so that he could see her face better. When he gently lifted one eyelid with his thumb he didn't like the look of her pupils, and liked even less the slight froth that had gathered on her lips.

He took her wrist, expertly placing two digits in just the right place – and found her pulse was too fast and reedy. 'Call an ambulance,' he said shortly over his shoulder to Mr Kempson, who nodded and ran down the stairs and out the front door. There was a telephone box at the end of the street, and he ran faster than he'd ever run since leaving school – and the rugby pitch – behind him.

'When did your daughter start to complain of feeling ill?' Clement asked the mother, as he gently put his finger to the side of the girl's neck to take her pulse again. He wished he had his stethoscope with him and a doctor's bag. Since he'd been a surgeon for most of his life, it had been some time since he'd done his stint as a GP, and he feared that there was little he could do for her until the ambulance came.

He saw a dirty glass on the bedside table, and automatically reached for it.

'She never said she was feeling poorly,' Shirley Kempson said, her voice wavering as she swallowed back tears. 'I didn't know she was off-colour till I called her down for her lunch, and she never came. I came up to see why she was dallying and found her moaning on the bed. Oh, whatever's the matter with her?' she added on a wail.

For Linda had now begun to convulse, and Clement, who'd

been sniffing the glass, put it hastily back on the table, and moved to hold her shoulders down. Fitting people could hurt themselves if left unrestrained. 'Mrs Kempson, help me, please,' Clement demanded. 'I need you to turn her head so that her mouth isn't pressed into the pillow at all.' If she began to vomit again, he'd have to act fast and turn her back so that she didn't inhale and choke, but right now, he was worried her airway might be obstructed.

If she wasn't getting enough oxygen into her lungs, he might have to do mouth-to-mouth resuscitation.

'Linda, can you hear me?' Clement said again, loudly in her ear, but she was unresponsive. 'Linda, I need to know if you've taken anything. What was in the glass, Linda?'

Her mother dragged her distraught eyes from her daughter to the glass on the table, shaking her head, unable to comprehend what was happening.

The girl's father came running back into the room just then, breathing heavily. 'The ambulance is coming …' He broke off as he saw his daughter jerking on the bed and the big old man who'd come to his door holding her down firmly.

Suddenly, he looked concerned. 'Here, who are you exactly, and what're you doing here?' he said. From the uncertain, slightly belligerent tone of his voice Clement could tell that he might become a problem, especially if he began to worry that Clement was hurting his daughter.

And he didn't have time for any nonsense right then.

'My name is Dr Clement Ryder. I'm currently the city coroner, but I was for many years a surgeon. I came to talk to your daughter about Mr Ray Reason's death. I held the inquest … Damn it!'

He broke off as Linda took a long, shuddering breath and suddenly went very still.

He shot up off the bed, turned her abruptly onto her back, bent down, quickly opened two buttons on her blouse and then bent down and put an ear to her chest.

Walter Kempson took a step forward as Clement undid his

179

daughter's buttons, and said uncertainly, 'Here, now what do you think—'

'SILENCE!' Clement roared, with not a trace of his earlier slurring. Shirley Kempson put two hands to her mouth, her eyes wide with panic. The girl's father froze, his face going chalk-white.

Clement heard her heartbeat with some relief. But it wasn't right … Not moving his head from its position over her heart, his eyes moved to look at the girl's father. 'Did they say how long the ambulance would be?'

'A few minutes they said,' Walter Kempson panted.

Clement grunted. 'It's possible I might have to perform a heart massage on your daughter, Mr Kempson. It involves me …' But just then they both heard the sound of a siren outside.

'Quick, go outside and point them in here. Tell them to be quick!'

Walter nodded and again shot out and down the stairs.

Beside him, he felt Mrs Kempson fall to her knees in an awkward heap, half pressed up against the wall, half against her daughter's bed and Clement's legs. She began to cry helplessly.

A few moments later, the ambulance attendants arrived and listened respectfully as Clement barked out his instructions.

Vincent arrived at the turning into the Kempsons' street just in time to see his father clamber into the back of an ambulance that had pulled up to a house halfway along, administering to someone lying on the stretcher.

He broke out into a run, but the ambulance wasn't waiting around and pulled out in a hurry, sirens clanging. A few moments later, a Morris Minor car pulled out very quickly, following on after the ambulance, and Vincent watched it disappear down the road, feeling at a total loss.

Chapter 28

Trudy, unaware of the drama playing out at the Kempson household, had her hands full herself dealing with the Pinney household.

She'd called and asked to speak to Delia. Mrs Pinney, rightly assessing Trudy's age as at least five or maybe six years older than that of her daughter, knew that she couldn't be one of Delia's friends and asked what it was all about.

Which was natural, but not ideal. Trudy, not dressed in her usual uniform, had a bit of a job convincing the protective woman that she was indeed a police officer, but even after she'd explained her errand, the girl's mother refused point-blank to believe that Delia had been attending a nightclub – let alone that there was any possibility that she could be a witness in a case of suspicious death.

By the time Trudy had managed to gain entrance as far as the front hall of the house, Mrs Pinney, a rather stout, well-dressed woman with permed blonde hair and large, slightly bulging pale blue eyes, was talking so loudly that her husband appeared on the scene.

Tall, lean and dark, he was the antithesis of his wife. Quietly spoken, he quickly calmed his wife down, listened to what Trudy had to say and took charge. For which Trudy was extremely grateful.

He called his daughter down from her bedroom, but the moment the young girl stepped into the living room, her face fell. She had no idea who the pretty woman was who was watching her closely, but she could tell by her mother's heavy breathing and red-tinged angry face, that trouble was in the air.

'This here young lady is with the police,' the girl's mother began ominously. 'And she says you've been sneaking off and going to some nightclub in town. Is this true?' she demanded.

Naturally, her teenage daughter immediately denied it.

Mrs Pinney turned a look of justified outrage on Trudy. 'You see! I told you so. My Delia is a good girl. She wouldn't have nothing to do with no nasty nightclubs. Now, I think you should apologise and be off. Disturbing people on a Sunday, and all over a mistake too.'

But Delia's father, who had been watching his daughter's face closely during this recital – and clearly had a better idea of her ways than had her mother – sighed quietly.

'I think we'd better all take a seat,' he broke in. 'WPC …?'

'Loveday, sir,' Trudy hastily introduced herself properly.

'Yes. Please sit down. Audrey, stop talking on so,' he added to his wife, who had started again to defend Delia's innocence and proclaim that there was no need for their visitor to stay, let alone make herself comfortable, all of which her husband ignored completely.

'We need to get to the bottom of all this and without any more fuss – please, Audrey,' he chided, raising his voice over the last few words in order to be heard over his wife's repetition that it was all a silly mistake.

After an awkward moment of silence, all of them took a seat – Trudy on an armchair, the man of the house in a matching one, whilst the teenager and her mother sat on the settee, side by side, clearly allied against her.

To his daughter, the only man in the room cast a stern but not angry look. He was a good-looking individual in an aesthetic, bookish sort of way, Trudy noted, and both his wife and daughter now obeyed him, as if realising that further argument would do them no good.

'Now, Delia, let's have the truth please,' Mr Pinney said with a no-nonsense brusqueness.

'Oh, John, how can you think ...' Mrs Pinney began, but her husband held up a hand for silence.

And got it.

'Delia?' John Pinney said, looking at his woebegone daughter's face steadily.

Delia began to cry. It was, Trudy thought a shade cynically, probably her usual first line of defence, but it wasn't going to do her any good this time. Neither Trudy – nor Delia's father, apparently – was in any mood to let things slide.

Her mother, however, instantly held her daughter's hand tightly, and bent her head close. 'Oh, Delly, what have you been up to?' she asked despairingly.

It took time, patience and plenty of tears and self-justification on Delia's part, but eventually the girl's parents were able to get the truth out of her. The story of her infatuation with a local pop group, and how she'd come to be spending her Saturday nights at the club instead of playing board games with some friends came tumbling out.

With this last admission, Audrey Pinney tried to throw the blame for her daughter's deceit onto Hilda, claiming the girl had always been a bad influence. But John Pinney would have none of it. It was hardly Hilda's fault, he'd pointed out dryly, if Delia had used her as an excuse!

Eventually, Delia's sobs subsided, and her father informed her that she would not be let out of the house except to go to school, for at least a month. Delia looked to her mother at this, but for once, her mother wasn't on her side, and only nodded her head vigorously.

'Serves you right, young madam,' Audrey said. 'Sneaking off to a nightclub! Oh what if the neighbours find out!' she suddenly wailed, seeing calamity of a different sort appearing on the horizon.

Trudy, having patiently let the family drama play out thus far, was not about to let Mrs Pinney have her head any longer, and finally broke in to get down to business.

Gently, she led Delia through the night that Ray Reason had died. And if her parents had been upset and surprised before, it was nothing to how they began to look as the story unfolded further.

Trudy took down the girl's faltering, frightened statement in her quick neat shorthand, about how she'd gone around to the back entrance of the building, where she'd earlier discovered a sneaky way in, and climbed in through a small, unlocked window. Of how she'd then found herself in the dimly lit back reaches of the club and approached down the narrow corridor until she saw the head of the spiral staircase. Then sensing movement there, she'd looked over the iron safety railing that ringed the entrance to the stairs and seen something that made her feel 'ever so sick'.

At this point, the girl's mother put her arm around her shoulder and shot a helpless, angry look at Trudy. 'Do you have to keep asking her things like this? Can't you see she's upset?'

'I *can* see that, Mrs Pinney,' Trudy said gently, 'but I'm afraid it's necessary we continue. Delia will probably feel better once it's all off her chest,' she added, hoping to placate her.

'A man died, Audrey,' John Pinney also put in flatly. 'And Delia needs to learn there are consequences to her actions. She also needs to bear up and do her duty. We all have to help the police if we can. Answer the police lady's questions, Delia,' he said calmly to his daughter.

Delia's pale, tear-streaked face tightened, but she took an obliging gulp of air and tried to rally her resources. 'I couldn't make much out at first,' she began unsteadily. 'It looked as if the stairs had been blocked by something soft and squidgy. Like bags of clothes or something. Then a door must have opened down below, because I could suddenly hear voices coming from down there, and this shaft of light appeared.'

She took another gulp and sighed. 'It meant that I could see things a bit better, and that's when I saw … I saw a man, lying sprawling down the stairs, sort of bent in the middle where the twist in the staircase was. His head was pointing down to the bottom, and his feet were pointing up to the top. And someone was crouched over him, all awkward like, because there wasn't hardly any room really for the two of them. She had one foot on the step above his legs, and another foot half-set in one of the gaps in the iron railings. She was sort of teetering a bit, as if she didn't have much balance. And then, I saw … her … look up.'

She swallowed hard. 'I was so scared, Mum. I just shot back and ran the way I came.' Delia half-buried her face in her mother's shoulder. 'I climbed back through the window and ran off down the alley. And that's all I know. Honest, and pinkie swear.'

'You were very brave,' Trudy said. No point saying now that she should have reported it and stayed on the scene to give a witness statement. She'd been a scared teenage girl. You couldn't expect her to think of doing anything except getting away, and then staying quiet. She wouldn't want her parents to know where she'd been, for one thing. And, as Duncan had said earlier, she'd been too young to have her first glimpse of death like that.

No wonder the poor kid had been having nightmares.

'Can't you leave her alone now?' Audrey Pinney said angrily, but Trudy had to reluctantly shake her head again.

'I'm sorry, Mrs Pinney. I just have a few more things to ask. But I'll be as quick as I can, I promise. Delia, you've been doing very well. Now there's just something else I need from you. Something very important. You said you saw *her* face. Who do you mean?'

'The woman who was crouched over him.'

185

Trudy nodded. 'Did you recognise her, Delia? Do you know her name?'

The girl shook her head vehemently.

'Could you see what she was doing?' Trudy tried next. Mindful of what Clement had said about Ray Reason having two distinct blows to the head, she added casually, 'Was she holding his head in any way for instance?'

But Delia immediately shook her head. 'No. She had her hands in his pockets, I think. Like she was looking for something in them.'

Robbery? Trudy wondered straight away. But she was sure, from her memory of reading the case notes, that Ray Reason had been found with his wallet still on him, and that it hadn't been empty of pound notes. He had also still been wearing his watch. Perhaps the thief had sensed or heard Delia above and had been scared off?

'You said there was a shaft of light. So you must have seen her face clearly?' Trudy stated firmly.

Reluctantly, the girl nodded. 'Yes, I saw her. Do you think she saw me?' she added, her eyes brimming over again. 'Do you think she's going to come after me next?' And she began to wail again in earnest. 'Wh-what if the k-killer comes after m-me now?'

At this, her mother gathered her tight in her arms, looking ferocious enough to fight off a whole squadron of killers.

It took some time for Trudy and the girl's father to calm down both mother and daughter, but eventually they managed it.

Trudy did her best to reassure them by telling them that there was no proof yet that a murder had indeed been committed, and that in all probability, what Delia had seen had just been another club-goer discovering the body and probably checking for signs of injury.

But even as she saw this calm them all down, she herself wasn't so sure. What if Delia *had* seen the killer? How likely was it that she had seen Delia's face as well? But after mentally going over the layout of the stairs and back corridor, she felt fairly sure that it was unlikely. The light coming from the basement room wouldn't travel far upstairs. And if Delia had been glancing over and had immediately shot back the moment she became scared, she didn't think, with the awkwardness of the angle and the limited light, that she would have been recognisable.

Nevertheless, when she reported to her superior tomorrow, she'd see what Inspector Jennings had to say about the possibility of providing police protection for her.

Having done a fair bit to relieve their anxiety, by the time she'd left the still shell-shocked Pinney family behind, she'd arranged for Delia and her parents to come to the station first thing tomorrow morning. She wanted Delia to sit down with a police artist and come up with a likeness for the woman on the stairs.

Would it be Lindy-Lou or Jenny Wren?

As she left the house and headed back to Clement's place, she had a bit of a skip in her step. At last, she felt as if they were finally getting somewhere!

*

At Clement's house, Vincent answered the door to her knocking, looking worried.

As he ushered her into the kitchen and put the kettle on, he told her what he'd seen. Trudy then returned the favour, and recounted what she'd learned from the Pinneys.

'It's looking as if the girlfriend did it, isn't it?' Vincent said eagerly, sitting opposite her across the table and watching her closely. 'I'm pretty sure it was her being carried away on the stretcher. Do you think she might have tried to, you know, do away with herself or something?'

Trudy frowned. 'Let's not jump to conclusions. She might have a burst appendix or any number of less dramatic things gone wrong with her. Whatever it was, it's lucky your father went to interview her, instead of you or me. We'd not have been of any use to the poor girl at all.'

Vincent nodded. 'Yes, good old Dad will have taken care of it all.'

Trudy swallowed a sip of tea, and then, her chest feeling tight, she took a deep breath and took the plunge.

'Vincent,' she said quietly. 'What's wrong with your father?'

For a moment, Vincent froze. 'Sorry?' he said vaguely, not meeting her eyes.

Trudy sighed. 'I heard him today. He was slurring some of his words. And in the past, I've noticed … things. He's not well, is he?' she said flatly.

Again, he wouldn't meet her eyes, and the tight feeling in her chest amplified, making her feel flushed and a little sick.

'I think,' Vincent finally said, 'you'd better ask him yourself.'

Trudy, her mouth dry, took another sip of her tea and forced herself to smile. 'All right. I'll do that.'

But she wondered if she actually would.

Because as she sat in her mentor's home, drinking tea with his unhappy son, Trudy knew that she didn't want to ask Dr Clement Ryder what was wrong.

For some time now – in fact, almost from the very beginning – she'd seen signs that all was not totally well with the coroner, but she'd persuaded herself that she was reading more into it than there was. Coming up with excuse after excuse to make herself feel better.

Old folks were sometimes unsteady on their feet.

They felt the cold more, and so of course they'd tremble with cold.

Maybe he drank a little bit too much sometimes, even if she couldn't smell alcohol on his breath.

It didn't matter what she told herself, so long as she could pretend it wasn't really happening. That it wasn't – couldn't be – anything really serious.

Because, deep down, something had always told her that the moment she knew the truth, her life would never be the same again.

And now, she felt as if that moment of truth was fast gaining on her, closing in, getting ready to clasp its teeth and jaws into her.

Her hand, when she raised the cup to her lips, was shaking every bit as much as she'd sometimes seen her friend's hand shake. But in her case, she knew the cause well enough.

It was fear.

Chapter 29

A tranquil Sunday evening lassitude hung over the city as Martin Cuthbertson and the rest of the Rainbirds met in a lock-up garage in Botley. It belonged to the uncle of the keyboard player and they'd begun to use it recently for rehearsals, as there weren't quite so many neighbours to annoy with their loud music.

Titus Crowther-Beauley, so he'd informed them when last they'd met, would be staying overnight in the city this Sunday, having been offered the loan of a friend's luxury flat overlooking Christ Church Meadow, so the whole band were nervously awaiting his arrival. They were due to audition the new band member that the star-maker and high-flying agent wanted them to consider, and excitement was running high.

Ian Scraggs, the bass guitarist, was chain-smoking and pacing about restlessly. 'It's got to be good news for us, right?' he said, not for the first time, as the drummer rolled his eyes at him. 'I mean, it stands to reason, right?' Ian persisted. 'He must be about to sign us for real, I mean, not just talking about it, if he's asking us to take on this Welsh guy.'

'Yeah, he wouldn't bother wasting his time otherwise,' Frankie Everett agreed. 'But stop pacing about, will ya – it's making me nervous.'

Ignoring him, Ian continued to pace and smoke. 'I can't sit still. This is it, don't you get it? Our big break. The moment when we stop being just another band in a provincial city and make it to the big time. We all know this guy can make it happen for us, don't we?'

He spoke to his bandmates in general, but he was looking at Marty.

Martin shot him a wan smile back, and nodded. The truth was, he was sure that Ian was right, and that it was all but a done deal that Titus was about to take them on. But unlike the rest of the jittery, excitable band, he wasn't feeling quite so upbeat about it. And the reason for his unease sat on an upturned tool chest, watching them with a grim little smile.

Jenny Wren, too, was awaiting the arrival of the 'big man' but not for the same reasons as everyone else. She was deeply suspicious about this new boy Titus wanted to join the band, and Marty wasn't sure that she was wrong to be concerned.

'I still don't see that it's up to him who you have in the band,' she said casually, addressing the group in general. 'He might be a big shot, but you can't let him influence your "sound". The fans'll be the ones who'll either make or break you, not him,' she pointed out, her voice as hard as the look in her eyes. 'And right now the fans love you just the way you are. Remember the reception you got at the club yesterday?'

Martin nodded. She was right, in a way. It was all about pleasing the fans. But he wasn't so naïve as to think that that was all there was to success. A lot of bands had a small following of loyal listeners. But it needed a shark like Titus to help them rise to the top and stand out above all the competition.

But he understood where she was coming from. Titus represented the big leagues, and they'd have to be careful. It was easy for people like them to get out of their depth. And, although he'd never actually admit it, he was rather glad to have Jenny's feisty, clever and shrewd support, backing him up. She might

191

be a bit much at times, but he never doubted her loyalty – or her fierce determination to stand by him and see him make a success of his life.

'And they were happy enough to have Marty fronting the band instead of Ray,' Jenny added, for the benefit of the other three members.

Pinky Rossiter gave her a grin and looked slyly at Martin. 'You've got a loyal bird here, Marty,' he said, half-teasing, half-sarcastic.

'Cut it out,' Marty said flatly. 'We can't start bickering amongst ourselves. We can't risk …' He broke off as he heard the unmistakable sound of Titus's big fancy car pulling up outside the open door.

Jenny knew when – and when not – to push her boyfriend, and saying nothing more, took herself off to the far back wall, where she leaned in the darkest shadows and watched the proceedings silently.

With the band set up in the light coming in through the door, she could see that Ewan Treadwell was even better-looking than she'd thought. She hadn't really been able to get a proper view of him in the dim lighting at the club, but now that she got a good look at him, she knew at once that he was going to be the teenage girl fans' new heart-throb. However, once she'd got Marty's teeth done and his skin sorted out, and given him a whole new look, that wouldn't matter so much. Titus would see that he could be both the voice behind the band and the star of the show.

She'd bloody well make sure that he did!

Titus was his usual self, full of bonhomie and charm, and when the Welshman began to play, it became clear that he was a decent enough guitarist but not good enough to be a threat to Marty. Annoyingly, it also meant they didn't have a legitimate excuse to turn him down.

And when they went through one of the Rainbirds' older songs, and Ewan began to sing with Marty, it was also clear that he had a weaker voice – another bonus. But even she had to admit that his voice and Martin's together did go well, and that the Welsh lad provided him with a good counterpoint. Loath though she was to admit it, Titus knew his stuff – and had a good ear.

Silently, Jenny cursed the agent under her breath. She'd been hoping that the newcomer would be a total washout.

After the garage fell silent, she could see Marty and the others exchanging looks, and listened, with growing anger, as Marty was forced to agree that he could join the band. She wanted to shout at him not to be so stupid, but she forced herself to keep quiet. Now was not the time to force a confrontation – not when the other lads were there to gang up on her.

No, she'd wait until she had Marty on his own, then go to work on him.

Titus, pleased with how things had gone, then immediately began to talk business, and Jenny really pricked up her ears.

At the end of ten minutes or so, it was agreed that Titus would have contracts drawn up and ready for the boys to sign tomorrow morning. They already existed in draft form and only needed tweaking. And he promised that before Christmas, the Rainbirds would be playing at venues in London.

After the excited outburst this produced had calmed down a little, he assured them that he personally knew several owners of famous clubs who'd be more than happy to take his word for it that he'd found the hottest new thing in pop music.

And the smug agent wasn't lying, Jenny knew, as she watched and listened and said nothing.

She had a fine tightrope to walk now, and she knew it wasn't going to be easy. The Rainbirds needed Titus – she knew that – but it had to be on *their* terms, not his. And key to this was steering Marty in the right direction and bolstering his courage when it flagged – as it inevitably would when Jenny persuaded him he'd have to butt heads with the super-smooth agent.

The Welsh lad, in the meantime, was elated to be with a band that was obviously going places, and was busy ingratiating himself with his new bandmates. All the Rainbirds were elated at being taken under Titus's wing, and only Jenny, it seemed, could see the writing on the wall.

But if Mr Titus Crowther-Beauley thought he was going to get rich off the Rainbirds' talent and hard work, she promised herself furiously, he was going to have to think again.

Marty would sign a stringent contract only over her dead body!

Chapter 30

The next day dawned bright enough with a warm, autumnal softness that brought smiles to people's faces as they left for work that Monday morning.

But Inspector Jennings' day didn't get off to the best of starts. He awoke to find his alarm clock had wound down during the night and had thus failed to wake him on time, forcing him to rush everything from his morning shave to his breakfast. His car started with an ominous cough, and didn't seem to be pulling as strongly as it should on the hills, foreshadowing a trip to the garage mechanics with, in all likelihood, a hefty bill to quickly follow.

And the moment WPC Trudy Loveday knocked on his door and stepped into his office, he could tell by the look on her face that things were afoot.

Since he'd already decided that it was about time to tell her that she and that interfering coroner couldn't play at 'murders' anymore, and to ditch the Ray Reason case, the last thing he needed to see now was that look of excitement and triumph in her eyes.

As if he didn't have enough work to do without bumping up an accidental death to murder!

So as she stood in front of his desk and began to relate the events of yesterday, he had to brace himself for yet more irritants. Clearly, the day that had started off badly, was only going to go downhill even further.

'And when Dr Ryder eventually came back home, he told us that Linda Kempson was seriously ill in hospital and had lost a baby. Her poor parents are still in shock,' she concluded, snapping her notebook shut with satisfaction.

Her mind, however, wasn't totally on the job, but still circling the problem of what was going to happen when she and Dr Ryder finally decided it was time to be honest with each other.

Although she'd tried to put it out of her mind, it kept coming back to haunt her.

Luckily, when Clement had returned to the house yesterday, he'd been too full of his news to notice that his son and his protégé were acting oddly around him. And before he could become aware of the fact, once they'd set out their strategy for today, Trudy had taken the decision to leave, thus limiting the chances of him catching on.

Vincent had looked relieved to see her go, as if he'd really thought that she'd choose *that* moment to tackle his father about whatever secrets he was keeping!

Seeing the Inspector look at her impatiently, she stopped wool-gathering and got her mind back to the business in hand. 'So Mr and Mrs Pinney and their daughter are due in any moment now, sir, to work up a likeness of the woman that Delia saw on the stairs. And Dr Ryder's got permission from the hospital for us to interview Linda Kempson later on this morning. She's out of danger now, apparently. Ordinarily, they wouldn't let us speak to her so soon, but Dr Ryder … Well, you know Dr Ryder, sir,' she said diplomatically. Nobody said 'no' to the coroner when he wanted to get his own way.

The put-upon Inspector snorted humourlessly at this. 'So, let's see if I've got this right,' he said wearily. 'You think this girl,

Kempson, killed her boyfriend in some sort of an argument, probably because he got her in the family way and refused to stand by her?'

Trudy shifted a little uneasily on her feet. 'Well, sir, that seems to be the most likely explanation at the moment,' she said cautiously. She wasn't totally certain, though, why she was being so pernickety with her words. Perhaps it was because she felt sorry for Linda, and was hoping there was some other alternative? She'd been through so much already, and now she might be facing a murder charge.

Or, more likely, a manslaughter charge? If Ray had died after an argument and Linda had just shoved him ... But no, that wouldn't work, she realised regretfully. There was that second blow to the head to deal with. Pushing a man down the stairs in a fit of anguish was one thing. Then cold-bloodedly lifting and banging his head again – or hitting him over the head with something else just to make sure the job was done – well, that was another thing altogether.

'Huh,' Jennings said, giving nothing away of his own thoughts on the matter. 'Well, better get on with things then,' he said briskly. At least this time, he mused sourly, the case seemed to be resolving itself satisfactorily and wouldn't require much more time spent on it. Once their witness was able to identify this Linda Kempson as the one who'd been standing over the dead body, getting a warrant for her arrest would be a piece of cake.

'Sir,' Trudy said smartly, then turned and left.

*

The Pinneys arrived on time, mother and daughter both nervous about entering a police station for the first time in their lives, whilst the man of the house hid his curiosity and fear much better.

The police artist, a PC who'd been to art school and had tried – and failed – to earn a living selling his canvases, quickly put Delia at her ease. His being rather handsome and kind helped,

Trudy noticed with a hidden smile. Her parents sat on chairs against one wall whilst Delia and the artist collaborated at a desk in one of the interview rooms. Trudy watched, fascinated, as the man began to draw.

Guided by Delia's comments, he erased lines and then added more, shading in hair a darker hue here, or altering the shape of the eyes and eyebrows there, as Delia instructed.

Trudy had heard from some of her colleagues who'd gone through this process that sometimes getting a good likeness could take a long time, since the artist had no visual references to help him, only the words of the witness and their (not always reliable) memories.

Before they were even halfway through, Trudy could already tell that the woman being gradually depicted on the sketch pad was not Linda Kempson. Nor was it Jenny Wren for that matter, but rather a woman she'd never seen before.

Inspector Jennings, she thought grimly, was not going to be pleased by this annoying little wrinkle.

After about half an hour or so, both Delia (who had been a bit unsure at first, but had quickly become fascinated and fully engaged in the process) and the PC were happy with what they'd achieved.

As he handed the sketch over to Trudy, the Pinneys rose and were allowed to escort their now slightly deflated offspring from the room. The teenager was very much still out of favour with her parents, it seemed, and was already beginning to feel the effects of her curtailed freedom.

Trudy walked through to the larger, outer office, and set about the process of getting some reproductions made of the unknown woman. Having done so, she returned to her desk and finished the necessary paperwork, and made sure to slip a copy of the likeness into her pocket before bearding the Inspector in his den.

It was as she was doing this that Walter Swinburne, the oldest PC at the station, walked past her desk, saw one of the copies, picked it up, grunted and said casually, 'I recognise this face, I think. So what's our Patty been up to now then?'

Trudy froze, unable to believe her luck. 'You know her?'

'If it's who I think it is, I've pinched her once or twice in my time over the last couple of years. Patty Nesbitt, bit of shoplifting and pickpocketing, upgraded into out-and-out theft and now earns her dishonest crust as a prostitute.'

'Don't suppose she hangs out at the Bootleggers Club does she, Walter?' Trudy asked hopefully.

'There, and any other dirty dive where she can pick up a desperate man,' the old constable said with a grin.

Trudy could have kissed him, but obviously didn't. Instead, she headed back to the Inspector's office, feeling a little less anxious. Although she had to give him the bad news that perhaps the Ray Reason case wasn't about to be wrapped up in a neat bow just yet, at least she had a positive identification for another suspect.

Jennings, on hearing the name, also recognised it.

'I know her. She and that club manager of yours are pretty tight,' he said, with the beginnings of a rather happy smile. 'He lets her pick up punters, and I wouldn't be at all surprised if she doesn't do him the odd crooked favour or two in return. Introducing some of her clients to drugs, for instance – all supplied by the Bootleggers' management. Well, well, I've been wanting to tweak Felix Simpkins's tail for some time, but up until now, haven't been able to.' Jennings straightened up in his chair, all but rubbing his hands with glee.

'The swine's always been too slippery for us to nab him, and too well protected by the bigwigs that run that club of his whenever he sails close to the wind. But this time … we're talking *murder*. This time, he might just have overstepped the mark, and his guardian angels will throw him to the wolves rather than get mixed up in it.'

He reached for the phone and barked down into it for his favourite sergeant, Mike O'Grady, to come to his office.

It didn't take the man long to appear. He cast Trudy a curious but affable look then fixed his gaze on the Inspector. He'd heard that the station's only WPC was liaising with the coroner again, but unlike his Inspector, he usually wished her the best of British luck.

'Mike, how'd you like a chance to lay Felix Simpkins by the heels?' Jennings said joyfully.

In response, the sergeant's face lit up. No words were needed.

'You know a Patty Nesbitt?' Jennings swept on.

'Sure I do. Her and Simpkins are birds of a feather,' the sergeant confirmed.

'Right. Well find her and bring her in. If we're lucky, she might just be able to help us bring down Simpkins at last.'

The Sergeant didn't need telling twice.

*

Trudy, feeling as though events were in danger of overtaking her somewhat, left the station – for once with her Inspector's wholehearted blessing – to catch a bus that would take her to the Radcliffe Infirmary on the Woodstock Road, where she was due to meet Dr Ryder and interview Linda Kempson.

She had the feeling that the Inspector, now that he had Simpkins in his sight, was glad to get her out from under his feet. Especially since, with the advent of this Patty Nesbitt character at the scene of the crime, it was looking less likely that Linda Kempson was their prime suspect. Which meant that he didn't mind letting a lowly WPC take a more active role in the proceedings than might otherwise have been the case.

The Radcliffe Infirmary, nestled up against Somerville College on one side, was a handsome building with classic columns and a haughty air, but once she'd stepped through the front door, she was assailed by that ferociously clean scent of bleach and soap that seemed to predominate all such medical facilities.

She enquired at the front desk for Dr Ryder, expecting to be given the usual run-around, but the receptionist had been primed by her friend in advance, and so knew all about her, and she was promptly directed to the right ward without any fuss.

It both amused and impressed Trudy just how much power the former surgeon still wielded in places like this. His medical reputation and social status opened doors to him as if by magic. How he must have missed being a surgeon.

As she approached Laburnum Ward, her footsteps started to flag a little. She felt, stupidly, a little nervous at meeting up with her mentor again. What did she think would happen? That he'd take one look at her face and know that something was wrong? Guess that she now suspected something was seriously amiss with him?

The man wasn't all knowing, she reminded herself crossly, no matter that he might seem to be at times!

Taking a deep breath, she turned the corner and saw Clement standing at the nurses' station, chatting amiably to a matron, a sturdily built, middle-aged woman with an impeccably starched apron and cap, and a calm, pleasant face. As he sensed someone approaching, he turned and looked at her, as did the matron, who noted Trudy's uniform with a look of approval. The latter surprised her a bit. Most people she met found her uniform troubling – and the combination of seeing it on a young woman doubly so.

But of course, the matron was a woman of power and authority herself, Trudy mused, which probably explained it.

'Ah, here's WPC Loveday now,' she heard Clement say. 'Trudy, right on time, as always.'

Trudy smiled briefly and nodded at the matron.

'Is Miss Kempson up to seeing visitors?' she asked, glancing between the two of them, so as to diplomatically make the question incorporate both.

'Yes, but only ten minutes,' the matron said firmly.

'Of course,' Clement agreed at once.

And from the look that passed between them, Trudy was sure that these two medical professionals understood one another perfectly.

Chapter 31

The ward held four beds, two of which were empty. In one occupied bed, a woman lay profoundly asleep.

'Post-op,' Clement said, glancing at her briefly with an experienced eye. 'Good. She'll be unconscious for quite some time. That'll give us more privacy with our patient.'

At this, they both looked at the curtained screens surrounding the far corner bed. Made of pale blue material, they circled the bed completely. Walking to it, Clement paused just shy of it and cleared his throat.

'Miss Kempson? This is Dr Ryder. I'm with WPC Loveday. Matron told you we were dropping by?'

A weary murmur, that Clement took to be an invitation, issued from behind the screen, and so he pulled aside one curtain and stepped inside.

Linda looked distressingly pale and haggard, and Trudy's heart fell a little as she took a seat and got out her notebook and a pen. She felt, for some reason, suddenly nervous, and it took her a moment to realise why.

She didn't want this poor girl to be the one responsible for Ray Reason's death, but if she was, the thought of playing a part in sending her to prison wasn't sitting well with her. Which, Trudy told herself sternly, she needed to hit on the head right away. She couldn't show bias. It wasn't professional.

'I've spoken to your doctors, Miss Kempson,' Clement began, drawing up a chair and sitting down beside Trudy. 'I was a surgeon for many years, and we're all agreed that you're out of danger now. But don't overexert yourself. I want you to tell us if you start to feel dizzy or breathless in any way, all right?'

He stopped there, waiting for Trudy to take over. They'd both agreed that Linda was more likely to feel comfortable talking to a girl of her own age, rather than an older, male authority figure.

He unobtrusively accepted Trudy's notebook and pen, which she handed over. Although he didn't have her shorthand, he was fairly confident that he could get down the salient facts. Later, Trudy could do her own notes from memory, using his efforts as a guide.

As Linda nodded in agreement to warn them if she felt too unwell to continue, Trudy edged a little closer. 'We just need to talk to you some more about what happened that night. To Ray,' she began gently. She was watching the other girl's face closely, and saw only weariness and resignation there, but no fear.

Not yet, anyway.

Which could mean that she had nothing to be afraid of. Or it could mean that recent events had drained her to the extent that she simply didn't have the energy left for any strong emotion at all.

'We know you lost your baby,' Trudy began as gently as she could. 'I'm so sorry – that must have been awful.' Clement had already told her that the doctors here had figured out that she'd taken some sort of home-made herbal concoction that had almost killed her as well as her foetus, but she wasn't about to go into that now. It was possible Linda might face another charge concerning these actions, but she hoped it wouldn't come to that. However, that was a matter for the prosecutors, and colleagues who held rank far above her own. 'It was Ray's, wasn't it?' she said instead.

Linda sighed and nodded, but didn't speak. Trudy didn't mind – she didn't get the feeling that the girl was trying to be clever or avoid being questioned. Rather that she was just too weary to speak much.

Which was fine with her. She could start off with things that needed very little effort on the part of her witness.

'Let me guess,' she continued gently. 'You told him about the baby, once you were sure?'

Again the girl nodded, her eyes fixed on the ceiling.

'But instead of being happy about it, he wasn't, was he?' Trudy tried next.

The girl shook her head. Her hair looked lank and in need of washing and her hands curled around the top of the bedcovers spasmodically. But it was the air of hopelessness about her that brought a lump to Trudy's throat.

She cleared her throat and hoped her voice would remain steady. 'You're doing well, Linda,' Trudy said encouragingly. 'I imagine you wanted to get married right away, yes?'

Linda nodded.

'But he didn't want to?'

Linda shook her head.

'That must have scared you.'

Linda frowned, sighed then nodded.

'That night, at the club. Did you argue about it?' Trudy asked, her voice now almost a whisper. Her mouth was getting dry now that they were coming to the serious stuff, but she didn't dare stop to get a drink of water from the jug sitting on Linda's bedside table.

Linda nodded.

'But you couldn't have done that on the dance floor,' Trudy mused out loud. 'I've been there on a Saturday night, and it's way too noisy to have a conversation – especially about something as private and … well … as delicate as the topic you must have needed to discuss. So did you go down to the common room?'

'No.' Linda spoke finally. 'It's always full of people too.'

'Did you speak to him in the corridor at the back of the club?' Trudy guessed.

Linda nodded. 'I saw him leave the bar and followed him.'

Trudy swallowed hard. 'Where exactly did you catch up to him, Linda?'

'Just as he was about to start going down the stairs.'

There had been something almost inevitable about the answer, and Trudy felt Clement stiffen slightly beside her, but he made no sound.

'These are the spiral stairs, yes?' she asked, needing to get things clear for the record.

Linda nodded.

'And you talked?'

Linda nodded.

'About the baby?'

Linda nodded.

'And you asked him to stand by you and marry you?'

Linda sighed. 'He said he'd help me. I thought, at first, that meant we were going to get married. But he meant ... he said he knew someone who could arrange things ... You know, how to get rid of the baby.'

Two tears began to leak from her eyes, but it was as if she wasn't aware of them as they rolled, warm and salty, down her face. She made no move to brush them away with her fingers, and her expression didn't alter at all. Nor did her voice, as she carried on in the same flat tone.

'It's ironic how that affected me, considering ... well, all this.' She lifted her hand far enough from the bedcovers to give a limp, general wave to indicate her surroundings. 'But at the time it made me so angry that that was his solution to it all. I thought he loved me you see,' she said helplessly, shifting her gaze from the ceiling to look at Trudy at last. 'Until that moment, I really thought we were in love. That it was mutual. Do you understand?' she asked urgently, some emotion finally coming into her voice and chasing away the dull, flat inflection that had been there before.

Her searching, pleading gaze made Trudy shift uncomfortably on her seat. But she nodded in empathy. 'Yes, I think I do.'

Linda sighed and returned her gaze to the ceiling. 'But he didn't love me,' she said sadly, 'and that was the moment I realised it. I mean, really *understood* how things actually were. What a mess I was in. How my life was about to collapse around me. At first, I just couldn't believe it – that I'd got it all so wrong. That he'd fooled me so completely – or that I'd fooled myself, I don't really know. But I got angry. I tried to make him see that the baby was a good thing. A positive thing. But seeing the look in his eye I could tell that he was … He was impatient with me. Annoyed. He blamed me for complicating his life and messing it all up. I just felt so … *stupid*. And angry, *really* angry. It was overwhelming. I'd never felt anything like it before. It was so all-consuming. There was nothing left but rage.'

Linda sighed. 'I started to shout at him – to really tell him what I thought of him. He tried to calm me down – he reached out and took hold of the underside of my arms with his hands, tried to pull me close to him. To *sweet-talk* me out of making a scene! Can you believe that?' she asked, shaking her head restlessly on the pillow. 'I could tell that he was only worried that his friends or the members in the other bands playing that night might hear us from downstairs and mock him. He kept glancing down there uneasily. It was the final straw. That he could be worried about something so … so … petty! When I was going through …'

Linda paused, and then shook her head helplessly. 'I yelled at him to get off me and pushed him away … and the next thing I knew he staggered and fell. He must have been off-balance or something, because I don't think I could have pushed him that hard. He is … was … a big, strong lad. Or maybe I'm just fooling myself again. I don't know anymore.'

Her voice, which had never been strong, trailed off weakly.

Clement cast a quick glance at his watch. He knew the matron would be back dead on time, and he cast Trudy a warning look.

Understanding it, Trudy pressed on. 'What did you do then?'

'Nothing. I don't know,' Linda said and gave a small, utterly sad smile. 'I think I just stood there for a while, waiting for him to get back up and start arguing with me again. Or maybe just get up and continue going down the stairs, cursing under his breath the way that he did sometimes, but going back to meet up with his precious band and friends and just leave me standing there on my own …'

Her voice trailed off, and a small frown appeared between her brows. She continued to stare at the ceiling.

'But he didn't move?' Trudy had to press her.

'No.'

'When he fell down the stairs, he never moved again?' Trudy reiterated urgently. 'Linda, I need you to think now. This is important. *Very important.* Once you'd pushed him and he fell, did Ray move? Perhaps try to get up, maybe hit his head on the stair above him?'

Linda frowned in puzzlement. She could sense something portentous in Trudy's voice, but she was too tired to try and work out what it was. Instead, she just shook her head weakly. 'No, I'm sure he didn't move. I was watching him, you see, waiting for him to … say something. Tell me off, yell at me, or … I don't know, maybe even get up and try and sweet-talk me into letting him get his way again. But he just lay there.'

'Did you go down the stairs to check on him?' Trudy asked quickly.

'No. There was no room. He was blocking the stairs.' She sounded puzzled by the question rather than wary, and for the first time, Trudy felt her heart lift a little as hope began to trickle back for the future of this girl.

'You didn't try and climb over him – to see how bad his injuries were?' she persisted.

'No. I didn't want to touch him,' Linda said, and two more tears leaked silently from her eyes.

'So what *did* you do?' Trudy asked.

'Do?' Linda looked at her, again with that puzzled little frown on her face. 'What should I have done? I just turned and walked away from him. We were done, weren't we? There was nothing more to do or say. I was on my own. I knew that then.'

Trudy was sure now that the girl had gone into shock. Probably stunned by the unexpected nature of what had just happened, her instincts would have been to creep away, like a wounded animal, and lick her wounds.

'You went back to the bar?' she asked quietly.

Linda paused. 'Yes. I remember seeing the lights, which were pretty, and the loud noise of the music and singing voices ... I wanted to hide in it, to drown in it, to let it engulf me. To block everything else out so that I could pretend, for a while, that I didn't really exist. Yes, I went back to the bar, and I waited until it was time for the Rainbirds' set,' she confirmed.

Trudy nodded. Just as she was about to open her mouth to ask the next question, the curtains parted and the matron looked in.

'Time's up,' the nurse said firmly.

Trudy risked her wrath by asking one more thing. 'All right, Linda, we're going to leave you to rest now. But there's just one last thing – and it's vital you tell me the truth now.' She said this as much for the older woman's benefit as the young girl's.

Matron's lips firmed, but luckily she didn't object.

'When you left him, did you see anyone else in the corridor?'

'No. I don't think so. I wasn't looking ... I can't really remember ...' Linda said with genuine confusion, and at this the matron took control.

Neatly, politely but firmly, they were ejected from her patient's bedside.

Clement thanked her courteously, and they left.

Once outside and able to speak without being overheard by anyone, Trudy said, 'So what do you think?'

'I think she pushed him and he fell,' Clement said flatly. 'And since by her own admission, he didn't move, I think he must have been rendered unconscious by the first blow.'

'But if she was telling the truth – and I think she was – then that must mean that she had nothing to do with the second head wound,' Trudy said hopefully.

'Perhaps. But, Trudy, she was in shock,' Clement felt he had to point out. He could tell that his friend was hoping that Linda Kempson was innocent, and he needed her to keep an open mind – for her sake, as much as anything. 'She said she didn't remember much after it all happened – only bits and pieces of it – and even then, what she did remember would have been hazy.'

'And you think it's possible she might have clambered over him and somehow delivered the second blow and either didn't remember it, or had blocked it out or something?' Trudy asked reluctantly.

Clement sighed. 'It's *possible*, yes.'

'But we've still got this second woman to contend with – the one Delia saw with the body,' Trudy insisted. 'That's something that needs to be cleared up, isn't it?'

Clement nodded. He didn't want Linda to be the killer either, but he was old enough to know that you couldn't always get what you wanted.

'If we're going to satisfy your Inspector that Linda was responsible only for Ray Reason's first injury, then we're going to need to find that other suspect. And prove that she also had a motive for wanting him dead.'

Trudy nodded. 'I just hope this woman, Patty Nesbitt, had one,' she said flatly.

Chapter 32

Felix Simpkins learned that the police were looking for Patty Nesbitt barely an hour after their search for her had started. People in his line of work had a network of spies who were only too happy to keep him informed about such things – for a price.

After the warning telephone calls started coming in, he got on the phone to his bouncer.

A sleepy voice answered after more than half a dozen rings. 'Dave?' Felix said. 'Get your arse out of bed. I need you to do a job for me.'

'Sure, Boss,' Dave said, yawning hugely. He lived in a basement flat not far from the Littlemore mental hospital (which had always made him feel both amused and alarmed in equal measure) and he'd had a phone installed as a little luxury. Now he sat up and rubbed a hand over his head. He liked to sleep late whenever he could. He yawned hugely. 'Whad'ya want, Boss?'

'I need you to find Patty Nesbitt and work her over,' Felix snarled.

In his bed, Dave froze. Then sighed. 'What for?' he asked, careful to keep his voice only vaguely curious.

'The cops are looking for her. I need her to be reminded to keep her mouth shut.'

Dave's eyes narrowed thoughtfully. 'Sure, Boss,' he said soothingly. 'I know a couple of places that she hangs out. I'll get on it right away.'

He hung up and dressed hurriedly.

*

Titus Crowley-Beauley cast a final glance over the contracts he'd had his legal team make up and courier over to him. It was in many ways standard, with most of the usual conditions in place, including his 'modest' cut. The devil, however, was in the detail – and in the case of the Rainbirds, was centred mostly around who owned the rights to any songs they recorded, and certain commercial clauses that looked innocuous enough on first inspection, but in reality weren't.

On top of that he also had an understanding with the owner of the record company that he used for all his singers, which involved the exchange of income that was not written down anywhere. So the taxman didn't need to know about it. And neither did his clients. Needless to say, it made both him and his record-company-owning friend a great deal of money.

Titus was not the sort to feel guilt, but even if he were, he could argue that the Rainbirds would be more than content with the leftovers, because, to them, it would be more money than they could earn in a lifetime's work at a factory. Peanuts, of course, to what he thought their potential earnings would be, but still enough to set them up for life (well, a modestly lived life) if they didn't blow it all on sports cars and lavish parties for all the inevitable hangers-on that they would attract.

It often amused him just how much money his clients from poorer backgrounds could get through. His middle- and upper-class performers, on the whole, were usually much more canny with their earnings, probably because they'd had it drubbed into them by their parents the value of comfortable, financially secure living. The poor, however, never having had any expectations of money, didn't realise, when given a large amount of it, that it needed looking after, and was finite. To them, money seemed to be for spending, for revelling in, and he'd seen it affect them in almost the same way as too much alcohol. A sort of devil-may-care euphoria swept through them.

He'd lost count of these working-class 'stars' who rose spectacularly, spent, lived big, then suddenly become yesterday's news, and had to go back to working on the docks or whatever, because they'd blown it all on holidays, wine, women and song. Good whilst it lasted, no doubt, but short-sighted.

He tried to tell them to buy real estate, or invest in safe bonds, sort out a pension or what have you, but very few of them did.

One young lad of his in particular stood out in his memory – a crooner in the Sinatra style, he'd been big for a while back in the late Fifties, but once the new pop phenomenon had taken over, Titus couldn't have got him a job singing at a cinema queue. Nobody's fault – it was just the way 'show biz' went. One moment you were solid gold, the next, not even nickel-plated alloy.

The silly sod had spent it all, naturally, so when the gravy train pulled out of the station, and his so-called friends had left to find another fool to suck dry, he'd jumped off a pier in the northern town where he'd grown up.

His death had made a big splash (no pun intended) in the local papers for a while, and some fans had cried and left flowers and now … Now probably, nobody would remember what his name had been. Stage name or real name. Well, except for his parents, of course.

Titus shook his head, wondering why he was in such a philosophical mood, and putting his latest potential money-making documents away, wandered vaguely to the window instead.

Oxford was a weird city. He'd chosen to go to the US for his education, managing to get into Yale on a scholarship. Even as a teenager, he'd known that his life was going to be all about making money rather than inheriting the lifestyle of a poverty-stricken 'gentleman' like his old man. And you had to hand it to the Americans, when it came to the acquiring of filthy lucre, they knew how to teach you all about that!

So the more genteel environs of Oxbridge had passed him by, and from what he'd seen of Oxford so far, he had no problem with that at all. It was so small, for one thing. Now used to the vast sprawling metropolis of London, the size of this place stultified him. And what was it with all the bell towers and the bloody clocks chiming all the time?

He shrugged, turned his back on the fabled dreaming spires and raided his friend's liquor cabinet instead.

He couldn't wait to get back to London. Tomorrow morning his latest acquisitions would all troop in here, with that usual mixture of excitement and fear that he'd seen so often, and Marty Cuthbertson would sign on the dotted line along with the others. And then it would just be a question of waiting to see if his judgement was still sound.

He had no real worries that it was though. Even when he'd first started out in the business, he'd signed very few duds. The Rainbirds were going to be big. He could just feel it.

He sat on the sofa and sighed. There was still only one potential fly in the ointment as far as his latest pop group went. And he'd seen her, lurking about at the back of the garage last night, wisely saying nothing but watching everything, as he'd successfully inserted Ewan into the group.

Titus Crowther-Beauley now considered Jennifer Renfrew with displeasure. It was clear she was not going to give up Marty easily. Why should she? The singer was by far her best shot at vicarious fame, not to mention her *only* shot at getting out of this backwater and living high on the hog. Parties in London, holidays in France, furs, jewels – as the wife of a famous pop singer (whilst it lasted) she would have a life that her parents couldn't even imagine.

And he'd seen the hot and hungry look in her eyes that

reminded him of a tigress on the hunt. Yes, she had all the hallmarks of becoming a right pain in his arse, all right. But he wasn't unduly worried. Life never would be all plain sailing and it would be bloody boring if it was. Besides, he had ways of dealing with the likes of little Jenny Wren!

Chapter 33

The next morning, as Titus made himself breakfast and waited for his latest prey to walk into his parlour, Patty Nesbitt approached the police station with the utmost reluctance. Her footsteps dragged and she kept looking nervously over her shoulder, wishing she was anywhere else instead – and *doing* anything else instead.

When Davey had called on her at her hidey-hole yesterday and told her that both the cops and Felix Simpkins were after her, she'd almost thrown up on his shoes.

Her first instinct had been to pack her bags and head for the hills – Scotland, maybe. Glasgow would be big enough to hide her, for sure. And she'd assumed that Davey was there to help her get away.

But Davey, it turned out, had been thinking and had other ideas.

At first, she'd barely listened to him. After all, what did the likes of Davey know about anything? Amiable, not too bright, he was hardly the sort she'd turn to for advice when it came to saving her neck.

But he'd surprised her. And the more he talked, the more she began to realise that he was not totally without guile after all. For a start, he clearly had the habit of keeping his eyes and ears open. Because, it soon turned out, that all the times the big bosses had met with Simpkins to discuss club business, he'd done more than just stand at the door looking stupid. He'd actually listened. And thus knew far more than she'd ever given him credit for.

She could still remember the pleased, self-satisfied and goofy grin he'd given her when he'd told her that he'd been placed there by one of the club owners expressly to report back on all of Simpkins's activities. It was probably standard practice for the bigwigs to have spies in the lower ranks, Patty thought, but even so, it was impressive that they'd chosen her Davey for the role.

And that he'd fulfilled that role without her (or better yet Simpkins) knowing about it, gave her pause for thought. There was obviously more to the bouncer than she'd realised. Mind you, she'd told herself, it was not rocket science what he did, and you didn't have to be a genius to figure out that it was better to run with the top dogs than with the runt of the litter. Even so, he had impressed her just enough for her to calm down and listen to what he had to say.

And what he'd said had made sense.

Simpkins was the one in deep shit, he'd made her see, not her. It was Simpkins who'd come up with the plan to deal with Ray Reason's blackmailing ways. It was Simpkins who'd asked her to do him the favour that might have put them all in deep trouble with the cops, if she hadn't thought fast and acted, thus saving everyone's bacon that night. And he'd make sure the big bosses knew it.

Which meant that it was now Simpkins who had the most to lose.

So, instead of running and hiding, Davey told her, she needed to turn the tables on him by feeding him to the cops.

Which *ordinarily* wouldn't have been a good move, except this time, Davey – being the faithful spy – would make it clear to the bigwigs how badly Simpkins had handled things the night Ray died. And that it was she, Patty, who was saving the day yet again by cleaning the house for them and getting rid of the incompetent Simpkins.

It was not as if any of the club owners cared who actually ran the Bootleggers – so long as the profits kept pouring in. And none of them owed Simpkins a thing. In fact, Davey assured her, nobody even liked him much. And they wouldn't be happy to learn Ray had only been able to put pressure on him at all because he'd been running some scam or other, and raking off *their* profits.

No, he'd insisted, the only way to get out of her predicament was for her to tell the cops exactly what she'd done the night Ray Reason had died. And why.

At this, she'd automatically balked. Glasgow, she'd told him, was better. The mere thought of talking to the cops sounded utterly crazy to her. In her experience, that was guaranteed to earn you a beating, or worse. It was rule number one – nobody snitched to the cops, about anything.

But Davey had been persistent. With Simpkins arrested, he could no longer pose a threat to her. He might howl for his 'protectors' to punish her, but none of them would bother. Why would they? When she'd been the one to keep them out of something that could have got very messy indeed.

And although it all made sense, and in the end she'd agreed to it, and was even now walking through the door of the police station, she couldn't help but feel as if she was walking into the lion's den.

What if the cops charged her with something? she'd asked Davey, in a last-ditch effort to change his mind.

But Davey had only laughed. What were they going to charge her with exactly? Anyway, they would be sure to overlook any little misdemeanours on her part, if it meant they got to put away Simpkins for a while.

And this, she had to admit, was probably true. The cops had had it in for Simpkins for a while now – everyone knew that.

So, even though her knees were shaking, every nerve was

stretched to breaking point and all her instincts were screaming at her that she should turn around and run, Patty Nesbitt approached the desk sergeant, cleared her throat and croaked, 'I'm Patty Nesbitt. I hear you've been looking for me? I want to talk to whoever's in charge of dealing with that bloke what died at the Bootleggers. Ray Reason. Yeah? I've got some important information they need to know.'

And she crossed her fingers and hoped that Davey was right about all this.

Chapter 34

As Patty Nesbitt was shown into an interview room, Jenny Wren was getting off a bus and heading towards Titus's temporary lodgings. She wasn't sure where the building was exactly, as she didn't often have cause to come to this posh, residential part of town, but she wasn't about to let that put her off.

If she had to traipse around and ask a postman, she was going to find him. She knew the lads were due to go and see him in just over two hours to sign the contracts, and she was determined to see them first.

Not that she thought she would be able to tell a good deal from a bad – she was realistic enough to know that. But she knew someone who would. She'd been putting out feelers to find a solicitor who specialised in that sort of thing, and she was willing to spend her own hard-earned money paying him to go over the contracts with a microscope.

And if Titus kicked up a fuss and refused to give her the contracts … Well then, when the Rainbirds showed up, she'd tell them what was happening. And ask them just why, if everything was so on the up-and-up and Titus could be trusted to do right by them, was the big man so reluctant to have an independent legal man giving the paperwork the once-over?

Although they might be mad at her at first for interfering, fearing that she might have queered the pitch for them, she knew that human nature would quickly take over. Suspicion was something that always lurked near the surface, because deep down, everyone knew that you couldn't really trust anyone or anything. And nobody liked to be taken for a ride. Nobody liked to be made a fool of, or cheated out of their dues. And once the boys were riled (and Jenny was good at stirring up trouble), the big man would find himself with a revolt on his hands.

A grim, determined smile lit her face as she stalked on, shoulders back and chin up.

*

Trudy, her DI and Sergeant O'Grady could hardly believe their luck when they were informed that Patty Nesbitt had walked into their arms, asking to speak to someone about Ray Reason's death.

It was decided that Trudy and the Sergeant would interview her. They thought the presence of someone as high up the chain as Inspector Jennings might give her second thoughts and make her realise just how serious things were. Every other time she'd had a brush with the law, it had been minor enough to be handled mostly by sergeants, and they wanted her to feel as comfortable as possible. For that reason, Trudy had managed to persuade her Inspector that a female presence might also be a bonus, and help her feel less intimidated.

So it was that when the door to the interview room opened and Patty Nesbitt looked up, she saw the stripes of a sergeant, and a pretty WPC who looked at her with friendly eyes.

Patty hadn't ever met a female plod before, but when this one offered her a smile, after a moment's surprise and hesitation, she gave a tentative one back.

Sergeant O'Grady, obviously, led the interview. Of Irish descent, he was in his mid-forties and had a slightly chubby appearance.

Pale blue eyes peered out from under a large quiff of sandy hair. He never tanned, even in summer, and he could be either terrifying or become your favourite uncle, seemingly at the flick of an internal switch.

Right now, he was in avuncular mode. 'Hello, Patty. Last time I saw you, you were up before the beak. Still being a naughty girl then?'

Patty smiled wanly. 'Not my fault, Sergeant, I swear. I've been trying to go straight, so help me.'

O'Grady grinned. 'Sure you have, sure you have. Thanks for coming in. Saved us another day of looking for you. What's been going on then?'

Patty took a deep breath, and prayed Davey had got it right.

'It's about that lad that died at the club. That's what you wanted to see me about, yeah?'

'This is the Bootleggers Club and Ray Reason we're talking about?' O'Grady said, giving nothing away, as Trudy busily got down every word in her notebook.

'Yeah, him. See, I do a bit of bus … I like to dance at the club,' she began, getting off to a nervous start, and shooting a slightly panicked look at the older man.

But O'Grady merely nodded reassuringly. 'It's all right, I know what kind of business you've been doing lately, Patty, but we're not here about that. Relax a bit, yeah?'

Patty took another deep breath, but she was beginning to sweat already. It was all right for Davey to be so sure that the cops would play ball with her, but it wasn't him who was facing doing time if they didn't, was it?

'Look, if I tell you all I know, you've gotta promise nothin' will come back on me, yeah?' she said anxiously, looking at O'Grady intensely, trying to read his eyes.

'Depends what you've got to say,' the Sergeant said cautiously.

'It's about Felix, and what he done that night,' she said, mindful of Davey's coaching. Mention Simpkins early on, he'd told her.

Dangle him as bait. If the cops thought they'd get a big fish, they'd be happier about letting a little minnow like her slip through the net.

She saw the Sergeant's eyes flicker, and for the first time she began to feel hope that Davey had been right – about everything.

Quickly, she pressed her advantage. 'I had nothing to do with that boy dying, Sergeant, but I knows stuff about what went on that night. Well, some of the stuff that went on,' she qualified hastily. 'I mean, I never saw the lad die or nothing,' she added truthfully.

'All right. Why don't you tell your story, starting at the beginning, and I'll do my best by you. How's that?' O'Grady said.

Patty bit her lip. It wasn't as much as she'd hoped for, but Davey had warned her not to expect too much too soon. Once they'd heard her story – and she'd promised to testify in court – that's when she could hold out for more iron-clad promises. Promises written down all fair and square and made by solicitors and stuff, not just the cops saying it'd be all right.

She sat up straight and nodded. 'All right, I'll trust you,' she said – this time, not altogether truthfully. But what choice did she have now?

'See, it were like this. That night, the Saturday when that lad died, I was at the club, having a drink at the bar, looking for company. You'd be surprised how many men in their twenties and thirties were there, trying to look trendy, you know? Anyway, I'm sitting there, sipping on my G&T, minding my own business, when Felix grabs me by the arm and hauls me off my stool, saying he wants a word.'

Patty paused and reached for the jug of water sitting on the table. She poured some into one of the glasses the duty sergeant had set up there. She took a nervous swallow.

'And you know how it is, when the boss wants something from you, well, you gotta go along, right? At first, I thought he just wanted a …' At this her eyes moved to the pretty WPC, who looked so young and innocent that her eyes moved hastily away

223

again. 'Er, I thought he just wanted the usual, you know. A bit of how's-your-father, like.'

Trudy's lips twitched, but she said nothing.

The Sergeant merely nodded. 'But that wasn't it?'

'No, it weren't. Wish it were! No, when he got me in the office he hands me this little slip of paper, see. All neatly folded into a tight square and tucked in like, so nothing could slip out.'

At this, Sergeant O'Grady's eyes began to sparkle. 'Dope?' he asked harshly.

But Patty was way too fly to fall for that. 'I dunno, Sarge. I didn't look, did I?'

'Come on, Patty, you're no shrinking violet. You must have seen plenty of the stuff at your "special" parties.' He could name off the top of his head quite a few 'respectable' citizens who liked to hold parties featuring girls and dope with like-minded friends.

'Yeah, well, I was surprised,' Patty said, in something of an understatement. 'I don't have nothing to do with that end of the business. I just give Simpkins a cut of anything I make picking up fellas at his club.'

O'Grady was inclined to believe her. The big bosses who owned the Bootleggers wouldn't be likely to trust prossies with dope. The two rackets were usually run on very separate lines.

'So what happened?' he asked, well and truly intrigued now.

'I asked Felix what the hell he was giving me some stuff for,' Patty said, sounding a little indignant now. 'I told him, I didn't use the stuff. It's a mug's game, that. I seen it happen. You get hooked on it, and then you're paying over every penny you got to a dealer to get your next fix. Sod that.'

'Very wise of you,' O'Grady said, but not without some sarcasm. 'So, you came here just to tell me just how virtuous you are, Patty?' he teased.

Patty Nesbitt gave out a surprised bark of humour – she couldn't help it – but then sighed. 'Nah. OK, I got the hint. You want me to get on with it,' she muttered nervously, and took a deep, fortifying breath. 'Yeah, anyway, so when I told him I didn't want it, Felix told me not to be such a silly tart and that he wasn't hooking me up. He said he wanted me to do him a favour with it, instead. Well, I can tell you, I didn't like the sound of that,' Patty said, again truthfully. 'But what could I do? You don't get on the wrong side of Felix, do you?'

O'Grady nodded in understanding and just a touch of genuine sympathy. She was right. People like her had no protection against predators like Simpkins. 'So what did he want?'

'Well, here's where it gets strange,' Patty said, frowning, shuffling a little on her seat. 'He knew I used to do a bit of pickpocketing see, when I was a nipper and fast on my feet like, and he said he wanted me to slip this little bit of paper into Ray Reason's jacket pocket whenever I got the chance.'

At this, Trudy's head came up in surprise, and she stared at Patty. At the same time, her Sergeant's jaw slackened just slightly.

Mollified at their surprise, Patty nodded. 'I know, right? You could've knocked me down with a feather too. I was so surprised that I asked him why he wanted me to do it, but it turned out, he had his reasons.'

Here's where she had to depart from the truth a bit, but Patty was sure she could put it across all right. She'd always been a good liar. 'Turns out, this Ray chap had overheard Felix doing a bit of private business on the side, something that his bosses didn't know about, and would have wanted their cut of, if they had. So, naturally, turns out this singer bloke had been blackmailing him into giving his band the best slots and what have you, and getting a bigger cut than all the other bands did. And Felix was getting fed up with having to toe Reason's line, and wanted Ray out of the picture, once and for all.'

Of course, Felix had told her no such thing. When she'd asked why he wanted her to plant the drugs he'd just sworn at her and told her to mind her own business, do as she was told and keep her mouth shut. Or else.

It was only last night that Davey had laid it all out for her.

'Anyway, I had to agree to do it, didn't I?' Patty said, sticking to the script her boyfriend had set out. 'He's got a nasty temper, has Felix, and I didn't want my chops getting smacked about. Can't pull in the punters with a messed-up face, can you? So I said, all right, all right, I'd do it. And then I scarpered, quick as I could, outta his office.'

She paused, then took another drink of water.

'Any idea what it was this singer had on Simpkins?' O'Grady asked greedily, but wasn't surprised when her face fell.

'No, sorry, Sarge. I'd tell you if I did. Honest. But Dav … this friend of mine, reckons Felix was always skimming here and hustling there. Filling his own pockets whenever he could, and not letting on to the people that actually own the club what he was up to. So …' She shrugged. 'I suppose Felix was scared this bloke would eventually drop him in it, and wanted to fix him once and for all.'

'But why the dope?' O'Grady said. 'Did he want to get Ray hooked or what?'

Patty shook her head. 'Nah, I don't think that was it. I mean, Felix couldn't be certain Ray would use the dope once he found it, could he? S'far as we knew, he was squeaky clean. What we reckoned was, Felix was gonna wait until after the club closed, then drop an anonymous call in to you lot, saying he'd seen Ray buying something off someone in the back of some pub or other. You'd then pick him up, find the dope on him and charge him. End of Felix's problems. He'd have a reason to ban the band from his club, and if Ray figured out who'd set him up and started telling tales on Felix … well, who'd believe a dopehead?'

O'Grady hadn't missed Patty's use of the word 'we' and he wondered who this Dav (probably short for David) was that seemed to know so much about things. He knew instinctively she'd never give him up if he asked – especially if he was the boyfriend – but it didn't worry him much. He didn't think it would take him long to find out, simply by asking around.

But right now, he had other matters on his mind. 'It sounds like you might be onto something there,' he agreed. It was the sort of twisted scheme that the likes of Felix might just have come up with. Whilst it might have been easier for Felix to have Ray shanked and his body dropped into the river, why should Simpkins take the risk of potentially facing a murder charge if he could get the cops to eliminate his enemy for him?

'But you never got to plant the dope on him, right?' O'Grady said, glancing across at Trudy. He knew that nothing compromising had been found on the dead man's body, or it would have attracted their attention at once. The presence of drugs on the scene would have been a total red flag, and Ray Reason's death would have been more thoroughly – *officially* – investigated, right from the start.

'Ah, well, see … that's why I'm here,' Patty said uncomfortably, and again reached for the water glass. Her mouth was getting really dry now.

O'Grady could see she was beginning to sweat in earnest, and raised a sandy-coloured eyebrow. 'Oh?'

He knew, of course, what was probably coming next, having read Delia's statement, but he wasn't about to let on to Patty about that.

'See, the thing is, I *did* get the opportunity to slip it into his pocket,' Patty admitted. 'I really wanted to do it last thing, after he'd done his singing and all that. There would have been less time for him to accidentally find the dope, see? Mind you, it was so flat and small and easy to get lost in that leather jacket pocket of his,' Patty said, then seeing the Sergeant's impatience, quickly went on. 'But I couldn't be sure I'd manage to get it on him if I left it to the last minute, and besides I got the perfect opportunity to do it when he was saying goodbye to his bird at the bar. I just pressed up behind him to pay for a drink and popped it in.'

'So why didn't we find it on him when his body was discovered?' O'Grady said flatly.

At this, Patty Nesbitt licked her dry lips. 'Well, see … I took it out again later,' she mumbled, eyes downcast.

The Sergeant and Trudy exchanged looks. *Now* they were getting to it!

*

As Patty Nesbitt gambled on her immediate future at the police station, Jennifer Renfrew finally found the large Georgian terrace where Titus was slumming it before going back to the Smoke.

She'd found the street name by simply tramping around in ever-decreasing circles, and now all she had to do was to scan the front doors for numbers. Titus had told Marty that he was in the penthouse, and had laughed when one of the boys had said that even his friends lived on the top of the heap.

Now that she was there, she could see that the heap in question was a lovely pale Cotswold stone, square-fronted edifice, consisting of a basement and three further floors above, which had each been converted into four luxury flats.

Presumably the top floor had once been the attics where the servants had lived, and she felt her lips twist at the irony. Perhaps she'd make some remark about it when she saw him in a few minutes. Maybe something along the lines of how did he like living in the servants' quarters? That might get under the posh sod's skin a bit!

With quick steps, she ran up the smooth stone steps to the main entrance and pushed it open.

Chapter 35

Back at the station, Trudy and her Sergeant were once again looking at Patty keenly.

'What did you do, Patty?' O'Grady said, his voice a soft, warning growl now. 'Plain and simple, let's just have it.'

Patty swallowed and nodded. 'Well, see, it was like this. After he left, I gave it a little while, then went out back to use the ladies' loo. Well, I did my business, and when I stepped back out into the corridor, I thought I heard a weird sound. At first, I thought it might'a been caused by the girl who must have come in and left the loo again when I was in one of the stalls. I could see her walking back towards the dance hall. But it didn't sound like footsteps – it wasn't so tap-tap-tap like, more of a sharp single thump.'

She paused, a small frown appearing on her forehead as she thought back. 'I know you're gonna ask me what kind of sound I mean, but I can't really describe it. It wasn't a hard, clanking sound exactly, like metal on metal. But I got the feeling metal was involved. There was a sort of softened "thunk". It wasn't very hard or loud, but for some reason it brought me all out in goose bumps.'

As she spoke, she absent-mindedly rubbed her hands over her forearms, as if trying to rub away the remembered irritation.

'I dunno whether it was being alone in the dark back there, or what, but I felt a bit shivery. Scared like. Anyway, I was about to head back to the main dance hall, but I was sort of curious, so I went around that little dog-leg bend in the corridor to have a peep, and something caught my eye – something at the head of those spiral stairs. It was the sole of a man's shoe.'

She shook her head. 'At first, I couldn't quite make out what was wrong with what I was seein'. Then I realised that I shouldn't be able to see the *sole* of a shoe – I mean, if someone was going down the stairs they'd be standing on it, wouldn't they? Stands to reason! So I crept forward like and saw it was the bloke I'd not long planted the dope on, lying sprawled down the stairs. Now, let me tell you, right away, the instant I saw him, I knew I was in trouble.'

She had too. Her mind had worked like quicksilver.

'He weren't moving, and I thought at first he'd just knocked himself out. I knew someone would call a doctor and, during all the argy-bargy like, that dope in his pocket was bound to come to light, and Felix would be furious with me. The cops would be called, and everyone would assume he'd got the drugs at the Bootleggers, and then Felix would be well in the shit! The bigwigs don't like it when you lot come sniffing around. And if you started running an investigation into dope at the Bootleggers …'

She didn't need to say more.

'You got it back, right?' O'Grady said flatly, pre-empting her.

Patty looked hard at her hands and shrugged helplessly. 'What else could I do, Mr O'Grady?' she asked pathetically. 'I sort of scrambled over him and slipped my hand into his pocket, which was hard to do, because his body weight was pressing it down. I thought my hand might get stuck if wasn't careful! It took ages to wriggle it out. At some point I thought I heard somebody above me, but I didn't see nothing.'

Delia, Trudy thought. Poor Delia, trying to sneak in and speak to her drummer boy.

'I could tell he was dead, once I was right on top of him and got a better look at him.' Patty swallowed hard. 'It were awful. I'd never been that close to a dead man before. Anyway, I managed to get the dope back, and then I scarpered.'

And that, she hoped, was what was going to save her from the wrath of the nightclub owners for shopping Simpkins. Davey was even now reporting back to the bigwigs, telling them what she'd done to save the club from being shut down and landing them all in the middle of a dope scandal. She only hoped that they would see her testifying against Felix – and Felix alone – as yet another favour that she was doing them. Getting rid of a man who had just landed them in the middle of a murder inquiry!

'No doubt you hurried back and told Felix all about it, and what you'd done?' O'Grady said, not even bothering to tell her that she should have called an ambulance, just in case there had been something that could have been done for the stricken Ray Reason. To Patty, it wouldn't have even crossed her mind. She was all about self-survival.

'Yeah. He swore, and threatened me to keep quiet. I'd just got out of his office, when this barman came rushing by and charged into Felix's office saying that he'd found Ray on the stairs. I thought, when the inquest brought in accidental death, it was all over. But Felix kept ringing me and threatening me about what would happen if I talked, so I knew he was still nervous. And then when I heard you lot was looking for me …' She shrugged. 'I thought I should do the right thing,' she concluded self-righteously.

The Sergeant looked at her knowingly, and she dropped her eyes quickly back down to the table, because they both knew she'd really only come in because she was scared Felix would follow through on his threat.

Then, following Davey's plan, she looked him straight in the eye again. 'Anyway, the thing is, I'm willing to testify to all this in court. That Simpkins gave me the dope to plant on Ray, and that he threatened me to keep quiet about it afterwards. And I'm willing to swear in court that he had this private vendetta with Ray, and that he told me about his plan to get him busted with coke on him. But I ain't saying nothin' about the ones who own the club,' she said flatly. 'And don't think I will, no matter what you threaten me with. They'd kill me,' she said, and everyone in the room knew that she was almost certainly speaking the truth.

Patty leaned across the table and stared the Sergeant straight in the eye. 'So, do we have a deal? I can give you Felix, but nobody else. Take it or leave it.'

O'Grady knew he'd have to run it past his DI, who'd then have to run it past *his* bosses, but he already knew they were going to take Patty's deal. They were too much the pragmatists not to.

Surrounded by solicitors, and with only hearsay evidence against them, there was no chance they'd be able to nab the club owners for anything. But Simpkins was definitely in their grasp at last.

Patty could see from the Sergeant's face that she'd won, and she breathed out a long sigh of relief.

And then Trudy spoke for the first time, surprising both Patty and O'Grady.

Although she'd been happy to have this girl's testimony against Simpkins, Trudy had quickly come to realise, as the interview progressed, that Patty had no motive for killing Ray. In fact, just the opposite. She'd want him to be alive and well away from the club so that her boss could complete the trap he'd set for him.

Which meant that the girl Delia had seen on the stairs was a dead end as far as helping to prove Linda's innocence.

But there had been one ray of potential light in Patty's evidence, and she was determined to follow it.

'You say when you left the ladies' loo, that you saw another girl walking down the corridor in front of you,' she said. She felt her Sergeant look at her in surprise, but he didn't interrupt her. 'Did you recognise her?'

Patty, now that her ordeal was over, shrugged. 'Sure, I think so,' she said casually. 'She was the girlfriend of one of the singers in the band – the Rainbirds, I mean. You know, the one with the silly nickname.'

Trudy felt her spirits sink once more. So Patty had seen Linda – or Lindy-Lou as she was known at the club – walking away just after pushing Ray down the stairs. She must have killed him after all. The strange sound Patty had heard must have been the sound of Linda finishing the job off – dealing him the second blow.

She'd lied to them all along, Trudy thought, feeling sick and foolish.

'For the record,' Trudy said grimly. 'You saw Lindy-Lou – Linda Kempson – Ray Reason's girlfriend walking away from the crime scene just before you found Ray's body?'

The Sergeant gave her an approving look. 'Well spotted,' he said under his breath.

But much as it cheered her to score points with her Sergeant, she was still feeling a little heartsick.

Until Patty Nesbitt spoke again. 'What? The dead bloke's girlfriend? No, not her – not the brunette. The other one – taller, with short blonde hair. Whadda they call her – Jenny Wren. Yeah. Jenny Wren.'

*

Jenny Wren knocked on the door of Titus's borrowed flat, her head back and prepared to do battle. When he opened the door and saw her, his face twisted sourly.

Jenny smiled at him. If he was feeling put out to see her now, just wait until he found out why she was here, she thought sardonically.

'Hello, Titus,' she said, refusing to be respectful and use his surname or call him 'Mr'. 'Aren't you going to let me in and offer me a cup of coffee?'

Chapter 36

Once she left the interview room, Trudy immediately rang the coroner's office and updated Clement on the events so far.

'So now we really need to speak to Jenny Wren again,' she concluded. 'If she hadn't just been to the ladies' loo and missed seeing Patty Nesbitt in there, then she's got some explaining to do. She can't have been coming back from the basement, because Ray was already blocking the stairs by this time. And if she'd been going *down* to the basement, she must have seen him lying there – so why didn't she report it?'

'Yes, I agree, we need to speak to her again.' Clement's voice came clearly into her ear – and with no trace of a slur, she was relieved to note. 'But that might not be as helpful as you think. She must have used the facilities, probably more than once, during the night, and there's no reason why she would have kept an accurate account of the times she did so. Would you? And even if she does know roughly the times she visited the conveniences, since we don't know *exactly* when Ray went down the stairs, the fact that she was in the area at the same time that Patty Nesbitt was needn't mean anything significant.'

'But Patty said she heard a sound,' Trudy said stubbornly.

'Which could have been anything,' Clement countered

234

reasonably. 'It was a busy, working nightclub. Perhaps someone was moving a barrel of beer about.'

Trudy sighed, and some of her adrenaline began to seep away. She'd been so sure she'd been onto something important. 'I still want to talk to her as a priority,' she said firmly, and heard the smile in Clement's voice as he responded.

'I'm not saying we don't need to interview her again. But speaking of interviews, I've been busy this morning also. I had my secretary call Titus Crowther-Beauley's office to arrange a time for us to speak to him, since he's the only one we haven't yet tackled, and we're in luck. He's not in London right now, but right here in Oxford. He's staying at a friend's flat – the friend is currently in Hollywood, she went out of her way to tell me. He's a rising star there, and is currently doing a film with Kirk Douglas apparently.'

Trudy couldn't help but laugh. 'And were you impressed by this news?' she teased, knowing full well the coroner couldn't have cared less.

'Oh, I was giddy with excitement,' Clement responded drolly. 'Do you have a pen? I'll give you the address and we can meet there. Or I can pick you up. Are you free right now?'

Trudy glanced across towards her Inspector's shut door. Sergeant O'Grady had gone in there to report on their triumph over Simpkins, and she was confident (well, *fairly* confident) that the two men would be wrapped up for a good hour or so if not more. Getting a warrant for Simpkins's arrest would need to be negotiated, not to mention arranging immunity for Patty Nesbitt in return for her testimony with the prosecution service, which would *definitely* take some time.

And since their priorities, right now, weren't fixed on the Ray Reason case, she was sure she could justify herself – if the need arose – in continuing to pursue that line of inquiry without first asking permission.

'Yes, come and pick me up. I'm sure the Inspector will be glad to get rid of me whilst he's so busy,' she said, crossing her fingers that she wasn't just indulging in wishful thinking. 'Let's go and see what the star-maker has to say for himself.'

*

The tenant in the flat below the top floor was trying to work. He was a music don at Wadham College and was trying to write a score for a new choral piece to be sung the following Easter in chapel, and he was beginning to get irritated by the gradually rising voices above him.

The tenant who lived up there was some actor chappie who was often away, and had thus left him with a spare key to his place in case of emergencies (water leaks and such like) so Dr Hubert Isherwood was used to having peace and quiet in which to work. Although his neighbour had informed him that he sometimes let friends and acquaintances use the flat when he was away, so far the musician had had no cause for complaint.

Now he winced as a voice – a definitely feminine voice – shouted something with growing fury, and a deeper, rumbling bass voice of a man shot something back in return.

Typical! A noisy lovers' tiff just when he was working on his descant for the sopranos!

*

Above him, oblivious to everything but their own battle of wills, Titus and Jenny were facing off over a small coffee table. Both were on their feet, both were leaning slightly towards their opponent. Both had their fists clenched in growing rage, and both were a little red in the face.

Titus was breathing heavily, as angry as he'd ever been in his life. Jenny, in contrast, held herself still, but her fury easily matched his.

It had started off coolly enough, with Titus asking her what he could do for her, and Jenny telling him she'd come to take the contracts for perusal by a specialist solicitor.

That, she had seen with satisfaction, had rocked him a little, but he'd quickly rallied, asking if Martin was aware of this.

That, in turn, had forced her to admit that he wasn't, leaving her on the back foot.

There had then followed an increasingly acrimonious to-and-fro volley of accusation and counter-accusation.

Neither was backing down.

'If you think I'm going to allow you to scupper my plans for the band, you're out of your mind,' Titus now snarled at her. 'And if you think you've got a strong enough hold over that poor sap Martin, then you're seriously deluded as well! Let me tell you something about the facts of life, girlie: men say whatever it is a girl wants to hear in order to keep her sweet, but when it comes down to the bottom line, they'll always look out for number one. And that lad wants fame so much he can taste it!'

'And he's going to have it,' Jenny snarled back, her voice as cold and hard and flat as the look in her eyes. 'He can sing, and play, and write songs, and *with or without* you, he's going to be a star.'

'Not on your life,' Titus spat back. 'Who do you think you are?' he howled, genuinely outraged by her gall. 'You're just a know-nothing little chit who thinks she only has to *want* something for it to happen. Do you really think success and all that entails will just drop in your lap, like manna from heaven?'

'No I don't then,' Jenny shouted at him, equally outraged by his arrogance. 'I expect we'll have to work hard for it, and have a bit of luck, but in the end it *will* happen, and do you know why?' she demanded, chin out-thrust in defiance. 'Because the times are changing. That's why! It's no longer the likes of *you*, with your lah-di-dah background and old-school-tie chums, who are running everything now. It's working-class lads from Liverpool and others like them who are running the show. It's people of *our* generation who are taking what's ours and we don't give a damn about the likes of you middle-aged, middle-class *has-beens*.'

In her diatribe, she'd leaned so far over the coffee table that she was all but in his face. In her eyes was a look of such total contempt and triumph, that Titus finally lost control.

Middle-aged? Middle class? He was neither, damn her impudence. And as for her ridiculous assertion that the balance of power was changing in the world, it was so pathetic it didn't even bear thinking about. If, deep down, he was not quite so sure about this as he liked to pretend, he was certainly not about to give in to those niggling little doubts now.

And what if society was going through something of an upheaval? As if the likes of this silly little working-class bit of stuff could ever aspire to being anything more than some shop-girl or cleaner, let alone have the intelligence or drive to make a success of any business venture – even something as fleeting and unimportant as a pop band!

How dare the silly cow challenge him! Demanding to see the contracts, threatening to take them to an independent party, which would indeed threaten his profits! He'd teach her what it meant to get ideas that she was something special.

Before he knew what he was even thinking of doing, he'd swung his hand, and with the flat of his palm, hit her mocking, annoying face.

He'd always had a violent temper when roused, and as a child had had difficulty controlling it. Now it felt good to let rip on somebody who wouldn't be able to do a damned thing about it.

The resounding 'slap' echoed satisfyingly around the room, and even more satisfyingly, put an end to her mocking, jeering, voice. And if she was stupid enough to threaten to have the law on him for assault … well, she'd soon see how expensive top-class solicitors could be.

Jenny's head snapped to one side, making her stagger in the same direction. But she quickly regained her balance, and when she turned to look at him, shock and something more, something much, much darker, swept across her face.

And for a moment, everything in the room went utterly quiet.

Then Titus Crowther-Beauley said, softly but venomously, 'If you don't back off, you silly cow, you'll end up like the last person who tried to come between me and my profits. Want to end up like Ray Reason, do you, little Jenny Wren?' he taunted.

And raised his hand again.

Chapter 37

Trudy and Clement had just climbed up the last set of internal stairs when they spotted the man standing outside the door to the top flat. He was a rather small, slightly portly man, with thinning dark hair, and was wearing half-moon spectacles. He was dressed in flannels and a tweed jacket with leather elbow patches and was so much of a type that both Trudy and Clement knew him instantly for an academic.

Sensing their presence, he turned and looked at them with wide, worried eyes that quickly changed to relief upon seeing Trudy's uniform.

'Oh, I'm so glad you're here,' he said, surprising them both. 'I was just wondering what I should do. If I should call you or just use my key and go in and see …'

He held up a small key as he spoke. 'But one doesn't like to interfere, does one? And I wouldn't, only … I am so worried, you see.' He looked so bewildered and uncertain, and was making no sense at all, that Trudy instinctively smiled and put on her most calming voice.

'What seems to be the trouble, sir?'

'Well, it's the people in there,' he said, nodding his head to the door. 'I think … Well, I think something very bad is happening in there. First they were talking to each other, very loudly, then they were shouting so much, I just couldn't put up with it any longer. *I'm trying to compose!'*

At this, Trudy blinked and shot a helpless look at Clement, but he only looked equally bewildered.

'So I got the key my neighbour left with me in order to keep an eye on his flat, because I didn't want to just ring or knock on the door. As I said, I think there's something not right going on in there, and I don't want to draw any attention or violence onto myself. I was just working up the courage to sneak in and take a peek and reassure myself that all's well. Well, not well, exactly but … Only, it's just this second gone so suddenly very quiet that I was having second th—'

But before he could complete his rambling sentence, a horrific feminine shriek of either fear or rage echoed from behind the door, making the academic literally leap back in fright. He dropped the key as he did so, and backed away, the eyes behind his half-moon spectacles going wide and wild.

Inside the flat, another howl came – this time definitely issuing from a man.

Trudy instantly bent down and picked up the key. 'Does this open this door?' she said, holding the key up to the man on the landing, and nodding at the door to the flat.

Wordlessly, he nodded.

Trudy wasted no more time, but thrust the key in the lock, turned it and stepped inside.

Clement was right behind her.

The door opened straight into the main room of the flat – a large living area, with views across the tree-lined wide avenue to a set of similar Georgian houses across the road. It was decorated in the modern style, but neither Trudy nor Clement were interested in the décor.

Instead their eyes went to the two figures in the room.

A slim, well-dressed man with dark hair and eyes was half

crouched on one knee, and was holding an arm up to protect his head.

Standing over him, holding a bronze statue of a female nude in her hand, was Jennifer Renfrew, and even as they watched, she swung it down, aiming for the man's head. But his raised arm took the brunt of it, and Clement clearly heard the bone in his arm snap under the pressure, and he winced in empathy.

The man howled again.

'You *stupid* man!' Jenny was screaming. 'Trying to scare me with your *stupid* threats! As if you killed Ray – you wouldn't have the guts, you pathetic worm!'

She raised her hand to deliver another blow; so intense was her concentration that she hadn't even heard Trudy and Clement enter the room.

But as Trudy hurtled across the room to try and stop the next blow before it had a chance to connect with Titus's head, Jenny screamed again.

'It was *me* who made sure Ray was dead, you idiot! And now I'm going to do the same for you!'

As Titus looked up at her, he felt death standing at his shoulder. The girl's face was so contorted by anger, triumph and, yes, madness, that she no longer looked like an attractive young woman, but rather like a modern-day Medusa. In her short blonde hair there were no snakes, but in her wild, mad eyes, there was hate and death.

His arm was too numb to lift and he knew the next blow would inevitably land on his unprotected head and finish him off.

And then someone clad in dark clothing leapt onto Jennifer's back, dragging her backwards, and Jenny screamed in surprise and rage, her arms flailing as she tried to keep her footing.

Titus collapsed onto the floor and closed his eyes. The pain in his arm was so intense, he found himself being helplessly sick, coughing up his recent breakfast and trying not to gag.

Jenny, struggling to rid herself of the weight on her back

twisted and turned, snarling and screaming like a banshee, but she couldn't seem to dislodge whoever it was.

As she and the person holding her staggered around, she saw the unmistakable figure of Dr Clement Ryder striding towards her. And that was when she knew it was all over. All her dreams, everything she'd planned – everything she'd done to make sure that her bright and wonderful future happened – was all gone. She began to curse and howl in earnest, the foulest words she could think of, mixed with threats of how she would kill the coroner too, and the policewoman she now knew was behind her, holding her back.

She felt the coldness of handcuffs slip over one of her wrists, but she didn't stop struggling, screaming out her defiance, telling the world that she would let nothing stop her from getting her prize. She *would* marry Marty. She *would* make him the greatest pop star in the world. She *would* be rich. She *would* be famous. She *would* be happy. She *would* have it all. She *would* kill anyone who tried to get in her way. On and on it went, in a stream of defiance and rage.

Eventually though, she found herself lying face down on the carpet, with someone sitting on top of her, both arms now secured behind her back.

And still she screamed on, swearing and howling in rage, spittle flying out of her mouth as her face contorted, her eyes bulging in her effort to buck Trudy off.

Trudy, panting slightly, her cap long since knocked off in the struggle, looked up at Clement a little helplessly. 'She's gone mad!' she said. 'What do we do?' Nothing in her police training had prepared her for this … this … insanity.

Clement bent down beside her to get a better look at the woman on the floor, but seeing him only made Jenny Wren scream louder.

'I'll kill you too! If you try and stop me,' she howled, literally foaming at the mouth now.

Clement nodded at Trudy. 'Yes, she's beyond reason right now.

I'll make a call to someone I know at the mental hospital. She's going to need specialist handling and sedation. It's no good you taking her back to your police station when she's in this state,' he said flatly. 'Your custody sergeant won't put her in the cells like this and would only call in the same professionals anyway.'

He got to his feet, staggered a bit as he tripped on his first step away, got himself steady again and then looked around the flat for the telephone.

In the doorway, the musician still hovered, watching, wide-eyed and silent.

He'd totally forgotten all about his descant.

Chapter 38

The next three days passed in a blur of activity for both Trudy and the coroner – but for different reasons.

Clement, whose letter of resignation had finally been very reluctantly accepted by the powers that be, had to set about starting the lengthy process of withdrawing from office. This would take some time, since he had no intention of going until his choice of a suitable replacement had been found and been broken in, but his life was no less difficult because of that. It seemed there were a hundred and one things that needed to be done.

For Trudy, she had to scurry to try and keep up with events as they happened, thick and fast – and fill in the vast amount of paperwork that accompanied each occurrence.

After seeing Ray Reason's murderer taken away in a straitjacket in the back of an ambulance, Trudy had returned to her station to report. For once, Inspector Jennings wasn't so inclined to haul her over the coals for doing things without checking with him first. Perhaps because he was still feeling jubilant over finally bringing down Felix Simpkins. Perhaps because it was finally beginning to dawn on him that Trudy, despite her gender, really did have what it took to be a good officer.

Or maybe that was wishful thinking on her part?

Whatever the reason, when she'd finished giving her verbal report, he'd merely sighed a bit, told her to write it all up and said that he would pass the information on to his superiors. Those superiors, he told her somewhat dryly, would no doubt consult with the prosecution service, who would in all probably consult with medical professionals about whether or not Jennifer Renfrew was fit to stand trial.

After all, he'd pointed out, with something of his old sarcasm reasserting itself, Dr Clement Ryder was a coroner and former surgeon, *not* a psychiatrist, and his opinions were only that. His opinions.

As it turned out though, the people who examined Jenny Wren at Broadmoor Hospital diagnosed a total mental collapse (or psychotic break, as they'd termed it) and declared she was certainly not fit to plead.

The report they submitted (in such torturous medical language that the Inspector had had to relent and ask Clement to come in and interpret it for them) basically boiled down to the fact that the young girl was suffering from a mania that was proving implacable.

Some people thought they were Napoleon. Others thought that they had special powers of telepathy or the ability to time-travel. Jenny believed that she should have been born rich, powerful and happy, and since she hadn't been, that it was all right for her to do whatever was necessary for her to gain her rightful place in the world.

Which included murder.

In some of her more lucid periods, she had admitted to seeing the argument between Linda and Ray, which had resulted in Ray falling down the stairs. And after Linda had fled in tears, Jenny had confessed to being curious, and had checked on Ray's condition. Finding him unconscious but still breathing, she'd told her doctors, seemed such an obvious gift from the fates that she'd felt almost obliged to lift his head and bang it down hard again on the metal stairs to make sure that he died.

In her mind, it all made sense. Ray Reason was trying to take over the band and push Marty into second place. Now, there he was, lying half-dead on the stairs, and all she needed to do was make him all-the-way dead, and her path to fame and glory would be assured.

Her statements made for chilling reading, and Trudy was glad that it was unlikely she'd ever be called upon to testify in court about those strange, terrible moments in the flat where she'd had to struggle to bring down a madwoman.

It was decided that Linda Kempson *would* have to face charges for pushing Ray Reason down the stairs, but her legal team seemed confident that, given the extenuating circumstances, she wouldn't face a lengthy sentence. And maybe, with a sympathetic judge, she might even be handed down a suspended sentence.

Titus Crowther-Beauley was recovering from his broken arm and other injuries back in London. And in spite of what had happened to him, he was still set on signing up the Rainbirds to his stable, and was anxious to have them sign the contracts as soon as possible – without, naturally, a neutral party casting an eye over them first.

Trudy, true to her word, had given Duncan his exclusive story, and a vivid description of her brave arrest of Jenny Wren had duly appeared in the press, embarrassing Trudy and putting a scowl on her Inspector's face that lasted for days.

*

So, what with all that going on, it was almost a week before Trudy was able to call on Clement at his house and properly catch up.

Vincent, it seemed, was no longer in residence, his holiday having come to an end, and he'd gone back to work in Cheltenham. His father passed on his apologies for not being able to say goodbye in person. He'd called at the station, apparently, but had been told WPC Loveday was too busy for a 'personal' visit.

It was six o'clock in the evening, and the autumn weather had arrived early. A fitful rain threw itself against his kitchen window as Clement made her tea, and a rising wind soughed through the trees outside, clearly audible through the old glass in the Victorian house.

When they were both settled down, and Trudy had finished filling him in on the tying up of all the loose ends of their latest case, Clement cradled his empty cup and stared down into it in silence.

Trudy, beginning to feel a little cold, sat hunched forward. 'Well, I suppose I should be going,' she said, but she made no actual move to go.

She'd known, from the moment she'd arrived and seen the sad look in her friend's eye and the tense set of his shoulders, that this was not going to be a routine visit after all.

And all the time she'd been chatting she was aware of feeling more and more afraid.

She could sense that something life-changing was about to happen, and now she felt a tightness start in the back of her throat as Clement leaned back in his chair and looked at her calmly. She felt a prickle behind her eyes, as he opened his mouth to speak.

And she felt her heart start to break, as he said gently, 'Trudy, have you heard of something called Parkinson's disease?'

*

An hour later, Trudy trudged forlornly into the police station, hoping that the tears she'd shed didn't show.

She'd barely stepped into the main office, however, when she heard her name being called.

'Ah, here she is, WPC Loveday. Congratulations.'

She looked up to see Chief Superintendent Whitting just coming out of DI Jennings' office, with Harry Jennings close behind him.

'DI Jennings has just been filling me in on the sterling work you and Dr Ryder did on that nasty nightclub business.' At this point, the Chief Super turned to her boss and grinned. 'You're lucky to have such a promising young constable as this, Harry.'

Her DI gave a rather sickly smile. 'Yes, sir,' he agreed weakly.

'I can tell you, we upstairs have been keeping a close eye on this young lady's progress over the last couple of years, Harry, and we're liking what we see.' There was, in his tone of voice, a certain hardness and warning that his DI picked up on at once. He'd been around long enough to know when he was being steered in a certain direction.

Satisfied that his man had got the message, the Chief Superintendent sweetened the pill a bit. 'We're also impressed with the way you've taken her under your wing and had the foresight to give her more and more responsibility, letting her blossom.'

At this, both Trudy and her boss blinked. It was hard to say who was more surprised.

'Not all DIs would have seen her potential and had the wits to encourage her as you have,' Whitting added with a twinkle in his eye.

DI Jennings managed another strained smile. 'Thank you, sir,' he muttered.

'So keep up the good work, Harry,' he said bracingly, then turned from Harry Jennings and nodded at Trudy. 'And I think it's safe to say that if *you* keep up the good work, WPC Loveday, in a few years' time your promotion to Detective Constable is all but assured. And after that, who knows? You might even rise to the rank of Sergeant.'

Trudy smiled tremulously. 'Thank you, sir,' she said.

In fact, she was determined to make it to Inspector one day. But perhaps it would be best to keep that to herself? At least for a while.

Dear Reader,

We hope you enjoyed reading this book. If you did, we'd be so appreciative if you left a review. It really helps us and the author to bring more books like this to you.

Here at HQ Digital we are dedicated to publishing fiction that will keep you turning the pages into the early hours. Don't want to miss a thing? To find out more about our books, promotions, discover exclusive content and enter competitions you can keep in touch in the following ways:

JOIN OUR COMMUNITY:

Sign up to our new email newsletter:
http://smarturl.it/SignUpHQ

Read our new blog www.hqstories.co.uk

https://twitter.com/HQStories

www.facebook.com/HQStories

BUDDING WRITER?

We're also looking for authors to join the HQ Digital family!
Find out more here:

https://www.hqstories.co.uk/want-to-write-for-us/

Thanks for reading, from the HQ Digital team